Deadly Obsession

Meaghan Pierce

Pierced Soul Publishing

Editing by Comma Sutra Editorial

Cover Design by Books and Moods

For Paula. Thank you for patiently answering all my questions so I could avoid weird ads on Facebook.

Dear Reader,

Please be aware that *Deadly Obsession* contains content that may be triggering for some. For a list of triggers, please see the next page.

Deadly Obsession contains the following content: descriptions of dating violence, stalking, panic attacks, sexual assault, pregnancy, and mentions of abortion

Chapter One

He was fucking insane.

Aidan had absolutely no explanation for what was happening right now other than Declan had completely lost his mind. That was the only thing that could make his ridiculous statement make sense.

His brother didn't look insane. He wore a cool, passive expression, one eyebrow slightly cocked and hands resting casually on the arms of his antique desk chair.

Declan Callahan looked like a man accustomed to getting his way. Because he usually did. But it wasn't going to work today. Aidan was not going to agree to this...this...death sentence.

"Well?"

Aidan's eyes were drawn to his sister-in-law. His lip curled at the word. He narrowly avoided the bond ten years ago when she left his brother at the altar. Until six months ago when she wormed her way back into Declan's bed. Aidan wondered if she'd stick around another ten years before disappearing again. He hoped not.

"Well, what?" he said, tone icy.

1

"No questions then?" Declan wondered.

Leaning back in his chair, Aidan crossed his ankle over his knee and gripped it, steadying himself for the assault that would definitely come with what he was about to say.

"I don't have any questions because I'm not doing it."

Evie snorted, but Declan smiled, his lips slowly parting to reveal his teeth. Maybe not a smile so much as a snarl that pretended at one.

"You say that like you have a choice."

Aidan jerked at his brother's sharp tone. "And you're saying I don't? You're saying you've decided, and that's that?"

Declan leaned forward, bracing his elbows on the edge of his desk, his eyes never leaving Aidan's. "That is precisely what I'm saying."

"This is my life," Aidan spat, his hand tightening on his ankle, barely checked rage threatening to bubble over.

"This is your duty," Declan replied. "To this family, to the syndicate, to the future."

"Exactly how long have you been planning this behind my back?"

Declan glanced up at Evie as if he couldn't remember. She shrugged. "Since we chose Falcone." Evie's voice was level, but she shifted ever so slightly at the look in Aidan's eyes.

"A month?! None of you thought to tell me you were going to sell me off like chattel for four *weeks*?"

"That seems a little dramatic," Evie countered.

"Oh, does it?" Aidan sneered. "What exactly would you call an arranged marriage to a fucking stranger, then?"

"A necessary evil," Declan replied. "I want a blood tie between the families to avoid future wars, and you're going to get it for me. This is not up for debate. You will marry her, you will fuck her, you will get her pregnant. The families will be joined forever."

"Now I'm just here to breed her?"

Aidan shoved to his feet. The idea of being both a husband and a father against his will had his heart thudding in his chest. He couldn't imagine a worse fate. He'd rather be buried in the ground next to…

"Finn wouldn't want this."

Pain flashed in Declan's eyes before they went blank again. "It was Finn's idea. We're having dinner with her family tonight." Declan pushed to his feet, the dismissal clear. "You will be there—on time—and you will behave yourself."

"And if I don't?"

Declan paused in his advance to the door, turning slowly. His expression was still carefully blank, but the muscle that ticked in his jaw when he was pissed off was beating a wild rhythm.

"You live under my roof, working for my syndicate, making my money. I've put up with your temper tantrums and your whining for far longer than I should have. You can marry this woman and give us the alliance we need, or you can leave Philadelphia and never come back."

Neither man reacted to Evie's sharp intake of breath, but Aidan knew if it surprised her that Declan was more than willing to make good on his threat. His brother turned toward the door again.

"I hope you make the right choice," Declan said before disappearing.

Aidan stared at the empty space where his brother had been, fingers twitching with the urge to break every goddamn thing in the room. Ironically, Declan's threat of marriage or banishment might be the first real choice Aidan had ever been given. His laugh was bitter.

The youngest son of the most powerful crime family in Philadelphia, he'd never been more than a prop for his brother's rise to power, and he'd been raised as such. He was considered a cog in the wheel—when he was considered at all.

Declan had amassed more money and power in the last decade than even Aidan thought possible. Declan's plan to remake the syndicate into a far-reaching empire had been set in motion long before their father died in a car accident three years ago. It would be truly impressive if he hadn't let the power go entirely to his head.

Leaving Declan's office untouched, Aidan stepped into the hall and climbed the stairs to his bedroom. The house was quiet save for the low hum of vacuum cleaners and conversation as the maids made their rounds.

At the top of the stairs, he turned toward his bedroom, stopping at the corner and staring down the long hall to the wing where his brother's suite of rooms was. If Declan was the king, then Glenmore House was his palace, and it was only a matter of time before he took that from Aidan as well.

Brogan, the third and last surviving Callahan son, still lived at Glenmore with his whore, the Italian princess who'd caused this whole mess in the first place. But Brogan was useful behind the screens of his computers. In an ever-growing digital landscape where fewer cops were interested in being bought, Brogan's skill set was vital to safeguard syndicate interests.

Apparently, the only thing Aidan brought to the table was fucking some faceless woman. Not something he really minded until his brother's announcement. In fact, nameless and faceless was the way he preferred to take his women. Nameless, faceless, and never more than once. Lovers didn't suit him.

He bared his teeth as he pushed into his room. Not that he intended to make a lover out of her. Marry her, fuck her, get her pregnant. That was his duty here, as Declan said. A duty he would apparently perform, albeit against his will.

Once she was pregnant, he fully intended to leave her to raise the kid while he went on with his life. He could set her up in a nice house and get the kid a nanny. Maybe a male nanny. Then she could have her fun too. Play house with someone who wasn't him.

Scrubbing a hand over his face, he flicked on the light, eyes narrowing on a garment bag on the bed. Crossing to it, he lifted the note off the top and flipped it open to read.

Wear this tonight. Scarpetta 7 p.m. Don't be late.

Gritting his teeth, he crumpled the note in his fist and tossed it into the corner. Now he was being dressed. How quaint. Out of sheer curiosity, he unzipped the bag. It wasn't a suit as he'd expected. Merely a pair of dark gray slacks and a green cashmere sweater.

He zipped the bag back up and crossed to the closet to change into running clothes. He needed a punishing distraction if he was going to get through tonight with a straight face.

Leaving Philadelphia was an option, but not one he liked. He could join any number of criminal organizations. Boston, New York, Chicago. He could probably even hop the pond and fit right in somewhere in Ireland. But Philly was his home, and the Callahan legacy was as much his as anyone else's.

Declan would get what he wanted like he always did. An alliance cemented by marriage and children and those blood ties he craved so much. But Aidan would do it on his own terms as much as he could manage. He might be a pawn, but he wouldn't be a puppet.

Chapter Two

He arrived fifteen minutes late simply because he could. After pulling up outside the restaurant and handing his keys to the valet, Aidan let himself in and gave his name to the hostess. She flirted heavily, and on any other night, he might have returned her advances. Tonight he felt like he was about to face a firing squad.

Declan had rented out one of the private rooms, larger than they needed for their party, probably to give people room to mingle, standing in groups with glasses in their hands and chatting in low voices.

It was odd that Declan hadn't insisted on meeting at Breá, his high-end steakhouse and bar. It had two private rooms and a ballroom on the second floor. Declan liked to meet on his own turf.

Aidan watched Declan's hand skim down his wife's back and rest on her hip. Tonight's dinner must be Evie's doing. His brother had been taking far too much direction from his wife in recent months.

Declan and Evie were chatting with an older couple. The

Falcones, no doubt. Aidan could only assume. He'd never been invited to any of the meetings they had with Falcone after choosing him to replace Giordano as the head of the Mafia. Ostensibly because they were keeping this whole marriage thing a secret and didn't want Falcone saying the wrong thing and ruining their sick game.

Brogan engaged another group of two men and two women he assumed to be their wives. When Brogan shifted, Aidan caught sight of Libby's blonde hair, and his stomach tightened. If anyone was responsible for the hell this family had endured over the last few months, it was Libby Giordano.

She'd brought this nightmare to their doorstep with her desperate pleas for help to stop her father's sex trafficking ring and save her sister, Teresa, from its clutches. A nightmare that had ended with his brother dead and buried, and now this travesty of a marriage he'd be bound to for life. He would give anything to go back to that hot August day and undo it all.

Aidan ordered a glass of scotch when the waitress stopped to ask if he needed anything, grateful no one had noticed him yet. Tearing his eyes away from Libby's swinging blonde hair, he found the last group of guests. His uncle Sean and cousin James tucked into the far corner talking to two men and a woman.

The man had his arm wrapped loosely around the woman's shoulders, and Aidan cocked his head. Had his blushing bride brought a date? Her back was to him, and dark brown hair hung straight to her shoulders. Slimmer than he would normally go for, but you didn't need to be physically attracted to someone to procreate.

The waitress pressed a tumbler into his hand and sent him a flirty grin. He didn't even have the heart to return it. Christ, something was wrong with him. After dinner he'd have to swing by the club and pick someone up, make sure Declan's missive hadn't permanently scarred him or something.

When he looked back at the room, he caught Declan's eye. Irritation at Aidan's tardiness flitted across his brother's face, but he masked it with a smile he usually reserved for schmoozing politicians.

"You made it," Declan said as he crossed the room. He clapped Aidan on the shoulder and squeezed so hard Aidan had to fight not to wince. "Let's make some formal introductions."

Aidan let Declan lead him over to the couple he'd been speaking with a moment before. The man was stocky, with hair going gray at the temples and a close-cropped beard to match. Aidan had several inches on him, but something about his future father-in-law told Aidan the man could hold his own in a fight.

"This is Adrian Falcone and his wife, Julia."

"Nice to finally meet you," Aidan said, his voice clipped.

"And you. Finally," Julia said with a tight smile, sipping her glass of wine when Falcone slid her a look.

Declan's smile was easy, but Aidan knew his brother's temper flared at Julia's disapproving comment in the tightening of his grip as he turned them toward the next group. Brogan was speaking to Falcone's two oldest sons and, as Aidan suspected, their wives. Leo, the heir apparent now that Falcone was in charge, was married to Marie, and Gavin, the second son, was married to Zara. If someone started reciting names of offspring, Aidan was going to scream.

Before Declan could haul him off and introduce him to the last group and his future wife, a waiter stepped into the room to announce that dinner was ready to be served. Aidan breathed a sigh of relief at the small moment of reprieve. Suddenly the room felt constricting, the sweater itchy.

They pivoted toward the table, and as Aidan approached, he noticed tented cards with names on them. Assigned seating. Wonderful. He found his in the middle of the long table, Brogan to his left and…Vivian to his right. He could only assume that was her. He'd never thought to ask her name.

Refusing to look around for her, he dropped into his chair and set his glass above his plate. When the brown-haired woman sank into the seat across the table from him, he frowned.

Not Vivian, then. Or they'd been placed across the table from each other so he couldn't say anything stupid. But then the man he'd seen with his arm around her shoulders leaned down and pressed a kiss to her temple, making her smile. If that wasn't her, then where the hell was she?

He felt movement to his right moments before she lowered herself gracefully into the chair. Her hair was long and black, and she wore it loose so it cascaded down her back and over her arms nearly to her waist. It took her a beat, but she finally turned to face him, dark brown eyes carefully meeting his gaze and wandering over his face before she smiled.

"You must be Aidan."

"I must be." When she extended her hand, he took it, squeezing it gently before letting it drop and ignoring the heat that singed his fingers. "And you're Vivian."

"Viv," she corrected, leaning back as the wait staff set a salad in front of her. "The only person who called me Vivian was my grandmother. Or my mother when she's angry at me."

"Viv, then," he agreed with a nod.

"You look positively thrilled to be here," she added, spearing a bite of arugula with a grin, and he grunted. "Can't imagine why."

Someone called her name, and she looked toward the

sound. His first thought was how annoyingly beautiful she was. If Declan was going to saddle him with a marriage he didn't want, he could have at least had the decency to do it with someone far less appealing.

She laughed at something someone said, and the sound tugged at something foreign inside him. He imagined having her underneath of him, pounding her until her breathy laughs faded into breathy moans. Well, at least fucking her wouldn't be a hardship.

She ignored him with a practiced skill through the salad course and most of the soup course. He couldn't fathom why that irritated him so much. It felt like she was grappling with the upper hand, waiting for him to break and speak first. Then she threw him off guard and turned to ask him a question.

"How long have you known?"

He waited until the staff cleared their soup bowls before turning to her. Her brown eyes were curious, her mouth rounded into an expectant O. He made the mistake of dipping his gaze down to her lips.

She'd painted them a bold red, and they stood out against the faint champagne shimmer of her dress. He had the sudden urge to reach up and rub his thumb across her lower lip, so he reached for his scotch and took a long sip instead.

"About the engagement?" She nodded. "Roughly six hours. You?" he asked when her mouth dropped open.

"Jesus," she breathed. "And I thought a week was bad."

She tilted her head and studied him carefully as the next course was brought out. Some kind of pasta dish.

"Why did you say yes?"

Aidan hadn't expected her to ask the question, and definitely not while surrounded by their family, but no one seemed to be paying them any mind. Except for Declan's occasional glances to make sure Aidan was behaving himself.

"Not much of a choice," he answered honestly.

Something like sympathy lit her eyes as she sipped from her wineglass. "Same. Well, we'll make quite a pair."

He didn't get a chance to respond because Declan cleared his throat from the head of the table, and conversation stilled. Aidan wanted to tell her they wouldn't make any kind of pair at all, but what was the point? She'd find out soon enough.

"Tonight marks a new beginning," Declan began. "An agreement between families to move forward together with the bonds of marriage and the promise of children."

Aidan thought he heard Viv snort at the sentiment, and he barely managed to swallow a chuckle.

"To the future," Falcone agreed, raising his glass in a toast.

Viv sipped her wine in toast and twirled pasta around her fork. They ate in silence, but conversation somehow miraculously slipped around them, leaving them in their bubble. If people noticed they said nothing more to each other, they didn't bother pointing it out. It wasn't until dessert had been served that Viv turned to him and started speaking again.

"I've spent the last week getting a crash course in your family history. For instance," she added at his confused frown. "That's your uncle Sean, your father's half brother. His wife, your aunt, died of cancer when James"—she gestured to his cousin with her fork—"was only seven. Which is very sad."

Her brows knitted together before her forehead smoothed again, and she again pointed at James. "James's wife Maura was killed a few months ago by Evie's evil twin sister, Nessa. The day after their wedding. It's like a Shakespearean tragedy."

He snorted softly, and he saw her tuck her tongue into her cheek.

"I heard about Finn. I couldn't imagine losing a brother."

Her eyes darted around the table and then back to his face. "I really am very sorry."

"It's not like you killed him," Aidan said, suddenly uncomfortable under her direct gaze and her sincerity.

"No," she agreed. "But I'm sorry it hurts all the same. So would you like one?"

He shook his head at her quick change of subject. The woman was impossible to keep up with.

"A dead brother? Already got one of those, thanks."

She laughed at his sarcasm, a smooth sound that had lust arrowing through him. Lust would make this a lot less excruciating to deal with. Not exactly pleasant, but less of a burden anyway.

"No, a crash course." Her eyebrows shot up when he only stared. "On my family."

Why the hell not. "Sure."

He angled toward her when she leaned in closer, and he tried to ignore the delicate floral scent of her hair as it brushed against his arm.

"You met my parents," she said, keeping her voice low. "They are as in love now as they were when they got married. It can be quite nauseating sometimes." Her words were teasing, but her tone was soft.

She shifted, her shoulder bumping his as she gestured to her two older brothers. "Leo and Gavin have seven kids between them. It's a wonder they're able to get any work done. I imagine they're just fucking like bunnies all the time."

"You imagine them fucking like bunnies?"

She looked momentarily horrified, but then she laughed again. "Gross. Not like that. That's my sister, Sofia." She pointed to the woman he'd mistaken for her. "And her husband, Tim. They've got two girls. And then Nico. The baby of the family. Barely twenty-two and hoping to play baseball in the major leagues when he finishes school."

"What team?"

She looked surprised at his interest. Not more surprised than he felt, though. "I wish I could say the Phillies, but he'd rather be somewhere warm. I think Atlanta, LA, and Houston are all at the top of the list," she added with an affectionate smile. "I hope he gets to."

"Why?"

"Because." She turned back to face him, eyes dropping to his mouth before dragging back up to meet his gaze. "Everyone should get to do the things they want, the things that are really important to them."

"And what do you want?" The question fell from his lips before he could stop it.

Her mouth curved up into a grin. "I'm not quite sure yet."

They lapsed into silence again, and he watched her with her own family. They teased and poked and laughed. He had similar memories with his brothers. Back when their father had been alive and before Evie had shattered Declan's heart. They felt like lifetimes ago. They were out of his grasp now, foggy.

Dessert was cleared and coffee poured, and slowly, finally, conversation began to ebb. Gavin and his wife, whose name Aidan couldn't remember, left first. They had four kids to get home to. Nico went with them. He had school and practice tomorrow.

Sofia left with her husband soon after, reminding Viv that she'd see her the following morning. Brogan took Libby home when she started rubbing her temple. She'd been getting headaches since her father's psychotic henchman DiMarco had kidnapped and nearly killed her, and Aidan was glad to be rid of her.

It was nearly midnight by the time they finally pushed back from the table, and when Viv stood, he got a good look at her from head to toe for the first time. He took in her soft hourglass curves and her long stretch of tan legs. She was taller than he'd expected, matching him for height in heels. Yeah, fucking her was definitely not going to be a hardship.

"I'll see you at the house tomorrow," Evie said to Viv, stopping in front of them.

"Yes," Viv replied. "For wedding planning."

Evie turned to Aidan. "Nine o'clock. Please don't be late."

Aidan seethed as she turned and walked away. If it wasn't bad enough that he was expected to go through with the wedding, now they wanted him to help plan the fucking thing too? What the hell did he care what flowers they chose or what music they danced to? All of it was a sham.

"Not much experience planning weddings, I take it."

When Aidan turned back to Viv, she was studying him carefully. "No desire to."

She gave a quick nod. "I can't say I've ever been one to dream of getting married myself. But we're in this together, so I guess we'll figure it out."

As quickly as the sentiment bloomed, he squashed it. They were not in this together. They would not be friends. To let her think otherwise was dangerous, if not cruel. She might be beautiful and captivating and intelligent, but he had one duty here.

"But we aren't, are we?" He kept his voice measured, cold. "This marriage has one purpose. Once it's fulfilled, we won't need to be anything else to each other."

He watched her closely. Noted the subtle straightening of her spine, the imperceptible lift in her chin, the way the light faded from her eyes and left them hard and unblinking. It was like watching all semblance of hope that this would be anything other than a business transaction leech out slowly, replaced by steeled indifference.

When she brushed past him without a word, he turned to

watch her go, ignoring the tightening in his chest as she slipped through the door. It would be better for them both this way. She clearly wanted affection, a connection he simply wasn't capable of. She deserved to know what she was getting into. Now she did.

Chapter Three

Viv let herself into the bakery the following morning. It was still dark yet, but she'd timed her arrival to after the early morning rush and before the late morning baking started. This way, most of the activity was over near the sinks and not in the main prep area.

She glanced around for her sister, hoping Sofia was busy with the line she'd seen snaking around the front of the building and wouldn't be in the back to play twenty questions. Viv tied her hair back in a low bun and bent to retrieve the ingredients she needed off the bottom shelf.

Her great-grandfather had opened Romano's Bakery in the fifties as an insurance policy for his family during the post-war boom while the Mafia underwent yet another fracturing reconstruction. He hadn't trusted the stability of the Mafia's top leadership as they fought among themselves for power.

He'd grown it carefully, going to great lengths to keep it as far away from Mafia influence as possible, and passed it down to his son, who'd passed it down to his daughter, Viv's mother. It had certainly seen them through rough periods in

Mafia history in the decades since. Only now she knew her parents worried it might be a liability, something someone could exploit or target to punish her father.

She hoped they didn't sell it. She'd grown up here, standing on a stool next to the counter while her mother and grandmother taught her every recipe they knew. She could make most of their family recipes from memory and loved developing new ones to see what would do well and what needed tweaking.

If they did decide to sell, maybe she could buy them out. Assuming being a Callahan bride gave her some kind of access to Callahan wealth. The alliance itself might dissuade people from taking such a direct public shot at them. Callahan retribution was always swift and merciless.

But she had no reason to expect anything from them, least of all to save a family-owned business that paled in comparison to their empire. The bakery was a drop in the bucket to what they controlled, and any hope that she might have been able to come to a mutual understanding, if not a partnership, with her future husband had been ruthlessly stamped out at dinner last night.

Temper flaring, she reached onto a high shelf for a stainless steel bowl and began measuring ingredients into it. She knew Aidan Callahan by reputation only. He'd fucked more than one of her friends, and the story was always the same. He was the best sex they'd ever had, but always gone by morning. Whether he was or they were, no one ever spent the night with him.

Not that she was a prude. She'd enjoyed a nice sweaty fuck with a guy whose name she didn't care to remember more than once. Aidan was exactly the kind of man she might like to have that nice, sweaty...she shook her head. This wasn't a one-night stand. It was altogether different. Unavoidable. Forever.

It had been too much to hope that he would be interested in at least meeting her halfway. She knew what was expected of her and that she had no choice. Her father might have phrased the option to marry Aidan Callahan as a question, but it hadn't been one. She imagined the same was likely true for him.

She wasn't harboring any delusions that they'd fall in love at first sight or even that they might fall in love over time. She wasn't a child, and this wasn't a fairy tale. What she did hope for was mutual respect. Something he clearly wasn't capable of.

That was fine. Once he'd fulfilled his *purpose,* she could busy herself with motherhood while he busied himself with whoever was willing to lie underneath him.

"What are you doing here?"

Viv winced as she finished mixing the ingredients and dumped the dough onto a baking tray to shape. Busted.

"I'm baking something."

"I can see that." Sofia came closer and pushed onto her tiptoes to peer over her sister's shoulder. Even with Viv in flat shoes, Sofia was several inches shorter than Viv's five-nine. "Can't you make biscotti at home?"

"I could." Viv turned and slid the baking tray into the oven. "But then I'd be trying to avoid having the same conversation with Mama. With less success."

"What conversation is that?"

Viv cocked a brow as she set the timer. "Well, if you're not going to bring it up, I'm definitely not going to bring it up."

"What did you think of him last night?"

"See?" Viv carried the bowl and spoon she'd been using over to the sink, dunking them both in warm soapy water. "That's the thing I'm avoiding."

"That bad, huh?"

Leaning back against the counter, Viv crossed her arms

over her chest. "Not bad. He seems to want this about as much as I do. Which, somewhere deep down, feels like it should be a good thing. It means he doesn't want a plaything to amuse himself with."

"But?" Sofia prompted.

"But this marriage is for life. Our family doesn't do divorce. His family certainly doesn't. I guess I was hoping for something a little...more."

Admitting it hurt more than she wanted it to and she rubbed at her chest to ease the ache. Neither of them had chosen this, but he'd snuffed out the only bit of hope she had that he had a vested interest in making it bearable.

"You don't always have to put yourself last, you know. Maybe Papa could—"

"No," Viv snapped. "He couldn't. And we both know that."

That had been Sofia's favorite argument since their father sat the entire family down and informed them of the marriage he'd arranged with Declan Callahan. A marriage that would forever tie the syndicate and the Mafia together in a way no two crime families were linked in the city.

Not that arranged marriages never happened. The Russians and the Greeks still relied on them heavily. But this one expanded Callahan reach in a very tangible way and, ostensibly, for generations. Blood ties.

She'd blanched when her father first used the term. She knew instantly it meant babies. Before she'd even met him, she was expected to bear his children, and if he had as much interest in being a father as he had in being a husband, then it was likely to be as lonely an undertaking as her marriage now seemed to be.

Motherhood had never really been something she'd dwelled on in the past, but for the last week it was all she could think about. Would she be a good mother? Did she even want to be one? Would she love a baby born out of necessity rather than love? She hoped so. She didn't seem to have any choice in the matter. It was this or risk her family's lives.

"You didn't have to make biscotti fresh," Sofia said by way of an apology. "We have some in the front case."

Viv offered a small smile. "I know. But Libby said cranberry orange biscotti are Evie's favorite, and I needed the distraction."

If Viv wanted to get at least one Callahan to like her, she'd go for the next best thing to her future husband—the matriarch and queen. Hopefully the way to Evie's heart was through her stomach.

Sofia dropped her off at Glenmore House and left her standing at the front door. Viv had been asked to come to this one meeting on her own, although Evie had assured her that her mother and sister could come to others. They were supposed to meet them later this morning to look at venues. The entire thing was painfully surreal.

Viv shook her hand to keep it from trembling and reached out to ring the bell. She felt awkward waiting in the early morning chill, cold fingers gripping the edges of the navy blue bakery box. She heard the dull thud of the deadbolt sliding out of the way moments before the door swung in. Her smile faltered when she realized it was Aidan and not Evie or a maid.

"You're early. Good for you," he said, stepping back from the door so she could enter. "Is that for me?"

She followed his gaze to the box in her hands. "No."

His expression faltered, but he said nothing as he closed the door and walked ahead of her toward the back of the house. He was wearing jeans and a long-sleeved sweater that hugged his chest and stretched tight over his shoulders. Did he have to be so hot? The asshole.

"This way," he called over his shoulder when she didn't follow.

Suddenly grateful she was several paces behind him, she let herself openly gawk. Glenmore House was as beautiful as she imagined it to be. A Gothic-style manor home that had been meticulously preserved throughout the decades. She imagined all the intricately carved woodwork was original, and if the plasterwork on the ceiling wasn't, it was a perfect replica. No one could say the Callahans didn't take care of their things.

She walked over rich, antique carpet past a formal living room with white couches and a huge fireplace, what looked like a smaller sitting room, and several closed doors. They turned a corner, and she had a quick minute to muse if they were in some kind of wing before he took another sharp turn into a huge solarium.

He stalled at her sharp intake of breath but kept going until he claimed one of the high-backed chairs flanking a large, rectangular coffee table. The room was beautiful. Big, wide windows were set in wrought iron frames.

It looked over the back of the estate and offered a panoramic view of the grounds. Two double sets of French doors, one on either side of the room, opened onto an expansive deck that seemed to stretch over most of the back of the house.

Beyond the deck, a manicured lawn spread in gently sloping hills to the tree line, alive with the bright colors of autumn. She imagined it would be beautiful in winter, blanketed in fresh white snow.

At a noise behind her, she looked up to see Aidan watching her carefully from where he sat in his chair. She felt heat flood her cheeks and deliberately turned away from the view to take a seat.

"Oh," Evie said as she rushed in, smoothing a hand over her curls. "You're both here already. Good."

She poured herself a cup of coffee from a silver pot Viv hadn't noticed and took a seat so they were arranged in a kind of circle around the table. Viv set the box she'd brought on the polished surface, feeling suddenly awkward about having brought a peace offering with the way Aidan kept staring at her.

"Biscotti," Viv said by way of explanation, pushing the box into the middle of the table. "I heard they were your favorite."

Evie's smile seemed warm and genuine. "That's very sweet. Thank you. Viv, did you want any coffee? Or tea?" Viv shook her head. "Okay, we might as well get started."

"About time," Aidan muttered, but Evie ignored him.

"The first and most important thing is Declan has decided to make this a society wedding. Politicians, business associates. Big. Splashy."

Viv frowned. "Why?"

The last thing she could think of making a splash over would be a hastily arranged marriage between two crime lords. Well, her father might be a lord. Declan was most definitely a king.

"Because it sends a message. In a century, the Callahans have never aligned with another family through marriage or anything else. They've deposed and installed leaders, but never established an outright alliance. Declan wants everyone in the city to know that this alliance carries the full weight of the syndicate behind it."

"Declan wants that, or you do?"

Evie ignored her brother-in-law's caustic accusation. "So, we go big and splashy. It's a lot to do in the time frame, but we'll figure it out. Your mom and sister are still available to go look at a couple venues later today?"

"Yes," Viv said with a nod. "Of course."

"Great. We'll also throw an engagement party next weekend. No need to worry about prep for that. I've got it handled. And I was thinking we could get an interview with the two of you in the society pages."

"What in the hell for?" Aidan snapped.

"I imagine," Viv replied, irritated with his snide remarks, "she'll tell us if you stop interrupting."

Aidan opened his mouth, then closed it again, jaw clenched as he swallowed whatever retort he'd been about to lash out with.

"Again, big, splashy. Declan and I did one. The questions are pretty simple, boring even. An hour of faking it for the paper, and you'll be in print as a happy couple. I hope I don't have to remind you," Evie added, eyes on Aidan as he continued to glare at her, "that this marriage has a lot riding on it. Now, let's do something fun. Engagement rings."

Evie pulled velvet jewelry boxes from a heavy paper bag, opening them up and setting them on the table between them. "These are family heirlooms." Evie twisted her own emerald engagement ring around her finger. "They're generally used by younger sons for their wives. There are others if you don't like any of these. Several generations back had eight sons, so they had to make quite a few."

Viv picked up the first box. A large oval diamond set in a plain gold band. Not really her style. The next was a little more ornate, gaudy even, with its large square stone flanked by two baguette sapphires and more diamonds laid into the band. The third one made her breath catch in her throat, though.

It was a single round ruby stone, deep set in a silver band intricately carved with a swirling and sweeping filigree around the stone and down either side of the band. The inside of the band had a single word inscribed on it. *Forever*. It would have been romantic under different circumstances.

She wondered suddenly if this was a test and there was a ring she was supposed to pick above the others. She cast a cautious look at Aidan, head tilted in question.

He pinned her with a bored stare, one dark eyebrow arched over ice-blue eyes. "Don't look at me. I don't have to wear the damn thing."

"Funny. Is that what people also have to say about your personality?"

She slid the ring onto her finger while Evie snorted into her coffee and decided she liked the look of it there.

"I love that one. It has a matching band, inlaid with alternating rubies and diamonds. Or you're welcome to pick out something new. We'll have to get one for Aidan anyway."

"I'd love to see it."

"I'll get Declan to pull it out of the safe."

"Pull what out of the safe?" As if summoned, Declan strode through the door.

"The matching band to that ring." Evie pointed at Viv's finger. "I remember there being one unless I'm remembering wrong."

Declan's brows knit together. "No, I think you're right. I'll check. I hate to interrupt, but I need to borrow the groom." His gaze slid to Aidan, but it was unreadable. "Something came up."

"Sure. We're through what I need him for anyway. Maybe you can give him more information on why you want to make this an event. Since he didn't seem to believe me."

Declan's smile was quick and razor sharp. "My pleasure. Viv," he said, gaze shifting to her, "good to see you again."

"Yes, ah, you too."

Declan turned back to Evie, and Viv had to bite back a

sigh when love lit his face. She chanced a quick peek at Aidan, who watched with a scowl, hands shoved into his pockets while he waited for Declan by the door. After a quick kiss on his wife's lips, Declan left the way he came with Aidan trailing behind him.

Viv was destined to marry a man who probably slept with a permanent crease between his brows, annoyed even by his dreams.

Chapter Four

"Something came up?" Aidan asked once they were in the car and beyond the driveway.

Declan made a non-committal noise in the back of his throat. "You know I'm doing this for your own good, right?"

"Mine? I thought it was for yours."

Declan's fingers tightened on the steering wheel. "You don't think this benefits the entire family? The Italians have been too explosive, too unpredictable, for too long. This brings them into the fold. It stabilizes the city in a way that lays a foundation for everything else I've wanted to build for over a decade."

Declan sighed. "If it was anyone else getting married, I know you'd see that. You always saw and understood far more than Dad ever gave you credit for."

Aidan was so shocked by his brother's words he almost said thank you. But there was something else, some other reason for the praise. There had to be. Declan always operated ten steps ahead of you.

"And yet here I am, relegated to stud for your alliances."

On a snort, Declan pulled into an alley just outside Little Odessa. "You're right. That's why I asked you to come instead of leaving you to discuss flower arrangements and place settings."

Before Aidan could ask exactly what he'd been invited along for, another SUV pulled into the opposite end of the alley, and he tensed.

"Relax," Declan said, reaching for the door. "Friendlies."

He indicated an earpiece on the dashboard before he got out of the car as Falcone and his two oldest sons did the same. Aidan slipped the piece into his ear and immediately heard keys clacking in his ear. Brogan. Aidan could add whatever the fuck this was to the list of things his brothers wouldn't share with him until it was absolutely necessary. It got longer by the second.

"Falcone," Declan said when Aidan stepped up beside him. "We have a problem with the Russians."

Aidan didn't miss how Declan emphasized the word we, and neither did Falcone, his brows ticking up a degree.

"I assume you know what he was doing with DiMarco?"

"I do." Falcone crossed his arms over his chest and flicked a glance at Aidan. "Buying girls from DiMarco's trafficking ring for his club."

"Yes. Even after strict orders from me not to. Ivankov doesn't appear to be very smart, but even the dumb need lessons."

Another car pulled into the alley behind Declan's Range Rover, and Aidan knew without turning around it would be full of syndicate men. Falcone's jaw set when the men stepped up behind them, but he said nothing.

Aidan followed Declan when he walked past Falcone's SUV, jogging across the street to keep up. They stopped in front of a restaurant with a dingy sign over the door, and the curtains in the front window pulled tight.

"Clear," Aidan heard Brogan say in his ear.

Aidan went in first, gun drawn before he even stepped over the threshold, and heard their men sweep in behind him. One Russian stood behind the bar, and his hands immediately shot up as he stepped out from behind it. Aidan wondered if that was the guy who earned the broken nose from Brogan the last time they conducted business with the head of Philly's Bratva.

Ivankov sat at a booth in the corner, looking as gaunt and ugly as Aidan remembered him. His usual bimbo, typically clad in a too-tight dress and teetering on impossibly tall heels, was nowhere to be seen. Today he was seated with his son, his only surviving child after the Italians murdered his daughter.

As syndicate men moved to flank the rear entrance and the door to the kitchen so no one would interrupt them, Declan stepped in, Falcone and his sons close behind. Ivankov had the good sense to blanch. Two visits from Declan in less than six weeks should definitely terrify him.

"Ivankov. Did you miss me?"

"It's good to see you again so soon," Ivankov said, getting up from the booth and reluctantly sliding into a chair across from Declan when he took a seat at an empty table.

Ivankov gripped his hands in his lap until his knuckles were white. He knew his penance had come due. No one betrayed the Callahan syndicate and walked away without paying for it. Usually with their life. But Aidan got the distinct impression Declan wanted to send a different kind of message and avoid another skirmish.

"You know I can't let what happened with the Italians go unanswered." Declan slid a cool gaze to Ivankov's son, who hadn't gotten up from the booth. "Someone has to pay."

"My daughter is dead. Isn't that payment enough?" Ivankov gritted out.

"Your daughter is dead because you placed your bets on the wrong man instead of remembering where your loyalties lay. But don't worry. I won't take your son. I want him to watch and to remember."

At the flick of Declan's wrist, two syndicate men rushed forward and gripped Ivankov by the arms, shoving his right hand onto the table and forcing his wrist down until his fingers were flat against the white tablecloth. When Ivankov's son shot out of the booth, Aidan pivoted, aiming his weapon at the kid's chest.

"Come here, boy," Declan said smoothly. "I want you to get a good look at the cost of betrayal."

When he didn't move, Aidan lunged forward to grab him by the shoulder, shoving him into a chair and leveling his gun at the kid's temple to keep him in place.

"Falcone," Declan said almost conversationally, turning in his chair. "Do you still carry knives?"

Falcone silently reached into his pocket and pulled out a folded knife, placing it in Declan's outstretched palm. Declan turned it over in his hand, pressing the mechanism that had the blade flipping out. It wasn't long, but it looked lethally sharp.

Declan tapped the point on the table between each of Ivankov's fingers before laying the sharpened edge against his pinky just underneath a small gold ring with the Bratva crest on it. Declan pressed the blade down until Ivankov yelped and blood welled from the cut.

"Don't," Aidan said, pressing the muzzle of his gun against the boy's head when he shifted toward his father.

"Your loyalty is not to the Bratva." Declan pushed the blade deeper, and Ivankov struggled against the hands holding him. "It's not to your son, not even to yourself. Your loyalty is to me."

He shoved the knife down until there was a thin snap, and

Ivankov screamed as the blood pooled under his hand and soaked into the white tablecloth, leeching out in thin tendrils.

"Because without my father's intervention twenty years ago and without our protection since, you would be dead. Let's hope you never forget that again."

When Declan pulled the blade back, glistening with blood, Ivankov's finger lay severed on the table, the small, gold ring glinting in the light. Declan wiped the blade clean on a napkin and handed it back to Falcone. When he stood, the men released Ivankov, who clutched his hand to his chest, sniveling.

"Don't make me come back here again, Ivankov. I have better things to do."

Aidan followed his brother to the door, gun still raised. He let the others file out and made sure he was the last one to step out into the bright light of late morning.

"Brogan," Declan said into his mic. "Watch to make sure they don't do anything stupid."

They jogged back across the street and into the alley without speaking. The men who'd come as backup climbed wordlessly into their car and drove off, leaving Aidan, Declan, and the three Falcone men alone in the alley. The tension was palpable, but no one dared break the silence. That had been a warning for Falcone as much as it was for Ivankov.

"Wh—" Aidan was cut off by the shrill ring of Falcone's phone.

"*Cara mia*, what…an accident? Where?" Aidan didn't like the way Falcone's voice became strained. "Is anybody hurt? Where are you?"

Declan's phone suddenly rang, and Aidan glimpsed Evie's face on the screen before he answered it. Whatever his wife was saying had Declan gripping Aidan's shoulder and backing toward the SUV.

"They were in the car together," Declan shouted at Falcone before climbing behind the wheel. "Stay there, love. Breathe. I'm on my way."

"What happened?" Aidan demanded as they peeled out of the alley to honks and rude gestures.

"I don't know. She said someone hit them."

"Hit them? On purpose?"

Declan's fingers tightened on the wheel as he weaved in and out of traffic. "I don't know," he said through gritted teeth.

Aidan wondered at the strange tightness in his chest. It's not like he needed to twist himself up over a fender bender. In fact, if something happened to Viv, he was off the hook. This could be his lucky day.

They weren't far from the accident, and when they pulled up, Aidan realized he could hardly call it a fender bender. The entire passenger side of the minivan was mangled, the sliding door caved in so severely it left a gap between the door and the frame. Glass littered the street.

Aidan jumped out after Declan, scanning the area. He didn't see any other mangled cars. So the one that had hit them must have driven off. Hit and run. Could have been for any number of reasons. Maybe it was a kid or a drunk who didn't want to get caught.

When Falcone screeched in behind them, it didn't take long for Aidan to hear more pounding feet on the pavement. Julia stumbled out of the driver's side door, looking a little shaken but no worse for wear. Falcone ran to her and scooped her into his arms.

Aidan saw Sofia through the glass of the front passenger side, but before he could react, Leo and Gavin were at the door, wrenching it open with a groan of metal. Evie came around from the other side of the van supported by Declan, and Aidan's stomach did a little flip. Where was Viv?

"She's in the back," Evie said in response to his unanswered question. "Viv is. I couldn't get her to wake up. I think she hit her head."

Before anyone else could, Aidan raced around to the other side of the vehicle and climbed into the open side of the van. Viv was slumped over in her seat, kept upright only by her seatbelt. Heart thudding a sluggish beat in his chest, he reached out to grip her chin, strangely relieved when he felt her breath warm against his fingers.

Not dead at least, but she had a nasty cut down her hairline from where her head had connected with the window. Bracing her shoulders, he reached down to release the seatbelt and gently rotated her until she was leaning back against his chest. He sank carefully down onto the opposite seat so he could draw her into his lap.

He brushed her hair off her face to inspect the cut. It didn't look deep. She probably wouldn't even need stitches, but she'd have a hell of a headache later. He tucked her hair behind her ear and tried not to think about how it was even softer than it looked. At the sound of approaching sirens, she stirred in his arms and looked up at him, eyes confused and a little hazy until she fully registered his face.

"What are you doing?"

"You were in an accident."

She rolled her eyes, wincing from the pain. "Yes, I was there. I remember the accident. I mean, why am I in your lap?"

His eyes narrowed, and he put a little steel into his voice. "I was making sure you weren't dead."

"Aww, Callahan." She laid a warm hand on his chest. "I didn't know you cared. Here I was thinking you'd be crossing your fingers, hoping to find me dead so you can get off the hook."

"Maybe you'll be less resilient next time," he said,

tone dry.

"You could only be so lucky."

He was saved from giving in to the urge to kiss her mouth —which she'd painted an enticing shade of plum today— when emergency vehicles pulled up to the scene. She slid carefully off his lap when the EMTs jogged over, holding onto the side of the van for support.

The police took a statement and arranged for a tow, and the EMTs confirmed what he suspected. No stitches but plenty of rest and pain meds and monitor for a concussion, though one was unlikely.

Once the official vehicles cleared out and the tow truck disappeared with the van, they gathered between the two SUVs. Evie curled into Declan's side, Julia into Falcone's, and Viv clutched her sister, a couple of butterfly bandages holding her cut closed.

"Declan, I didn't tell the cops this, but…" Evie paused, eyes meeting Julia's, who nodded. "I don't think that was an accident."

Aidan's body went rigid, and he found he couldn't tear his eyes away from Viv, who looked equally shaken.

"It was too fast," Julia agreed. "They didn't even try to brake. It was almost like…"

"Like they sped up. Gunned it," Viv finished, her voice small.

"Who the fuck would do that?" Leo demanded, wrapping a protective arm around Viv's shoulders.

Aidan glanced up at the traffic lights stretched over the intersection and counted one, two, three cameras. He shared a look with Declan.

"Whoever it is, Brogan is going to find him for us," Aidan said.

"And then we're going to fucking kill him," Declan added.

Chapter Five

Alone in the fitting room of the bridal boutique while the consultant scoured the stock for dresses that fit her mother's specific parameters, Viv studied her reflection in the mirror. She wouldn't normally consider herself a vain person, but the stark white bandages holding the angry red of her cut closed looked unsightly against her dark hair.

Add that to the purple bruise on her forehead she hadn't quite been able to disguise with makeup, and she'd been forced to endure everyone with working eyeballs asking questions about it. Or staring. She wasn't sure which one was worse.

She prodded at the bandages with a gentle finger. The pain meds she'd taken this morning had worn off, and the cut and the accompanying bump where she'd hit her head on the window pulsed with a dull ache that was more annoying than painful. She took the meds more to try and forget it was there than to ease the pain.

The wedding was a few weeks away. She had a million things to do, and she'd only met her unwilling fiancée twice.

She didn't have the time or the energy to wonder who was trying to take cheap shots at her father. Or the Callahans.

Just like she didn't have time to wonder about that look she'd seen in Aidan's eyes when she'd come to on his lap. Concern tinged with possessiveness. She didn't have time to wonder why it had sent a little thrill through her either.

He'd made it very clear what he intended this marriage to be, and he had no business looking at her in a way that made her want to wrap herself around him and see what all the fuss was about. The prick.

The consultant swept into the room, interrupting her thoughts and lugging dresses over her shoulder, and carefully hung her selections on hooks on the wall. Viv tried not to wrinkle her nose at the obscene amounts of tulle and lace that had gone into making skirts with so much volume. Her mother wanted to see a princess walk down the aisle, and Viv felt like anything but.

She didn't argue as she undid the belt of her satin robe and let the consultant help her step into the gown, zipping it up the back and securing it with clips to fit her frame. What would be the point? There was too much to do, too many things to think about to be picky about this.

She only needed something pretty and presentable that would look good in pictures. Liking it wasn't a requirement.

Gathering the skirt, she swished her way out from behind the curtain to gasps and excited whispers. Her mother's eyes were big and bright when Viv stepped onto the dais. Most everyone seemed to like it, but Evie's eyes were shrewd, locking on Viv's face in the mirror before dragging down her body to appraise the dress.

"What do you think?" her mother asked.

"It's...nice," Viv replied, tracing her fingertip over the delicate beading on the bodice.

"It'll be beautiful with the flowers I'm thinking of. But,"—

Viv caught her mother's eye in the mirror—"I want you to love it, and you don't love it. Try on something else."

Viv forced a smile and stepped off the dais. She hadn't put enough thought into getting married to envision the perfect wedding dress. She had no idea what she would or wouldn't love, and she didn't have time to try on every dress in the store to find out. They had to leave with a dress today. And they were due at the florist in two hours.

She paraded three more dresses similar to the first in front of her mother, her sister, her friends, and her future sisters-in-law. None of them were hideous, they were couture after all, but she didn't feel like a bride in any of them. Even though that thought was laughable. She wasn't a bride. She was a negotiation.

Preparing to show off the fifth dress, she paused at a knock on the door, surprised when Evie poked her head in.

"Hi. Can we talk for a minute?"

Viv nodded, and the consultant slipped out, closing the door behind her without a sound.

"Is everything okay?"

"Why wouldn't it be?"

Evie rolled her eyes. "Oh, I don't know. In less than a month, you'll be marrying a man with the emotional depth of a thimble in order to secure an alliance my husband wants. And while I can agree it's in the best interest of the *families*, I can appreciate it's pretty shitty for you."

Viv felt relief flood her chest. At least someone understood. Someone who didn't insist on painting a happy, smiling face on it.

"I know we don't have much time, and I'm sorry for that. But I want you to have as much of what you want as I can get for you. You deserve at least that much." Evie gestured toward the pouffy ball gown. "Is this thing what you want?"

The disdain in Evie's tone had Viv laughing. "God, no. I

look like I'm floating in cotton candy. But…" Viv caught her reflection in the mirror. "It's what my mother wants, and I'm her last daughter. She won't get to dress another bride like this."

When Viv turned away from the mirror, Evie's eyes were sad. Viv suddenly remembered that Evie's own mother had been murdered barely six months ago. In a blink, Evie's face cleared.

"Even still. Whatever you want, as long as I can get it for you. I can get this for you. I have an idea. Trust me?"

Surprisingly, Viv found she did. Or she was at least resigned to pleasing someone today, even if it wasn't herself. She nodded.

"Good. I saw a dress on the floor I think would be stunning on you. Let me grab it."

The consultant didn't come back in when Evie left, and Viv couldn't get out of the fluffy monstrosity on her own, so she waited. There were aspects of the dress she liked. The lace overlay on the bodice and the beading at the neckline that caught the light when she moved.

Evie slipped back in without knocking and hung up two dresses, neither of them white. She unzipped the first one, an ivory mermaid dress covered in delicate beading and embroidery. It had simple lace cap sleeves and a sweetheart neckline.

"Let's try this one first."

Viv turned so Evie could help her out of the ballgown and into the more fitted dress. It hugged every curve from breast to hip until it fell away at mid-thigh in a puff of tulle. It flattered, and she liked it better than the others, at least.

"This isn't my pick, but I'm trying an experiment. Ready?"

Curious, Viv nodded and followed Evie out to the waiting area. Sofia's eyes widened, and her mother's jaw dropped. Viv had to hide a smile as she stepped onto the dais.

"You don't like it?" Viv wondered when no one spoke.

"It's not what I was picturing," Julia admitted. "But you look beautiful. Do you like it?"

Viv caught Evie's eye before answering honestly. "It's not my favorite. There's one more I want to try on."

She hopped down and headed for the dressing room. This time the consultant helped her strip off the dress and pulled out the other one Evie had brought in. This one was more of a champagne color. The beading over the lace appliqué made it sparkle in a way that really made you think of bubbles in a glass of champagne.

It had a high neckline, not something she normally would have gone for, but the back swung low, exposing her shoulders and spine in a way that was more flattering than she would have anticipated. Lace sleeves hugged her arms to her wrists, and the dress was fitted to her knees until it flared out into a long train.

Steeling herself, she turned toward the mirror for the first time, breath catching at her own reflection. The idea of finding something she actually liked, let alone something that made her feel like a real bride, had seemed an impossible dream. But Evie had done it.

Viv didn't care what anyone on the other side of that door thought. She was going to get married in this dress. Smoothing her hands down over her hips, she smiled and turned for the door.

The silence when everyone saw her was so palpable her resolve faltered. Could she really go through with this dress if they all hated it? She stepped in front of the three-way mirror and gave a little twist to see the dress from all angles. Yes. She could.

"Well?" she asked when everyone simply stared.

"You look…" Sofia's words trailed off, and Viv's heart thumped in her chest.

"Incredible," Julia finished.

When Viv met her mother's eyes in the mirror, they were bright with tears. So were Sofia's. Even her friends were dabbing at their eyes. Only Evie's were alight with something that looked like triumph.

"That's it," her friend Felicity said. "That's the one."

Viv turned back to the mirror and smiled. At least she would get one thing she wanted on her wedding day. She was going to feel like a goddess.

Chapter Six

I t had been three days since the accident, and Aidan knew Brogan was no closer to finding out who rammed the minivan. Not because it was a difficult task, but because they'd been nonstop busy with a million other things. Word of the impending alliance and wedding had skirmishes popping up all over the city.

Smaller, less powerful groups hoped this was a moment to expand their territory or take a shot at the syndicate while their attentions were elsewhere. But syndicate eyes were always watching, and Aidan had seen more field action in the last week than he had in months. It was nice to get his hands dirty again.

Plus, he didn't mind the distraction. Anything to get that woman out of his thoughts. She'd invaded them like a nightmare, and if he wasn't careful, he'd catch himself thinking about her soft hair or the shape of her mouth or the way her legs would feel wrapped around his waist. It was infuriating.

He was already resigned to marrying her; his brain didn't need to torture him with thinking about her too. On top of that, he'd been reluctantly fielding questions about wedding shit all week. Tuxes and boutonnières and what did he think about the food. He didn't give a damn about any of it. Least of all his bride and her perfect ass.

He wasn't worried about her. He hadn't been worrying about her. Plucking her out of that car had been about nothing other than instinct. Plain and simple. If there was something to be found, Brogan would find it and they'd deal with it. Otherwise he wanted to think about her as little as possible.

He tugged a blood-splattered shirt off over his head and debated whether it was worth saving. On a shrug, he tossed it into the laundry bin instead of the trash. The maids were usually good at getting out blood. And discreet.

He chose a fresh shirt and pulled it on, noticing Declan in the doorway when he crossed back into the bedroom, eyes glued to his phone. He glanced up when Aidan cleared his throat.

"Successful raid, I'm told."

"No casualties. For us anyway."

Declan nodded. "Good. Let's go. I've got another assignment for you."

His brother didn't wait for acknowledgment or agreement before turning on his heel and taking off down the hall. Aidan rolled his eyes and grabbed his leather jacket off the back of the chair where he'd slung it, checking that his weapon was still secured to the waistband of his jeans.

He caught up with Declan on the stairs, but his brother still didn't say where they were going even as they loaded into his Range Rover and pulled out of the driveway. They were halfway to Center City before Aidan got sick of the silence.

"Is there going to be a time in the not-so-distant future

where you'll freely offer up details for whatever you keep hauling me off to?"

Declan's shoulders jerked like his mind had been far away, and he turned sharply to look at Aidan. "What?"

Aidan sighed. "Where the hell are we going?"

"We've got a supplier who keeps stepping out of line, and I want to remind him who the fuck he's dealing with."

"And you need me to do that? Why?" he asked at Declan's nod.

His brother grimaced before his features smoothed again. "I've got a hole in the family now, Aidan, and I need someone to fill it."

Finn. This would have been exactly the kind of thing Declan would have tapped Finn for. They were barely ten months apart, Finn and Declan, and from Aidan's earliest memories, they'd been thicker than thieves. Always reading each other's minds and finishing each other's sentences. You'd have thought they were twins.

Finn was a natural choice for Declan's right hand. No one had ever assumed it would be anyone else. If Declan was going to replace Finn, and he needed to because the syndicate required a clear chain of command in case the worst happened, Aidan had always assumed it would be Brogan. Or Evie.

"And you want that someone to be me?" He couldn't keep the doubt from his voice.

"I can't spare Brogan from the tech, and I'm not putting Evie in the field like that."

"So honored to be your first choice."

Declan sighed. "What in your recent history would have led me to believe you should have been?"

"I've never not followed an order." Aidan's hand curled into a fist on his knee. "Not once."

"No," Declan conceded. "That's true. Your defiance is death by a thousand paper cuts of attitude and sarcasm."

"You act like Finn never disagreed with you."

The click of the turn signal was deafening in the silence that stretched between them. Declan's voice was tired, strained when he spoke again. "Of course he did. He always pushed back when he thought he needed to. But he always had a reason."

Aidan scoffed. "So when Finn did it, he had a reason, but when I do it, it's just annoying? Thanks for clarifying."

"Finn always put the syndicate first. Do you have a strategic reason to hate my wife as much as you do?"

"She left once. No telling when she'll do it again. Next time she'll take a lot of sensitive intelligence about us with her."

Thanks to you, he wanted to say, but he bit his tongue.

Declan pulled into a rundown strip mall and parked in one of the last spaces, far away from any entrances. The parking lot was littered with garbage that would skid along the broken pavement when the breeze kicked up, and most of the shop signs were either hanging by a single bolt or missing entirely. The only evidence they'd ever been there was a dark spot where the sun hadn't faded the brick.

"I hope you never find yourself in a position to hurt the one you love. You'll crush her, and she might never forgive you."

"I won't," Aidan replied. "I don't ever intend on falling in love."

With a shake of his head, Declan climbed out of the SUV and waited for Aidan to join him. They walked in silence toward the pawnshop on the far corner of the strip mall. It was the only one on the entire strip that looked like it was still open for business.

"He's been jerking us around for months trying to negotiate a higher rate," Declan explained.

Aidan looked over at the change in his brother's tone. All the emotions he'd seen swirling on his brother's face in the car had been locked under a hard mask. His jaw was set, his eyes cold. He was ready for business.

"How much higher?"

"Thirty percent."

Aidan snorted. "He's insane."

"And we told him as much," Declan agreed, the corner of his mouth ticking up. "We replaced him with two other suppliers who give us better quality and faster delivery."

"So why are we bothering with this guy, then?"

"Because he's trying to blackmail me. And because we can."

Aidan followed Declan into the shop at the tinkle of a bell, swallowing a grin when the lanky man behind the counter paled at the sight of them. He had a distinct look of regret about him. At the attempted blackmail or getting caught, Aidan wasn't sure. Either way, he had to know why they were there.

"Declan, what brings you by? Finally ready to do business again?"

Aidan turned and flipped the lock on the door, finding a cord for a set of blinds and tugging it until they fell in a cloud of dust. He could almost hear the man's throat click when he swallowed from across the room. Aidan let his hand rest on the butt of his gun while Declan wandered the shop as if he was a browsing customer.

"You would think with all the money I've spent with you over the years, you'd stop doing business out of such a shithole."

"Old habits," the man said. "Did you...did you rethink my offer?"

When Declan turned, the man shrank back, stumbling backward when Declan advanced. Aidan almost felt sorry for the guy. Almost.

"Which offer are you referring to? You'll have to be more specific. Your offer to gouge me for weapons I can get cheaper and faster somewhere else? Or your offer to pay you off or you'll leak my name in an anonymous tip to the cops?"

Aidan hissed out a breath, and the man flinched at the sound. The son of a bitch.

"I only want what's fair."

Something in Declan's eyes had the man lurching back until he was pressed tight against the wall behind the dirty glass case. Aidan took a step forward so he could see the guy's hands clearly and make sure he wasn't going to reach for anything.

"You're not entitled to what's fair, only what we agreed on."

The man's chin ratcheted up in defiance even though he was clearly trembling. Either he was very brave or very stupid. Probably the latter.

"If you kill me, Wendy knows. She'll go to the cops for sure."

"Wendy is dead." Declan's smile was ruthless when the man whimpered, and he made a show of checking his watch. "Or she will be in about twenty minutes. Car accident, very tragic. It was a pleasure doing business with you, Ollie."

Before Ollie could protest, Declan drew his weapon and fired one round into his chest, holstering it as the man collapsed to the floor with a gasp.

"Make sure he's dead. I'll call McGee for cleanup."

Declan didn't spare Ollie a glance as he dug his phone out of his pocket and let himself out. Aidan stepped around the counter and stared down at the man clutching his chest. Still alive, but barely.

45

He drew his gun while the man looked up at him, eyes pleading. Aiming at his forehead, Aidan put him out of his misery with a bullet to the brain. When the man relaxed fully into death, Aidan turned on his heel and followed his brother into the street.

"McGee is close. Brogan is going to scrub the cameras."

"Threatening to give you up to the cops was a bold move."

Declan glanced back at the door as McGee's white panel van pulled into the parking lot and around the side of the building.

"He's not the first one to do it. I imagine he won't be the last."

Declan explained to McGee what happened and the level of cleanup he wanted, and they left the men to their work, jogging back across the parking lot to Declan's Range Rover. Once inside, Declan put the keys in the ignition but didn't start the engine.

"So…"

"So what?" Aidan replied.

"Can I trust you enough to have my back even when you don't agree with my choices?"

"Did you ever think you couldn't?"

Declan reached for the keys, and the car roared to life, but he didn't make eye contact as he pulled out of the parking lot and headed for home.

"A lot has changed in the last six months. I need to know you can do more than just follow orders. I need to know you want this, that you can put the needs of the syndicate ahead of your own."

"I thought I was already doing that by agreeing to your arranged marriage, your terms."

"And so willingly." Declan snorted.

Aidan gritted his teeth. "And you'd have gladly given up

your freedom to marry someone if Dad had demanded it? Someone who wasn't Evie."

"Yes," Declan said without hesitation. "I would have. The syndicate is bigger than all of us. It always has been. I'm giving you an opportunity to prove you're not as careless and reckless as you seem. Do you want it?"

"Yes," Aidan said after a beat. "I do."

Chapter Seven

Viv handed the customer their receipt and turned to help the next person in line, startled when she saw Evie and Libby across the counter.

"Everything okay?" Julia wondered, appearing at Viv's elbow. "Did something happen with the wedding? The accident?"

Evie waved a hand in the air and smiled. "Everything's fine. We were actually wondering if we could borrow you." Evie pointed at Viv. "For the day."

"Borrow me? I thought we weren't meeting until Friday to go over the last-minute stuff for the party."

"We're not. This has nothing to do with the wedding. Call it sisterly bonding." Evie glanced up when Sofia pushed through the swinging door that connected the kitchen to the front of the store. "Callahan sisters," she amended. "Unless you're too busy."

Viv glanced at her mother's nervous face, then back at Evie. She didn't know Evie well; they'd only met a handful of times, but she seemed nice enough. A little reserved, very no-nonsense. She reminded Viv a lot of Sofia in that way.

And Viv knew Libby from their years that overlapped at school and Mafia functions. She had no reason not to trust them, no reason to wonder if there was a wrong answer here. Maybe, at the very least, she could get some insight into her future husband by spending time with them outside the perfectly choreographed production wedding planning had become.

"Can you spare me today, Mama?"

Julia hesitated but ultimately smiled. "Of course. If we really need some coverage, Zara can help until the kids are out of school."

Viv slipped her apron over her head. "I have to grab my stuff from the back. I'll meet you in the parking lot."

She pushed into the kitchen and hung her apron on a peg, grabbing her purse from the drawer in the office. She had no expectations of how this day might go or what might be expected of her. She only hoped she wouldn't say the wrong thing or push the wrong buttons.

Evie was leaning against the hood of a royal blue Maserati, Libby at her side, when Viv rounded the side of the building. They looked friendly with each other. No, more than. They looked like friends, and it surprised Viv how much she wanted that too. These women would be a big part of her life from now on. She wanted them to like her.

"Sorry if we put you on the spot," Evie said, tipping her sunglasses down her nose and shooting Viv an apologetic look. "It was a last-minute decision over breakfast."

"Sisterly bonding?"

"Yeah," Libby said. "We've decided to make it a thing. And we're not even going to make you strip naked."

"I'm sorry, what?" Viv wondered what the hell she'd gotten herself into.

"Libby," Evie said, tone dry but teasing at the edges.

"Don't scare the poor woman. Besides, we took you shopping. We didn't make you streak across the front lawn."

Libby chuckled. "That's true. Though Brogan would've gotten even more of an eyeful if you had."

Evie grinned and shook her head. The easy, teasing banter had the tension draining from Viv's shoulders. She was used to this after growing up in a family with four other siblings and everyone vying for attention. Viv had learned to be the calm in the center of the storm, the steady one, the one who gave more than she took. It's how she'd learned to survive.

"So," she said, drawing Evie and Libby's attention, "what's on the itinerary?"

"I was thinking mani-pedis first." Evie twirled her keys around her finger. "Then maybe some lunch."

"Sounds good to me," Viv said when Evie and Libby both slid her an expectant look.

"Perfect. First, some pampering."

"Shotgun!" Libby yelled when Evie hit the button to unlock the car, and Viv chuckled.

They drove away from the bakery and toward the shops that, to Viv's mind, announced the wealth of the people who lived on Philadelphia's Main Line. Boutique stores with cream fronts and wrought iron accents, exclusive restaurants that only opened for dinner service, appointment-only salons and spas. A playground for the filthy rich.

Evie pulled into the parking lot of a salon and led the way inside. It was bigger than it looked from the outside, with soaring ceilings and ornate chandeliers hanging from long, thin chains. She thought the sound of a babbling brook was being piped in through speakers until she noticed the wall behind the receptionist's desk was actually a waterfall, the water cascading over iridescent blue and green tiles into a narrow pool below.

"Can I help you?" A woman with brown hair twisted into

a simple braid pinned around her crown looked up from the desk.

"I called earlier about a private room if you have one. Evie Callahan."

The woman's serene smile was at odds with the way she shot out of her chair and moved around the edge of the desk. "Of course, Mrs. Callahan. We were very happy to accommodate your request. Right this way."

The woman led them past a row of white tables fronted by wide leather chairs, past one room with pedicure stations and another with massage tables, and down a narrow hallway to a door marked Private Guests. Twisting the knob, she opened the door to reveal a large room set up with the same manicure and pedicure stations they'd just passed.

Ushering them in, the woman gestured to a bottle of champagne chilling in a bucket next to a row of expensive bottled water and a tray of artfully arranged finger foods. "Please help yourself to whatever you like, and if there's anything else I can get for you, don't hesitate to ask. My name is Janelle, and your technicians will be right in."

"Is that something you ever get used to?" Viv wondered once the door was closed.

"What?"

Viv turned to Libby. "Being treated like royalty when you introduce yourself as a Callahan?"

"Oh." Libby grabbed a bottle of water from the side table and claimed one of the pedicure chairs. "I don't know. I'm not a Callahan."

"Not for Brogan's lack of trying," Evie said, and Libby's cheeks flushed pink. "And no, you don't get used to it. Or at least I haven't. It was weird ten years ago, and it's weird now. But this salon is syndicate owned, so I suspect that has something to do with it."

Viv waited for Evie to sit before sinking into the last available chair and twisting to face Libby. "Has Brogan proposed?"

Libby's blush deepened. "A few times."

"But you don't want to say yes?"

"I do, but I…I'm not ready yet."

Evie cocked her head. "Why?"

Twirling a strand of blonde hair around her finger, Libby gave a frustrated huff. "I keep thinking he'll change his mind and decide it's not what he wants anymore." Libby winced. "Sorry, I probably shouldn't have said that."

Viv's stomach tightened, and she glanced at Evie, who gave her a sympathetic look. This was her path, and that was that. No point in wasting time feeling sorry for herself over it. "We all make choices. This one's mine. You have to make the right one for you."

"Still. I am sorry," Libby said again, voice going soft and thin. "About everything. If not for me, you wouldn't be here and—"

They all looked up when the door opened, and three women in identical smocks stepped in, smiling and carrying supplies on silver trays.

"Let's just have fun," Evie said, and Viv was grateful to steer the conversation in a different direction.

Everything seemed so much easier to manage when she was singularly focused on getting to the wedding. She didn't want to think about how she got here, whose fault it might be, or what would be expected of her after.

"The biscotti were delicious," Evie said into the silence while the technicians filled the basins of the pedicure chairs and motioned for them to dip their feet in. "I refused to share a single crumb."

Viv chuckled. "I can make more so you can share."

"That seems unlikely," Libby said. "She guarded those like a dragon. Not even Declan got a bite."

"I share a great many things with my husband. Biscotti is not one of them. A wife's prerogative."

"I'll keep that in mind."

Evie slanted Viv a look. "This is going to sound like a loaded question, but it isn't. How are you feeling about everything?"

Viv's spine straightened, and she fidgeted in her seat while the technician added a fragrant oil to the gently swirling water. How could that not be a loaded question? "I feel fine."

"I think it might be nice to just soak for a little bit." Evie caught the eye of one technician, and the woman nodded. Evie was silent until the last one filed out and closed the door with a soft click. "No one knows better than us what being in a relationship with a Callahan man is like. But you're a unique case and not just because this whole thing has been arranged."

"Because Aidan hates me, you mean." Viv wanted to claw back the words as soon as she said them. She didn't know if it was safe to speak the truth with these women.

"He doesn't hate you as much as he hates the idea of you. I wish it could be different. I wish this war had asked different things of all of us."

"But this is the price of peace," Viv murmured.

"Yeah," Evie sighed. "This is the price. But I meant what I said at the bridal boutique. I want you to have as much of what you want as I can get for you. For the wedding and beyond. You're family, or you will be, and family is everything."

Viv was saved from having to respond when a technician poked her head around the door, and Evie motioned them inside. Not like she had any idea what to say anyway. But Evie's words nestled down deep and took root.

Family. That's what you gained when you got married,

right? A new family. Aidan might hate her, but Evie didn't seem to, and Libby was eaten up with guilt for decisions that were far beyond her control, however responsible she felt.

Evie was offering far more than Viv ever expected, a place carved out in the Callahan family, and she was going to try to make the best of it. She'd been doing that her whole life. What was another sixty years or so?

Chapter Eight

Aidan sat in one of the chairs flanking the fireplace in his room, a series of files and papers spread out on the low table in front of him. They maintained just enough records to keep things straight and be able to pinpoint if anyone was screwing them, but not enough that they'd sink the whole damn ship if they ever got raided.

The syndicate was a business as much as a criminal enterprise, and Aidan was getting a peek behind a curtain he'd never expected to see. The hardest part wasn't memorizing dealers or suppliers or their long list of buyers that kept them in business. It was reading through page after page of Finn's looping script.

It had been over a month since he'd been killed in the raid, sliced open from the middle of his chest to the waist of his jeans. Finn had left behind a wife Evie's age, one of her best friends, and a young son. Evan wasn't even four.

Finn's absence was a heavy, dark cloud that hung over them, impossible to escape. For Aidan especially, because Brogan blamed him for Finn's death. He blamed him then for not acting quickly enough, and the way he wouldn't meet his eyes and barely spoke to him showed he blamed him still.

What Brogan didn't know is no one could blame him more than he blamed himself. Every night when he closed his eyes, he saw Finn's lifeless body dripping blood onto the dining room floor, and he wished he'd done something different. Anything to get upstairs faster, to cover Finn and his team.

Libby might have brought the nightmare to their door, but he was the one trapped in it, the one who jolted out of sleep in a cold sweat most nights with Finn's face swimming in his vision.

He dropped the paper he'd been reading on the table and rubbed his eyes before squeezing the bridge of his nose. He needed to focus. He only had a few more hours before he had to get ready for this stupid engagement party tonight.

At a noise in the doorway, he turned to look over his shoulder and found Brogan framed there, his eyes fixed on some point over Aidan's head. Aidan sighed.

"Got something. Upstairs in five." He was gone before Aidan could respond.

After shuffling the papers into neat stacks and sliding them back into their folders, Aidan stood and followed the hall to the stairs, taking them up to the third floor. It was mostly storage and staff rooms up here for the few permanent staff who were always in residence, but Brogan's tech lair was here, as well as a library Declan had renovated after Aidan had been outvoted on putting in a home theater.

The door was open when Aidan rounded the corner, and he could hear the hum of the machines and the wall-mounted air conditioner as he approached. Stopping in the doorway, he was greeted with the crunch of metal and glass breaking. Declan bit off a curse.

"Find something on the accident finally?"

Aidan ignored the way Brogan snorted under his breath as he pulled up the footage from another angle and displayed it on the largest screen over his head. He tapped a button and the footage played, this time without sound.

The van drove toward a red light, slowing slightly until the light changed and they picked up speed. Just as they pulled into the center of the four-way intersection, a black Jeep came careening from the cross street and rammed the van, making it spin a full 360 and teeter on two wheels before stabilizing itself.

The Jeep paused for a fraction of a second to see if anyone got out of the van. When no one did, they sped off in the opposite direction. Pedestrians and other drivers called the cops, while the women inside called their husbands instead. Brogan hit pause when Declan's SUV lurched to a halt and they both jumped out.

"So...not an accident."

"Doesn't look like one," Declan gritted out.

"Unfortunately, I don't have anything on a driver," Brogan said, tapping the keys and bringing up another angle. "The car has no plates on it, and if I had to guess, it's probably stolen."

"Can you get a good look at anyone inside the car?"

"No. The clearest shot I have is when they're sitting still after they ram them. And the sun is glaring off the windows too much to make out any kind of person, let alone get a clear image of their face."

"How did they know?"

"What?" Declan looked over his shoulder at Aidan.

Aidan stepped forward and reached out to point at the screen, dropping his hand when Brogan glared at him and shoving it into his pocket.

"The direction the Jeep comes from is lined with trees. There's no way they'd be able to identify exactly which car was coming through the intersection next, let alone time it perfectly to hit them. So how did they know?"

Declan turned back to the computer while Brogan typed furiously, searching for wider camera angles.

"A spotter?"

"Maybe," Brogan agreed. "Or they were hacked into cameras too. I'm not the only guy who knows how to hack things in the city. If they were going to spot, they'd have to be over in this area, which is cut off by most cameras. Let me see if…"

He lapsed into silence, and Aidan watched his fingers fly over the keyboard at a dizzying speed. Brogan's affinity for technology had always awed and impressed him. Except for the times he used it to cheat at video games. Then it just pissed him off.

"Here," Brogan finally said, bringing up a new video and enlarging it on the big screen with a couple keystrokes.

This angle caught two women walking together, one with a dog on a leash and the other pushing a stroller. Just before the intersection, they had to shift to single file to go around a man in a baseball cap who refused to move so they could pass.

He looked like he had a phone in his hand, but the footage was grainy, so it was hard to really tell. As the minivan approached the intersection, the man's head kept darting from the van to whatever he was holding in his hand. Until finally the van passed by in the bottom of the frame and then spun into the middle of the intersection.

The man pivoted toward the crash as if he was communicating with the Jeep, and once the Jeep disappeared from the top of the frame, he turned and walked quickly from the scene before cutting onto a side street and vanishing completely.

"How did they know where they were going to be? If you

plant a spotter, you know exactly where someone will be and when."

"I'm sure at least a dozen people would have known Viv was coming to the house and then going to look at venues. It wouldn't be hard to map out a couple of routes."

"Awfully lucky," Brogan replied.

"Or they were being followed," Aidan murmured.

"I don't like either fucking option. The question is, who was the ultimate target? Evie? One of the Falcone women? Or Viv specifically?"

Aidan frowned at Declan. "Why would anyone want to target Viv specifically?"

"Maybe they think if they take her out, they take the alliance out."

"Wouldn't they?"

Aidan forced himself not to think about how conflicted that made him feel. He might not want to marry the woman, but that didn't mean he wanted her to actually die to get him out of it. He wasn't that heartless.

"No," Declan replied matter-of-factly. "There are plenty of single women in the Mafia. Brogan, print out a picture of the spotter. Maybe one of the Falcones will recognize him."

As Declan walked out, Brogan tapped a few keys, and the printer in the corner behind Aidan whirred to life. When his brother turned and saw him standing there, his eyes narrowed.

"You can go."

Aidan sensed Brogan following him to the door, and when he turned to say something, the door closed in his face with a loud crack. Aidan dropped his head back with a sigh and stared at the ceiling before heading back to his room to punish himself with more of Finn's looping handwritten notes before the party.

Chapter Nine

Viv smoothed the fabric of her dress and clenched her hand into a fist to keep her fingers from shaking. For reasons she could not explain, her anxiety had been building to a fever pitch over this party all week.

So she'd kept herself busy with wedding planning. She had a dress that was currently being altered. They'd chosen the flowers, selected the bridesmaids and their dresses, and secured a beautiful location that was as close to a dream as she'd ever hoped for. Turns out you really could manage quite a lot if you could write enough zeros on a check. The Callahan name on said checks didn't hurt.

It opened doors for her she didn't even know existed, let alone were closed. When Evie had mentioned to the florist that Viv wanted a flower that was rare this time of year, one of the few things she'd ever seen clearly about her wedding day, the woman all but pledged to fly to South America to prune it herself. Similar promises happened at the venue when Viv mentioned her groom by name.

But those things only kept her busy during the day. At night Viv was left with entirely too much time to think. Lying awake in the dark, staring at the ceiling and thinking about all the terrible ways this party could be a disaster of epic proportions.

The whole thing felt more manageable when it existed behind closed doors. She'd expected a hastily thrown together ceremony in front of close family and friends before being deposited wherever Aidan intended to keep her until his purpose had been fulfilled. Not an event that landed her on the front page of the society pages next to a man who seemed less than willing to play his part at all, let alone convincingly.

"You look beautiful."

Turning from the full-length mirror, Viv smiled at Sofia standing in the doorway. She ran a hand over the hair she'd swept into a loose chignon. She'd wanted to wear it up to keep herself from thinking about Aidan's fingers in it all night.

"Is it too much?" Viv wondered, glancing back to survey the long white gown.

"No." Sofia shook her head. "You look positively bridal."

"I figured since my wedding dress wasn't white, I'd give Mama some kind of traditional look." Viv eyed the box in Sofia's hand. "What's that?"

"A courier just dropped it off for you."

Sofia held out the small, neatly wrapped package and Viv looked at it warily. Who the hell would send her gifts at this hour? Tearing away the paper and letting it flutter to the floor, she lifted the lid, eyebrows raising at the small velvet jewelry box nestled among white tissue paper.

"More jewelry from the family vault?" Sofia wondered, stepping closer. "I hope it's not as heavy as that thing they want you to wear for the wedding."

"Seems too small for another chandelier necklace," Viv said, popping open the lid.

Secured to a satin cushion was a delicate pair of pearl and diamond drop earrings. Simple but beautiful and perfectly to her taste. She ran a fingertip gently over the bauble, making it sparkle in the overhead light. Had Aidan sent her jewelry to wear tonight? And was it a gift or a command?

Sofia let out a low whistle. "Those are gorgeous. Is there a note?"

Passing the earrings to her sister for closer inspection, Viv dug under the tissue paper in the box and found a carefully folded slip of paper. Pulling it out, she tossed the box on the edge of the bed and unfolded it, smoothing the creases with her fingers.

You don't have to wear these tonight, but I thought they might go with your dress, and I wanted you to have them. -Evie.

Viv couldn't explain the swift feeling of disappointment that flooded her knowing the gift was from Evie and not Aidan, but she shrugged it off. Aidan had no reason to send her gifts of any kind, let alone earrings as beautiful as these. It was a sweet gesture from her future sister-in-law. That was enough.

Sofia was lifting them out of the box when Viv reached up to unhook the earrings she'd already fastened in her ears. She replaced them with the pearls and moved closer to the mirror to study them.

"They are exactly the kind of thing you'd pick out for yourself," Sofia said.

They danced when Viv turned to slip on her heels, and she smiled. "They are." She took a deep breath, reaching out to stop Sofia's retreat with a hand on her arm. "Sof...tell me this is going to be okay and I'm not going to crash and burn tonight."

Her sister reached out to grip her elbows, giving them a reassuring squeeze. "Of course you're not going to crash and burn. If you can get the two of you to mostly stick together throughout the night, you can make up the story as you go along. It'll be fine."

Viv nodded and followed her sister into the hallway and down the stairs on legs she willed to stop shaking. Her parents, Nico, and Sofia's husband, Tim, were waiting for them at the bottom.

"How do you feel?" her mother asked, concern knitting her brows.

"Like I might throw up everything I've eaten for the last three days at any moment. But..."

"But?"

Viv slid her gaze to her father and forced herself to smile. "I'm sure it'll be fine."

For the first time since he'd asked this of her, Viv saw guilt in her father's gaze. She didn't think she'd get through the night in one piece if he said whatever he was about to say.

"It's fine, Papa. Really. Let's go so we're not late."

They took two separate cars, and Viv was glad she wasn't the one navigating the snarl of Saturday traffic in Center City. Evie had insisted on neutral territory for tonight's party, neither Callahan nor Mafia owned. A place with no bad blood, signifying a fresh start. After all, they were making history.

The guest list had been carefully curated with representatives of the syndicate's original five families and their wives invited. Well, original four now that Evie's father was dead and she had no brothers. Plus the men who had shown the most loyalty to her father since he'd stepped up as Don. If criminals were going to rub elbows with the city's elite, they needed to be ones they could trust.

The event staff was still putting the finishing touches on the room when they arrived, but Viv found herself impressed that Evie had pulled together a party this fast. Then again, the woman didn't really take no for an answer—about anything.

"God, you look incredible," Evie said from behind them, spinning her finger in the air to indicate Viv should twirl. "Very bridal." When her eyes caught on Viv's earrings, her gaze softened and she smiled. "You wore them."

Viv reached up to finger one of the pearls. Something in Evie's tone sounded sad. "They're stunning. Something I'd have picked out for myself. Are they from the family vault?"

Evie reached out to squeeze Viv's arm. "They were my mother's."

Viv's eyes went wide. "Oh. Well, I'll make sure I get them back to you at the end of the night."

"Of course not." Evie waved the offer away as if it was an insult. "They were a gift. I want you to have them."

Emotion tightened Viv's throat, and she nodded. "Thank you. That's very sweet."

They shared a long look, and Viv thought Evie nodded ever so slightly before turning to Falcone. "The men are on their way. Something came up last minute they wanted to look into. I think they might want your help with that."

"However I can."

"Good. Now, I'm going to borrow the bride for a quick minute before everyone else arrives." Evie led Viv away under the guise of showing her something and waited for Libby to join them before speaking. "You're nervous."

"Oh God." Viv pressed a hand to her stomach. "Is it that obvious?"

"No. I'm just very good at reading people. Don't be nervous. You'll be fine, and Aidan has been warned to be on his best behavior. If he gives you a hard time, just remember it's easier to fight fire with fire where he's concerned. Give as good as you get," Evie added at Viv's raised brows. "Though I don't imagine you have any difficulty with that."

Viv started to respond but was interrupted when the door to the far end of the ballroom opened for the Callahan men.

First Declan, then Brogan's unmistakable form. Even in a suit, he looked like a bouncer.

"He's coming," Declan said in response to Evie's frown, leaning down and pressing a kiss to her lips. "He's… regaining his composure."

"Great," Viv muttered.

"Don't worry. He's been reminded of what's good for him. A vision, Viv, as always," Declan added before leading his wife away.

Viv watched them go, stopping in front of her parents to make small talk. Her eyes tracked to where Libby and Brogan were standing, Brogan rubbing Libby's arms and murmuring against her forehead. Libby looked as nervous as Viv felt.

She'd only heard snatches of what happened to Libby when she faced DiMarco. None of it good. It took a certain kind of strength and resilience to be here tonight to support the family. A show of commitment even if she and Brogan weren't legally bound yet.

At another click of the door, she steeled herself, mentally preparing to greet guests on her own until Aidan was *composed* enough to join her. But when she looked over, it wasn't guests. It was him.

He'd skipped the suit his brothers were both wearing, whether as a tiny rebellion or to stand out, she wasn't sure, but he was still imposing in dark gray slacks and a navy blue sweater that stretched over his broad shoulders. She imagined it did wonders for his eyes.

He paused as the door closed behind him, eyes dragging down the length of her body and back up again. When he advanced, she found she couldn't move. The only sensation that registered was the tingling in her spine from the way he wouldn't stop looking at her and the dull thud of her heart.

He stopped in front of her, his eyes tracing over the swell of her breasts under the draped neckline, the dip of her waist, the curve of her hips, lingering on the top of the slit that exposed her left leg up to mid-thigh before trailing down to her feet and back up to her face. Christ, she was in trouble.

Closing the distance between them in quick strides, he threw her so off balance that she had to brace a hand on his chest to steady herself. She knew touching him was a mistake the moment she did it, the heat of his chest flooding against her palm and shooting up her arm. The man was a walking pheromone.

Eyes locked on hers, he leaned down to slowly press a kiss against her cheek, and the spicy notes of his cologne enveloped her. Leave it to him to smell exotic and forbidden. He trailed the tip of his nose across her cheekbone and whispered against her ear, his breath hot on her skin.

"If this dress is supposed to make you look virginal, it isn't working."

She jerked back to look up at him and the wicked grin that spread across his face. Fire with fire then, if that's how he wanted to play it.

"Not virginal, Callahan," she said, shifting so her body pressed against his in a way that had something flickering in his icy blue eyes. "Like walking sin. Seems like it might be working just fine."

His mouth set in a hard line when the doors opened behind them, and the hum of conversation drifted through as guests arrived. His eyes dipped down to her lips, and she traced her tongue across them, satisfied when his eyes darkened before darting back up to meet hers.

They stood in the center of the room and let people come to them like some choreographed receiving line. She recognized all the syndicate men and their wives—she'd been studying—but she pointed out all the Mafia people to Aidan, and they let the socialites introduce themselves, although some she recognized from the media. Declan really knew how to rub elbows with the rich and famous—the very rich.

When a waiter passed by with a tray of glasses, she reached for his hand, lacing her fingers through his and gripping it tightly. She did not want to know the stupid things that would come out of his mouth if he had too much to drink tonight.

He leaned down to whisper against her ear, jaw clenched. "What are you doing, *darling*?"

She looked up at him with a sweet smile, pressing into his side as if he'd just said something romantic. "It's probably best you remain perfectly sober tonight. Don't you think?"

He lifted a single brow. "I don't know what's more insulting. That you're trying to control whether I drink or that you think one glass of champagne will get me drunk. Both. They're both insulting."

He plucked the flute she'd taken a single sip from out of her hand and set it on a nearby table. "If I'm not drinking, neither are you."

Irritation flared in her chest, but she tamped it down. Fair was fair, after all. "Whatever you say, *sweetheart*."

When the next couple came to greet them, he shook her hand free and slid his arm around her waist instead, fingers drawing small circles on her hip in a way that was very distracting. She couldn't even remember the wife's name by the time they stepped away.

"What are you doing?" she asked through a forced smile.

"I'm just pretending, honey. As instructed."

Over the next hour, he snaked his arm slowly up her torso, first drawing lines up and down the back of her arm, then draping it across her shoulders, until he finally had his hand wrapped loosely around the back of her neck, his thumb rubbing small circles over the sensitive spot behind her ear.

She wanted to both melt into his touch and knee him in the balls for making her legs so wobbly. She turned to tell him to knock it off when the sound of clinking glassware got her attention.

Declan stood at the front of the room and motioned for the music to be turned down, smiling one of those million-dollar smiles when the crowd quieted and turned to face him.

"I want to thank all of you for coming tonight. Marriage is one of the hardest things I have ever done, and even though I wasn't sure my baby brother would ever find the woman who could put up with him for the rest of his life, he somehow managed it."

Viv felt Aidan stiffen beside her, and he dropped his hand from her neck. She looped her arm through his as much to anchor him and his temper as to touch him again.

"Viv," Declan continued. "I couldn't ask for a better partner for my brother, and I know you two will do every-thing in your power to make a strong, lasting relationship. To a lifetime of happiness."

"To a lifetime of happiness!" The room cheered before downing their glasses.

"Well, that wasn't very subtle," Viv muttered, and Aidan huffed out a laugh.

Someone in the crowd started chanting for a kiss, and all eyes pivoted from Declan to where they stood in the center of the room. Jesus Christ, she couldn't catch a break.

She turned to him and kept her voice low. "Just make it quick, Callahan. A brief moment of suffering."

But he wouldn't make it quick. She knew the moment she met his eyes, knew it in the way his hand slid up to cup her jaw. He could have given her a quick, innocent peck to satiate the crowd of hungry onlookers. He didn't.

He took with an intensity that left her breathless. Some-where in the recesses of her mind, she thought she should care that a room full of people was watching them right now, but she couldn't force herself to. Not as his tongue teased against hers and his hand tightened on her jaw, his thumb pressing under her chin to ease her head back.

He was igniting a fire he would refuse to extinguish. She'd have to remember to hate him for it later. Right now, she was busy.

Chapter Ten

W hen he pulled back, her eyes fluttered open and were cloudy with want. Her lips were swollen from his kiss, her lipstick slightly smudged. He heard chuckles from around the room as the music and conversation resumed. She finally looked as unsettled as he'd felt since seeing her in that damn dress.

"Might want to go touch up your lipstick, princess. Oh, that's the one, isn't it?" he asked when her eyes narrowed.

"You can *not* call me that."

"I can. I will." His eyes glittered as she met his gaze without flinching. "It's fitting, I think." He slid his hand down to the small of her back, grinning when she shivered.

"I need a break, sugar lips." His lip curled, and she grinned. "Don't like that one? I guess I haven't found the perfect one for you yet. I'll have to keep trying. I'm going to make a quick run to the restroom. But you'll have to actually let go of me first."

He released her slowly and watched her go until she disappeared around the corner to the bathroom. Exasperating, headstrong, sexy woman. She'd painted her mouth an enticing shade of dark pink that stood out in stark contrast to her white dress—her very tight white dress.

He'd wanted to taste her lips from the moment he'd seen her across the room, could think of little else while he smiled and nodded through their string of polite exchanges with couple after couple. Quick and chaste had been the goal when Declan backed them into a corner, but temper had snapped through him at his brother's speech, and rather than lashing out, he'd funneled it into her mouth instead.

Her tempting, kissable, heart-shaped mouth. She'd hardly resisted. If they hadn't been standing in the middle of a room full of people, it wouldn't have taken much more before he had her dress shoved up around her waist and his cock buried deep inside her.

That was the problem. He shouldn't want her. He didn't want to want her. Wanting her was not in his plan for how this marriage would go. And yet he couldn't seem to stop himself. The sooner he scratched the itch, the sooner he could get it out of his system.

Without her there to stop him, he flagged a waiter down for a glass of scotch and crossed to where the two people he knew as well as his own brothers stood, watching him with knowing expressions.

"That was some kiss," Rory said.

"Declan wanted a show."

Liam snorted. "Is that what that was?"

"Shut up."

He accepted the glass of scotch from the waiter, irritated at the quick pang of guilt in his gut before he brushed it away. The insufferable woman wasn't his mother. He was allowed to drink at his own engagement party.

"The date of your impending nuptials draws ever closer. Feeling claustrophobic yet?" Liam wondered.

"You two make marriage sound like a punishment," Rory scoffed, eyes finding his wife across the room.

"It is," Liam and Aidan said together.

"At least I'm well adjusted enough to date. This one is jumping right from hundreds of one-night stands to marriage. I honestly feel bad for the woman."

"Don't," Aidan drawled. "She'll have plenty of money to occupy her time."

"Because that's what women want when they get married." Rory snorted. "Cash."

"So you're saying Bridget married you for your charm and good looks and not your sizable bank account."

Aidan tuned out their same old bickering argument when he saw Viv round the corner from the bathrooms again. He expected her to search for him across the room, but she didn't, smiling instead in the opposite direction. He frowned, following her gaze to her family.

Viv made her way to them and hugged both her parents and then her siblings. She looked truly relaxed for the first time all evening. Her smile had lost that forced sharpness, and when she laughed, it was quick and easy.

She looked up and caught him staring at her from across the room, and her smile took on that hard edge again. Rather than motioning for him to join her, she gave her mother's cheek a kiss and made her way to him instead. Something stirred in him at the way her eyes always found him even when she stopped to greet people until a man he didn't recognize stepped into her path.

When she registered him, she took a step back. It was subtle but deliberate, and it put every sense he had on alert. The man was animated, waving his hands in the air and jabbing his finger at her. Whatever he was saying, she shook her head and took another step back. The man advanced.

When she turned and caught his eye again, she didn't

look bored or annoyed; she looked terrified. Instantly he veered away from Rory and Liam, ignoring their confused questions. Weaving his way through the thinning party goers, he jerked to a stop at her side.

"Is everything all right here?"

The relief was obvious in her face, her voice. "Oh, there you are. I was just catching up with an old friend."

Her voice caught on that last word, and Aidan shifted, subtly placing his body between them and forcing the man to take a step back.

"It's nice to meet you…"

"Collin," the man said, forcing a smile though he was gritting his teeth. "Collin Milano."

"Nice to meet you, Collin. How do you know my fiancé?"

He used the word deliberately and watched as it had the desired effect. Collin's eyes flashed with anger and possessiveness. He felt Viv's fingers grip the back of his sweater. Collin scared her, and Aidan wanted to know why.

As if suddenly remembering where he was, Collin's face smoothed into a polite mask. Something that had Viv stepping even closer.

"We've known each other a long time. Intimately at one point. We were practically engaged."

"Lucky for me you didn't go through with it."

Collin's head tilted, his grin tight. "Looks that way. Would you mind giving us some privacy? I'd love an opportunity to catch up with Viv. Alone."

"No," Aidan replied, tone deadly. "I don't think I'll be doing that."

Collin's eyes darted over Aidan's shoulder. "Come on, Viv. For old time's sake."

Aidan looked back at her, noting the way she swallowed hard. He reached back and slid his palm against hers, lacing their fingers together. Collin's eyes dropped to their joined hands, narrowing on her engagement ring.

"A ruby doesn't seem like something you would wear. You deserve a diamond."

"I…" She cleared her throat. "I picked this one out. I like it."

"Well, no accounting for taste. You always did need me to show you what was best," Collin said, gaze sweeping over Aidan. "You're making a big mistake here, Viv. You'll realize it eventually. Maybe I'll even be gracious enough to take you back when you do."

Aidan moved to step forward, but Viv's fingers tightened on his, holding him in place. Declan would hate a scene, but it would be for a supremely good reason. Not wanting to take his eyes off Collin for long, Aidan glanced up to where her family had been standing, catching Leo's attention and lifting his brows.

Her brother instantly recognized Collin, and the look on his face was pure murder. He didn't hesitate to make his way toward them.

"I think it's time for you to leave," Aidan said.

"And how are you going to make me without causing a scene?"

"Collin." Leo's voice was low and made Collin visibly cringe. "What the fuck are you doing here?"

Collin pivoted so he could see both Aidan and Leo and smiled wide. "This is a party, isn't it?"

"Not for you," Leo said. "Remember what happened the last time you showed up at a party you weren't invited to?"

Collin's gaze flicked to Viv, and he dragged his tongue across his teeth. "I fucked your sister in a bathroom?"

Leo's hands balled into fists at his sides, and Aidan felt Viv press against him.

"And then I broke your nose. I would be happy to do it again."

Collin flinched when Leo reached up to grip his arm but quickly recovered, trying and failing to wrench his arm away.

"Let go of me."

"If I do, you'll find my fist in your face. And I'm sure his won't be far behind." Leo nodded at Aidan.

"Count on it."

Leo signaled to Gavin, who appeared on Collin's other side in an instant, and resigned, Collin shot an ugly smile at Viv, laughing when she cringed away from him.

"You never did know what was good for you," Collin said as they led him across the room and out the doors.

As soon as he was gone, Aidan felt Viv start to shake, her breath coming in shallow gasps. Ignoring the confused stares, he tightened his grip on her hand, leading her away from the crowd and around the corner opposite the bathrooms.

When they were out of sight of the party, he eased her back against the wall and released her. She pressed her palm to her chest, and he watched tears form at the corners of her eyes.

"Viv." She jerked at her name on his lips, and he softened his voice. "Viv. He's gone, and you're okay."

"He's...he's..." Her breath sawed in and out of her lungs and her fingers trembled.

"Listen to me. He's gone, and he's not going to hurt you. What do you need?"

"Just...I just..."

She reached out and gripped his hips, pulling him closer and wrapping her arms around his waist. Bracing his forearm against the wall, he reached up to cradle the back of her neck when she dropped her forehead against his shoulder.

When she pressed closer, he slipped his free hand around

her waist and drew her body tight against his. The minute he did, she relaxed ever so slightly, her fingers tangling in the fabric of his sweater as she sucked in deep, shuddering breaths.

"You're okay," he murmured against her ear. "You're safe."

He could tell the minute she eased all the way out of her panic attack when her body froze. Her head snapped up, and she dropped her arms from his waist. Reluctantly, he slid his hand from around her and stepped back to put the space between them she hadn't wanted moments earlier.

"I'm sorry. That was...embarrassing." She puffed out her cheeks and then blew out a slow breath. "Collin and I...we were..."

"You don't have to explain it to me."

She dropped her gaze to her hands and fidgeted with her engagement ring. She didn't look at him when she continued.

"We used to date. For a few years. He asked me to marry him this spring, and I said no. We did fuck..." She flinched even though he said nothing.

"We did have sex in a bathroom. Then he asked me to marry him, and I said no. When I did, he hit me."

Aidan fought to keep his voice even despite the rage that burned like a fire inside him. "He hit you?"

She nodded. "When Leo saw the bruise, he broke his nose. I'm sorry. I didn't think...I didn't know he was invited tonight."

"Was that the first time? That he hit you?"

Her answer was in the way she wouldn't meet his eyes. He reached up to place a single fingertip under her chin, tilting her head up slowly.

"He will never touch you again. Understand?" He waited for her to nod. "If he does, I will kill him."

"There you are," Leo said, appearing around the corner.

"Collin's gone. I regret I did not get to break the fucker's nose again. You okay?"

Viv nodded, plastering on a small smile. "Yeah. I'm fine."

Leo flicked a glance at Aidan, who nodded confirmation before he said, "Good. There are a few more guests we're trying to shepherd out the door, but then we should be okay to take you home. Come on. Mama wants to make sure you're all right."

Viv glanced at Aidan before skirting the corner with her brother. Aidan shoved his hands deep into his pockets, clenching them into fists to keep from punching a hole in the wall. Or three.

The fear in Viv's eyes, the way she'd clung to him while she panicked, the knowledge that anyone had ever laid a hand on her had unlocked something inside of him. He knew Collin wouldn't have to lay another finger on her for him to make good on this threat. He was already planning on killing him.

It didn't take long for the last of the guests to finally leave, and they were left with just the Callahans and the Falcones in the ballroom while the staff began breaking things down around them. Someone had already briefed his brothers on what happened.

"He wasn't on the guest list. I don't remember the name Milano being on it anywhere," Evie said.

"He wasn't," Julia agreed. "The bastard."

"I'm sorry he—"

"Stop apologizing," Aidan snapped, glad to see some fire come back into her eyes at his command. "You have nothing to be sorry for."

"Is he going to be a problem, this guy?" Declan wanted to know.

"I didn't think he would be. He's an asshole who likes to

hit women when he doesn't get his way." Falcone's gaze landed on his daughter.

"Maybe she should move into Glenmore House," Evie suggested. "Until the wedding."

"I think that's a little extreme," Viv countered. "He crashed a party and said some mean things."

"He terrified you," Leo pointed out.

"I've been afraid before. That doesn't mean I need to be under lock and key."

"What about a protective detail, then?"

Viv rolled her eyes at Gavin. "I have a million and one things to do before the wedding. I hardly need someone to follow me around the whole time. Collin is an asshole, but we don't need to overreact about it."

They let the conversation drop as they shrugged into coats and made their way to the parking lot. Aidan was so busy keeping a careful eye on Viv that he nearly ran into the back of Brogan when he stopped short.

"Son of a bitch," someone muttered.

Aidan turned in the direction of their collective gaze and sucked in his own breath. Both Falcone vehicles had their windows smashed, one windshield caved so violently into the front seat it was a wonder it was still attached. When Aidan shifted, he could make out words carved into the paint. Whore, slut, bitch.

"A protective detail," he bit off. "No arguments."

"But—"

"Please, *passerotta*," Falcone said.

Viv visibly softened, then sighed. "Okay. But who?"

"I'll do it," Leo said.

"No." Falcone shook his head. "I can't spare you right now."

"I will," Aidan said before he could stop himself. "Unless you object," he added, turning to Declan.

Declan's stare was curious, but he shook his head. "No objection. Maybe we can coordinate a few meetings around whatever you have to do for the wedding." He looked to Evie, who nodded her agreement. "Fine, then."

"You do not want to follow me around for the next two weeks," Viv said when the group moved forward to handle the vandalized cars.

Except he did, and that was a problem. "Well, someone has to keep you alive. You seem to have no sense of self-preservation."

She snorted. "I thought we already decided you should be happy if I die. Then you're free from this obligation and from me. Unless you plan to be a piss poor bodyguard and get me killed anyway."

She stepped away from him, and his hand shot out to grip her wrist, tugging her back against him. He snaked his arm around her waist to keep her from wriggling away.

"Don't worry, princess. You'll be safe with me."

"I'm not so sure," she murmured, stumbling back when he suddenly released her.

She backed away from him slowly before turning and joining her parents, who'd already arranged for rides and someone to come junk the cars before the event staff saw them and called the cops.

He rubbed at the back of his neck as he watched her, ignoring the unfamiliar ache that tightened his chest. He wasn't so sure either.

Chapter Eleven

By the third stop on Monday, Viv was beginning to regret agreeing to this arrangement, and she had a headache blooming behind her left eye to prove it. At this point, the idea of Collin murdering her sounded like a vacation.

Her main goal when Aidan picked her up—late—had been to get through the laundry list of tasks Evie emailed over the night before as quickly as possible. There was only one appointment today she was actually looking forward to. Cake tasting.

They'd sent in a design late last week but couldn't make their schedules match up to set up a cake tasting. So Viv had graciously—or selfishly—volunteered to go on her own.

She was looking forward to having this one blissful thing she got to pick all by herself without having to ask or pretend to care about the opinion of half a dozen other women. And her stupid fiancé was ruining it.

The man had been in a mood all afternoon, and she was ready to punch him in the throat. Nothing was more irritating than having a man follow you around complaining about how much there is to do while simultaneously doing none of it.

After approving the final proof for the programs, place cards, and menus at the printers, Viv followed Aidan back into the sunshine and climbed into his truck, rubbing at the ache behind her eyebrow.

"Please tell me we're almost done."

She squeezed the bridge of her nose. "One more stop. You don't even have to come inside for this one. You can wait in the car."

"That hasn't worked at the last two places. I doubt it's going to work at the next one." He pulled away from the curb and followed the directions she gave.

"If you were just going to whine the entire time, why did you volunteer?"

"I do not whine," he snapped, and she snorted.

"Sorry, I'm not familiar with a more manly term for what you've been doing all day. It isn't as if I enjoy dragging you behind me planning a wedding we're both dreading. Just drop me off at this last place, and I'll take a cab home or something."

"Absolutely not. I gave my word, and I'm keeping it."

"You know, Callahan, sometimes the execution of the thing matters as much as simply doing it. I appreciate you making sure I don't get assaulted on the sidewalk, but I don't see why you have to make us both miserable in the process. Unless miserable is your default setting. Lucky me," she muttered as he pulled into the parking lot of the upscale bakery.

He put the car in park and studied the elaborately decorated cakes in the display window.

"I thought you already picked out a cake."

She paused with her hand on the door, eyebrows shooting up. "How do you know that?"

"I do listen when Evie rattles off the long list of things she insists I know about this wedding."

"Begrudgingly, I'm sure. Tell me, then."

He looked over at her. "What?"

"What do you know about the wedding?"

"Is this a pop quiz?"

"Yes. Come on, Callahan." She shifted so she was fully facing him, a smile tugging at her lips when his frown deepened. "I'm on the edge of my seat here."

"Forget I said anything."

"Oh, no." She reached over and snatched the keys out of the ignition, holding them against her chest. "Tell me two things you know about the wedding."

"Don't think I won't come over there and get those," he said, eyeing where her hand clutched the keys between her breasts.

"Two things," she repeated, ignoring the way his stare made her blood hum.

He heaved a dramatic sigh, and she fought hard not to roll her eyes. "The flowers are orange and red. Expensive. Being flown in from Costa Rica or something."

"Brazil," she said, trying to mask her surprise. "And the second thing?"

His fingers tapped a quick beat on the steering wheel, and she thought she had him until he finally said, "There are two flower girls."

She cocked her head and held his gaze. "Why?"

His eyes dropped to her breasts again and lingered. "You said two things. I gave you two things. But it's because you have two five-year-old nieces and couldn't pick which one, so you picked both."

Without another word, he held out his hand for the keys, and she reluctantly dropped them into his palm.

"Color me surprised, Callahan. You do listen. Now are

you going to ruin this cake tasting experience for me? Because I've been looking forward to it all day."

"That's what we're doing here? Cake tasting?"

She cast her eyes to the ceiling before climbing out of the truck. "I've mentioned it no fewer than three times today," she said when he joined her.

"Yeah, but I wasn't listening all those other times. I like cake."

"That's great," she said, starting across the lot. "But I don't want your opinion. You can eat cake in silence." She ignored him when he scoffed. "I haven't been able to make a single goddamn decision about this wedding on my own. I want to make this one."

He held up his hands in surrender while she pulled open the shop door and motioned for him to go ahead of her. When he refused, she took a deep, calming breath and brushed past him.

As they approached the counter, she watched the woman standing next to a case of cupcakes rake her eyes over Aidan from head to toe. The vicious stab of jealousy caught her so off guard that when the man closest to them asked how he could help, she jumped.

"We're here for the cake tasting for the Callahan wedding."

"Oh, of course. Have a seat, and I'll get you set up."

The woman continued to stare as they claimed a table by the front window, and Viv grit her teeth. The fucking nerve.

"What is wrong with you?" Aidan asked, glancing up from his phone. "You look like you're about to punch someone."

"That woman is practically eye fucking you," she replied, trying to keep her voice light.

He set his phone on the table and casually glanced over his shoulder. "Jealous, princess?"

83

"Oh, please. It's just rude. I mean, I'm sitting right here, and we're tasting wedding cake flavors. Catch a clue, lady."

He scratched his fingertips across his jaw. "I don't know. You seem jealous."

"I am *not* jealous. I'm sure you've spent plenty of time getting your dick wet since finding out about our unhappy union." She ignored him when his eyes narrowed on her face. "Which reminds me. You should probably get tested and try to restrain yourself before the wedding."

Before Aidan could speak, the man pushed a cart up next to the table and set silverware, napkins, and glasses of water in front of them.

"These are our most popular flavors," he said. "But if you want to try any other combinations, let me know, and I'd be happy to make you a sample. And if you have any questions, just give a shout."

When they were alone again, she reached for a piece of chocolate cake, pretending not to notice how Aidan was staring at her even though it had butterflies doing somersaults in her stomach.

"Chocolate cake with chocolate buttercream and raspberry filling." She read from the card next to the slice, jerking back when his fork shot out and smacked hers away with a metallic clunk. "What are you doing?"

"Get tested for what, exactly?"

Viv blinked. "I know the nuns don't give a thorough sex education, but surely they talked about STIs."

He dropped his fork on the plate and slid it away from her across the table. "I do not have an STI."

"This is not a personal indictment of your very active sex life, Callahan. But considering condoms are not an option for us, I would appreciate a little consideration on your part."

She reached for the cake, scowling when he knocked her fork away again and took a big bite.

"You see this?" she said, gesturing to him with her fork. "This is you ruining the cake tasting for me."

"You just accused me of having a venereal disease," he replied.

Viv lifted another piece of cake off the cart and sighed loudly. "I did not. I merely said you should do the smart thing and get tested. I did when I went off birth control."

His eyebrows shot up. "Having a lot of sex?"

"A topic that is hardly any of your business." She took a bite of the lemon chiffon cake and nearly groaned at the sharp tang of citrus. Lemon was the superior cake flavor.

"And yet here you are assuming I have herpes or something."

"You are so dramatic. Try this one." She pushed the lemon cake to him and reached for the red velvet. "Oh my God. Never tell my mother, but this is the best red velvet cake I've ever had."

"Does your mother have a monopoly on red velvet cake?"

"She considers it her specialty, and it's one of our best sellers at the bakery. What?" she asked when his brows drew together.

"I forgot your family owned a bakery. Why aren't they making your cake?"

The fact that he said your cake and not our cake didn't escape her, but the quick stab of hurt irritated her, so she brushed it away.

"It's a lot of pressure. If we were going to ask someone from Romano's to make it, my mother and probably my sister and maybe my sister-in-law would insist on helping, and then it would be a whole thing. This makes it easier."

"And it means you get more of a say."

She licked frosting off her finger and grinned. "Exactly."

He slowly slid the chocolate cake back across the table and took the red velvet. "Red velvet is my favorite."

She silently ticked the box for the top tier to be red velvet. "What about the lemon?"

It wasn't the silent, indulgent cake tasting she'd imagined, but they managed to pick the last three flavors without too much bickering, and the man behind the counter even boxed up the remaining slices for her to take home. Cake heaven.

Viv moved to the door while she waited for Aidan to adjust the collar of his jacket, studying the cakes in the front window. Paulie could probably recreate some of those for the wedding and special occasion cakes they sometimes made. She'd have to try and sketch some of them up for him.

"You would think working in a bakery would make you hate dessert, but—"

Without warning, Aidan stopped beside her and yanked her up against the hard plane of his chest. His mouth was on hers before she could even form her next thought, hot and hungry, his tongue dragging across her lower lip.

He tasted like chocolate and sin as he nipped her bottom lip with his teeth, and she very nearly dropped the bakery box she was holding so she could wrap her arms around his neck and explore his mouth a little more. But then he released her, and she sucked in a sharp breath, instantly annoyed at the smug look on his face.

"What the hell was that for?"

He reached up to grip her chin, dragging his thumb over her bottom lip. "Had a little frosting right there."

"So you licked it off?" she hissed, following him outside.

"You didn't seem to be complaining. And besides, now your friend behind the counter is staring for an entirely different reason."

She turned back to see the woman watching them with a pinched expression, barely swallowing a grin as the door swung shut. "You have a weird sense of humor."

He studied her for a long moment before pushing his

sunglasses up his nose and hiding his eyes. "Is that what you think that was? Humor?"

"Sorry, I forgot. You're not very funny."

He huffed out a laugh, and they walked to the car in silence. From the moment he poisoned her hope for a partnership under the sharp sting of his cold indifference, she figured she knew exactly what to expect from him. It hardly seemed fair that the man continued to surprise her. She hated surprises. Especially ones that looked like Aidan Callahan.

Chapter Twelve

"What the hell are you still doing here?"

Aidan looked up from his study of the document he was holding to stare at his brother framed in the doorway to the conference room. He'd commandeered the big, oblong table they kept in the sparsely furnished meeting room underneath the nightclub to better understand what Finn had been responsible for.

It was a lot, but Aidan finally felt like he was getting a handle on it. If he'd been impressed by the ease with which Finn negotiated deals, he found himself floored by the obscene number of details his brother had somehow carried around in his brain, because he hadn't committed much of it to paper.

"I think I found a better way to catalog shipments for faster delivery." Aidan reached for a paper he'd set on top of a stack to his left. "Right now, Sean earmarks different types of weapons for specific warehouses and then goes around to each one, tallies inventory, and creates shipments. A process that takes days."

He held the paper out to Declan. "But we could cut that in

half at least if we ran inventory at a main warehouse and then farmed it out. Do all of it in a single day instead of over multiple. Plus, less traffic to the smaller warehouses. I'd maybe put on more security at the main hub, but we'd be able to turn product over much faster."

Declan read through Aidan's hastily scribbled notes, eyebrows raised. "This is good. We'll definitely talk more about this later, but right now you need to go."

"What? Why? Go where?"

"Home. You have your interview today. With Viv. For the paper."

Aidan's sigh was instantaneous; he couldn't stop it even though he knew it would cause Declan's disapproving frown. "Is that interview really necessary? Can't we just put an announcement in the paper or something?"

"Yes, and no."

"Is it, or do you just enjoy watching me squirm under all this?"

Declan tossed the paper on the edge of the table and slid his hands into his pockets. "Maybe a little bit of that too. Hurry up, or you'll be late."

He left without a word, and Aidan shoved a hand through his hair. He had a million things still to catch up on. He wanted to look into some of their buyers and see which ones had contacts outside Philadelphia. Then there was the list of open deals Finn hadn't been able to close that he wanted to take another pass at.

"Now, Aidan!" Declan shouted from down the hall.

With an irritated grunt, he grabbed his jacket off the back of his chair and slammed the door to the conference room behind him. He checked his watch as he climbed into his truck. He wouldn't be that late. If he hurried.

Frankly, he didn't see the need to parade this whole thing in front of the entire city. It should have been a quick ceremony in front of family and then back to life as normal. Instead he'd gotten himself stuck trailing behind a woman whose ass was made for staring at and lugging the occasional box. Like an idiot.

It didn't help that he wanted to kiss her every time she wielded her quick wit like a dagger. Which is why he'd acted on impulse at the bakery the other day. The way she'd been pushing his buttons like someone had given her a manual. It was nice to know he could push hers back.

He technically wasn't late when he pulled into the driveway. He still had three minutes to spare, but all three women were waiting for him like a firing squad when he let himself into the living room.

"There you are." Viv stood in the center of the room next to a woman Aidan assumed would be doing the interview. Irritation was evident in the way she fiddled with the bracelet she wore. "Meeting go okay?"

He crossed the room and pressed a kiss to her cheek, ignoring the pinch she gave his arm. "Meeting was fine. Sorry I'm late."

"Oh, not at all." The blonde assured him, holding out her hand. "I'm Diana, and this is June."

The photographer gave him a quick once over while she slipped the camera strap over her head, which had Viv pinching him again. He gave her a sharp squeeze on her hip. Despite what Viv might think, he hadn't slept with anyone else since Declan had announced the engagement. An uncharacteristic change in behavior he'd decided not to think about too much.

"Are we ready to get started?"

"Almost," Diana said. "We'll finish getting some lights set up, and then we'll be ready to go, I think."

"Perfect." Viv smiled. "Can I get you anything to drink?"

"Some water would be great."

"I'll help you," Aidan offered when he caught the look in her eye.

"Could you possibly rein it in, lover boy?" Viv hissed once they were out of earshot of the living room. "I know it's out of character for you, but it's bad form for you to flirt with the photographer."

"Dear God. I was not flirting with the photographer. She smiled at me. I had no idea you were such a jealous person."

She yanked open the refrigerator door with such force it nearly smacked him in the forehead, and he had to put out a hand to catch it.

"I am not a jealous person. I am a pissed-off one. You were supposed to be here an hour ago."

"I know. I lost track of time. What are you worried about, princess? That I'll embarrass you?"

She shoved two bottles of water at him, eyes flashing. "No, Callahan. That you'll disappoint me. Although maybe I should get used to the sensation. I imagine I'll have to live with it often enough for the next several decades."

He glared at her back when she stalked off down the hall. Well, someone was in a mood. Clearly the only way to shut her up would be to put on a very convincing show.

Smoothing his features, he followed her back to the formal living room, handing a bottle of water to both women and taking a seat on the couch next to Viv, who felt stiff as a board. The photographer had set up big umbrella lights and was taking test shots that had the lights strobing brilliant white. Jesus, he'd be blind by the time the damn thing was over.

"Relax," he whispered against her ear while the interviewer took out a notepad and the photographer snapped candids.

She twitched at his side, but her posture didn't change much, so he slid his hand up her back and cupped the back of her neck, rubbing circles over the spot just behind her ear. No doubt she'd give him hell for it after, but if she didn't relax, she was going to blow this for both of them, and then he'd have sat through this torture session for nothing.

"Well, a Callahan wedding is always big, exciting news," Diana said, smiling at Aidan. "I was so happy when your sister-in-law called and asked me to come interview the two of you. If you're ready, we can get started."

"Whenever you are," Aidan said.

Diana's gaze slid to Viv, whose spine was still rigid. "It's normal to be a little nervous, so I always like to start with some easy ones. How did the two of you meet?"

"Through a mutual acquaintance," Viv said smoothly, and Aidan gave her neck a light squeeze, moving his hand to rest on the back of the couch.

Well, it wasn't a lie, and it wasn't the whole truth. Somewhere in between. A perfect tone for an article that would gush about a blissfully happy engagement between two near-total strangers.

"It was pretty unexpected," he agreed. "I don't think either of us saw it coming."

Viv laughed, and the photographer snapped a quick photo. "That's an understatement."

"Sometimes those are the best love stories," Diana said. "The ones that catch you by surprise. Here's another easy one. Where did you go on your first date?"

"To dinner," they said in unison.

"At Scarpetta," Viv added, relaxing a little more, though she still clenched her hands in her lap. "The veal pappardelle was delicious."

"I think dessert was the best part," Aidan said with a cheeky grin that flustered Viv just enough to give them the wrong idea.

Diana cleared her throat to hide a laugh. "Okay, last little icebreaker. What's something you learned about the other person that first night that surprised you?"

He felt Viv tense ever so slightly, and he gave her shoulder a reassuring rub with his thumb.

"How forgiving she is." He leaned forward when she slowly turned to face him, laying it on thick. "I kind of made an ass of myself, and she was gracious enough to give me another chance."

"And you, Viv?"

"How willing he was to admit he made a mistake." The smile she sent him was almost smug, and he quirked a brow before she turned back to Diana. "It's very refreshing when a man can admit he's wrong, don't you think?"

Diana laughed. "You might have yourself a unicorn there."

"He's certainly something," Viv said, relaxing a bit more and giving his thigh a firm pat.

"Here's the one thing readers always want to know. How did he propose? Was it romantic? Funny? Did it catch you by surprise?"

Viv tilted her head, and he knew she was considering how to weave this particular lie.

"It was definitely a surprise," she began. "He knows I hate being the center of attention, so he came over and we made dinner together." Her voice went dreamy, and he wondered if she was recounting her ideal proposal or just doing it for added effect. "I turned around from taking the chicken out of the oven, and he was on one knee right there in the middle of the floor. It was...very sweet. I couldn't have asked for a more perfect proposal."

Diana jotted down some notes and smiled at Aidan. "Were you nervous?"

He chuckled. "Nervous is one word for it. I wasn't sure if

she'd say yes or if she'd like the ring I picked out. But I knew I'd regret it if I didn't go for it."

"Your family has a bit of a tradition of using family heirlooms to propose, if I recall."

He reached for Viv's hand with a nod, lacing their fingers together and staring down at the ring while the photographer snapped pictures of their joined hands.

"They're usually pretty big and gaudy. You've seen Evie's. That used to belong to my mother. This one seemed like it fit her. It has an…understated elegance."

That, at least, wasn't a lie. It did seem to suit her perfectly. When he looked up, Viv was staring at him, eyes soft and unreadable.

"That is just so precious. To know someone that well. But if I'm not mistaken, this is a pretty fast courtship, isn't it? What's the rush?"

"When you know, you know," Aidan said, finally dragging his eyes away from Viv to smile at Diana while the photographer continued snapping away. "We didn't want to wait, and our families were okay with a short engagement."

"Viv, your family owns Romano's Bakery, right?"

"Yes, that's right."

The rest of the interview flew by in a parade of questions about their families, the ceremony, and the reception. The woman wanted to know every detail down to the number of guests, which, truthfully, neither of them could remember.

The whole thing was mind numbingly boring, and they both played their parts well. Viv looked every bit the excited bride and he the enraptured groom. Diana was practically eating out of the palms of their hands.

The photographer directed them through some posed shots for the lead photo of the article, and as they were packing up, Diana asked, "So what are your plans for the honeymoon?"

"Oh, well, we—"

"We decided to delay until the summer. When it's warmer," Aidan interrupted.

"We did? I thought we agreed we weren't going to take one?" Viv added in a rush. "You're just so busy with work and everything…"

He made a show of running his hand down her back and hooking it around her waist, pulling her in closer and pressing a kiss to her temple. He smiled against her skin at the way she squirmed ever so slightly against his touch.

"Well, it was going to be a surprise, but…I thought you'd enjoy Rome more in June than November."

"Rome?"

"Yeah." He shifted his hold on her waist to turn her toward him. "Haven't you always wanted to go there?"

"I have, but—"

He pulled her in for a quick kiss on the lips and gave her hip a pat. "Now that the cat's out of the bag, I'll tell you about all the details later."

She studied him for a moment before forcing a smile when Diana gave a breathy sigh.

"You really caught a good one, Viv."

"Apparently so."

"We're under a pretty tight deadline for this since the wedding is coming up very soon, but you should see it in the paper on Friday. I'm rooting for the two of you and wishing you every happiness."

He waited while Viv walked both women to the door, and when she stepped back into the doorway of the living room, she had her arms crossed loosely over her chest.

"That was great, wasn't it?"

"It was something."

"Oh, come on," he said. "You were perfect. She was practically a puddle on the floor with that proposal. Did you see that in a movie or something?"

"It's actually the way that…" She waved a hand in the air. "Never mind. Yeah, I guess you could say it was a movie. What about you with Rome, though? That was an interesting last-minute addition."

"Heat of the moment, I guess. Why? You don't think she bought it?"

Viv paused to wind a scarf loosely around her neck and slip into her jacket. "No, you were very convincing. She definitely bought it. I guess we can write the whole thing off as a big success."

Something about her tone struck him as off, and she wouldn't meet his gaze as she crossed to the front door.

"I think it went really well."

"It did."

"Then why do you look upset?"

"I don't know because I'm not upset." She forced a smile with that same sharpness he recognized from the party. "I just still have a million things to do. Oh, speaking of, you don't need to worry about taking me for my final dress fitting on Friday. I'm going to ask Sofia if she can take some time off from the bakery to go with me."

He frowned. "Why?"

"Because it's bad luck for you to see me in my dress, and we've got enough working against us already." There was that thing in her voice he couldn't quite place again.

"I don't have to actually see you in it. I'll wait outside the room."

"There's no need to risk it when my sister is available. We'll be fine for this one thing. No one has heard from Collin since the engagement party anyway. I'm sure he's gotten bored and found someone else to harass by now."

He should be grateful she was letting him off the hook.

They had three shipments coming in this weekend, and Declan wanted to work overtime to get things squared away before the wedding. He didn't want any product sitting while they were distracted. He should let the whole thing drop.

"Ever think he isn't bothering you because I've been with you every step?"

"No, I think he got bored. Either way, I shouldn't have a ton of errands next week anyway."

"You're sure nothing's wrong?"

"I'm sure." She jerked open the door and stepped quickly into the cool afternoon. "You did great today. Enjoy the break from following me around, Callahan."

Before he could stop her, she turned on her heel and practically sprinted down the front walk to her car. He thought the interview had gone really well, all things considered, but something about it had rattled her. He should leave it alone, but before he even closed the door, he knew he wouldn't.

Chapter Thirteen

She'd gotten caught up. That's what she kept telling herself. Caught up in the show they'd been putting on, the romantic story they'd weaved for the interviewer and the photographer. Caught up in the nearness of him, in faking it too well.

He'd thrown her off with his comment about honeymooning in Rome and how she'd always wanted to go there. She had, but of course he didn't know that. How could he? She was Italian; Rome was an easy guess. The fact that she'd let it mean anything more, even for a split second, was stupid. It made her feel stupid.

They'd spent too much time together over the last week. That's all it was. Between being around him nearly every day while they ran errands and Evie giving her a crash course in being married to a Callahan man, she was steeped in him. It was ridiculous. She was being ridiculous.

Viv had no more formed a connection with Aidan Callahan than with the tech she saw at the nail salon every two weeks. Honestly, Lina probably knew more about her than Aidan did anyway.

Taking a deep breath, Viv reached for the newspaper her mother had left folded in the middle of the table. She had a few more minutes before her sister arrived to take her for this fitting, then she would come home and take a nice long soak in the tub, maybe even indulge in a glass of wine.

She unfolded the paper and pressed it flat with her fingers, flipping past the headlines and the advertisements until she got to the society section. There it was, above the fold on the first page.

Youngest Callahan Son Engaged After Whirlwind Romance, the headline announced. She shook her head with a derisive snort at the message that rang through loud and clear. She was a nobody engaged to a somebody. And only the somebody got mentioned in the headline.

Her eyes dipped down to the large photo of them that covered the entire right side of the page, and she choked on her coffee, sputtering as the liquid burned her tongue.

The photographer had made them sit through a dozen posed shots at least, and in the end, they'd gone with a candid photo of them instead. That moment just after Aidan had taken her hand and given his line about the engagement ring.

He was looking ahead, smiling at Diana. He practically oozed charm. The asshole. But while he'd been busy schmoozing the photographer, she'd been staring at him like a lovesick puppy. She looked besotted. Embarrassment swamped her, and she prayed he hadn't cared enough to read it.

Disgusted with herself, she set her mug on top of their faces and forced herself to skim the article. Diana had clearly gone for the Cinderella story, making it sound like Aidan had plucked Viv out of the gutter and handed her the world on a silver platter.

She'd even spun the surprise trip to Rome into some kind

of Make-a-Wish moment, insinuating Viv couldn't possibly know how lucky she was to be chosen by the likes of Aidan Callahan. As if she should be grateful to be shackled to a man who wouldn't spend a single minute mourning her if she got run over by a truck.

The entire thing was fucking insulting.

When the doorbell rang, she shoved back from the table and stalked across the kitchen, yanking it open while muttering to herself about reporters and journalistic integrity. The figure at the door only served to darken her mood further.

"What the hell are you doing here?" she demanded.

"Why does everyone keep asking me that?" Aidan mumbled, huddling on the shallow stoop out of the rain. "Are you going to let me in or what?"

Viv moved to block the narrow opening. "No. What do you want? I told you Sofia was going to ferry me around today. She'll be here any minute."

"No, she won't. I called her and told her not to come."

She crossed her arms over her chest to keep from wrapping her hands around his throat and squeezing until his eyes bugged out. "And why would you do such a thing?"

"Because I volunteered. It's my job. Deal with it," he added when she still didn't move.

"Your hero complex is insufferable, Callahan. Go away. I'm not your responsibility for another eight days, and I can take care of myself."

When she moved to slam the door in his face, his arm shot out, holding it open enough for him to wedge his foot in against the frame.

"You are really trying my patience, princess," he said through gritted teeth. "Now either you can get your coat and get in the damn truck, or I can throw you over my shoulder and do it myself."

Like hell. She was done being ordered around. She'd had her fill of doing exactly what she was told just to keep the peace. For once, she wanted to be in control of something in her crazy, upside-down life. If this was her hill to die on, she might as well make a scene.

Before she could talk herself out of it, she opened the door enough to stomp down on his toes, enjoying his quick hiss of pain. When he jerked his foot out of the door, she shoved into it with her shoulder, but he was faster, slamming it open so hard she stumbled back two steps.

He left it hanging, the rain falling in sheets and whispering through the trees as he advanced. She let her irritation at being ordered around by him, of all people, simmer into anger. Anger was better than feeling like an idiot.

She thought she'd anticipated his lunge, but he feinted when she tried to dodge around him to the right and hooked his arm around her waist. Lifting her off the ground, he held her tightly with one arm while he snatched her jacket and purse off the bench by the door.

In any other circumstance, she'd be impressed that he could lift her so effortlessly with one arm, but right now she just wanted to claw his eyes out.

"Put me down, you asshole!" She slapped and scratched at his arm as he dashed out into the rain, slamming the front door behind him.

"Christ's sake, woman, what the hell is your problem?"

He set her on her feet under the overhang in front of the garage, blocking her from making a run for it by laying a hand on either side of her shoulders. Not that she wanted to in this downpour. She was already half soaked from being hauled this far.

"You are my problem!" she shouted, drilling her finger into his chest. "You can't just manhandle people when you don't get your way!"

Meaghan Pierce

"I gave you your options," he growled. "It's hardly on me that you chose the difficult one. Now are you going to get into the fucking truck, or do I have to do that too?"

She reached up to brace her hands on his chest, but instead of shoving him back, she gripped the lapels of his jacket and tugged him forward, tilting her head up so his mouth crashed into hers. It didn't take him long to respond, his arms wrapping around her waist and molding her against him.

He tasted like coffee, and she caught herself wondering how he liked to drink it. She shoved that thought aside and focused on the steady onslaught of her tongue against his. She didn't want to get lost in the details of him. She wanted to throw him off. She wanted him to know what he did to her.

When he backed her up against the garage door, she arched against him, making him groan as she sucked his bottom lip and then dragged her teeth across it. His hands slid down to her ass, cupping it, squeezing it, and she sighed.

His hands slid down farther, wrapping around the tops of her thighs. He was going to lift her up against the garage door, and she'd let him do it, and whatever came after if she didn't get a grip.

Capturing his lip between her teeth, she pulled back, tugging it as she leaned her head back against the cold metal and gave him a gentle shove, though she didn't loosen her grip on his jacket. His chest rose and fell rapidly under her fingers, and she tried not to shiver when his breath blew hot against her collarbone.

His light blue eyes had gone sapphire, and she couldn't bite back the smug grin that had them narrowing on her face. Before she gave in and kissed him again, she wriggled out of his grip and bent to retrieve the jacket and bag he'd dropped by their feet. Pushing past him, she climbed into the truck and waited.

He didn't speak as they drove toward the bridal boutique, but his fingers gripped the steering wheel, and every so often, he sent her a searing look that she avoided with practiced ease. She had three brothers. She knew how to irritate a man with feigned disinterest.

The boutique was busy. Bustling with brides and bridesmaids picking up their dresses and last-minute necessities for weekend weddings. It made her feel even better, steadier that he looked both out of place and uncomfortable.

"Can I help you guys?" A short blonde with a gold-edged name tag stepped around a group of women examining a display of fake tiaras and smiled.

"I'm here for my final dress fitting. Vivian Falcone."

"Oh, right. I saw your interview in the paper." Her eyes slid to Aidan, and she smiled. "You two look so cute together."

She heard Aidan clear his throat from behind her, and she grinned. "Thank you so much. Is there somewhere he could wait so he doesn't see me? I want it to be a surprise."

"Of course. If you'll both follow me this way."

She led them toward the back, leaving them next to a display of lingerie to check on the availability of a fitting room. Viv turned to see Aidan eyeing the rack of lace and satin, lifting a brow when he slid his gaze to her.

"In your dreams, Callahan," she mumbled.

"Are you saying you haven't bought anything for our wedding night?" He fingered the lace cup of a corset-style top. "What am I supposed to take off you?"

"Don't worry," she replied, forcing the mental images he was purposely painting to the recesses of her mind. "The dress has plenty to keep you busy."

When the consultant reappeared, Viv left Aidan in the

waiting area and stepped into the dressing room. Slipping out of her clothes, she left them neatly piled on a chair and let the consultant help her into the dress. She loved it as much as she had the first time. She ran her hands down the length of her arms to adjust the sleeves and wriggled while she tugged the satin underskirt to make it lay flat under the lace.

The consultant held her train as she stepped out into the main section of the fitting area and around the corner to one of the raised platforms so the seamstress could check the fit. While the woman adjusted and pinned, Viv tried hard not to think about Aidan removing it next weekend or what would happen once he did. She didn't need something else to torture herself with.

"You're a vision in this dress," the seamstress told her, adding one final pin at her hip. "Just make sure you stay that way and don't do anything crazy."

"How crazy can you get with one week to go?"

The seamstress chuckled and helped her step down. "One time, I had a bride decide to do a juice cleanse. She lost eleven pounds of water weight in five days and in all the wrong places. The dress hung in such a way that she looked pregnant. So, I repeat, don't do anything crazy."

Viv chuckled. "I can promise you I don't care enough to do anything drastic. About my weight, I mean," she added quickly when the seamstress's eyebrows shot up.

"I figured as much. I've seen your fiancé."

Biting her tongue, Viv made her way back to the dressing room and carefully stepped out of the dress so the pins didn't poke her. The consultant zipped it back into its protective bag and left Viv to dress.

Aidan rushed over the minute she stepped through the curtain that separated the waiting area from the fitting rooms. His eyes roamed over her, but they were more worried than anything else.

"Viv, what kind of car does Collin drive?"

Her gaze immediately shot over his shoulder, scanning the people still milling about the store. Had Collin been there? Was he watching her? She'd been too busy getting ready for the wedding and sparring with Aidan to think about him much over the last week. She'd prefer to never have to think about him again.

"Viv. What kind of car?" Aidan repeated.

"Um. A black one. A Jeep. Why?" she asked when he swore under his breath.

"I thought I saw him standing by the door while you were in the back, but I wasn't sure, so I got up to check. By the time I made it outside, the only thing I could see was a black Jeep peeling out of the parking lot."

"He was here?"

"I think so. But you're fine," he added, giving her arm a quick rub. "You want to tell me what the fuck this guy's problem really is?"

"What's there to tell? He's an asshole who didn't like to hear the word no. And he disagreed with his fists. Or with a well-aimed slap to the face. We hadn't really progressed to fists yet. Not until I told him I wouldn't marry him."

"And he's been bothering you ever since?"

She shook her head. "No, actually. I haven't heard from him since Leo broke his nose. I figured my father or brothers warned him off. Papa thinks he's just trying to break up the alliance by scaring me off."

"Declan thinks the same."

"But you don't," she said at the skepticism in his tone.

"I don't have a reason not to, but…"

"But?"

"Do you have anything else to do today? Are you lying to me?" he asked and she shook her head. "All right, then I'm going to take you home."

Viv unfolded the jacket she'd draped over her arm and slipped her arms through the sleeves, frowning when her fingers brushed a piece of paper that shouldn't be there. She gripped it in her fist, forcing it through the opening and looking up at Aidan, who was studying it.

She hadn't even opened it all the way when she saw the thick slashes of a black marker bleeding through the page.

You have one week to do the right thing.

Before she had time to process all the words, Aidan snatched it from her hands and read it through again, lips moving as he scanned it. He balled it into his fist before shoving it violently into his pocket.

"Excuse me," he said, voice calmer than he looked, stopping a passing consultant with a light hand on her arm. "Is there another way in and out of the shop besides the front door?"

The woman frowned, looking from Aidan to Viv and back again. Something in Aidan's gaze had her answering his question.

"There's an employee entrance that opens into what I guess you could call an alley. There are dumpsters back there and a little loading dock for deliveries. Is everything okay?"

"Yeah. Everything is fine. Thanks."

He put his hand on the small of Viv's back and led her out into the parking lot. His hand never left her, forcing her to keep pace with his long strides around the side of the building and toward the back. When they rounded the corner, he stopped short, gripping her hip to keep her close.

There were two employees leaning against the side of the building, one smoking, the other bent over their phone. The door was propped open with a plastic container. Anyone could slip in through that door if someone wasn't paying attention or made a quick run to their car and left it unattended.

"What are you looking for?" she asked when she noticed his eyes darting around the perimeter of the buildings.

"Cameras. This is the direction I saw the Jeep pull out from."

That's right. Libby had mentioned Brogan was good with tech. Viv tracked Aidan's gaze around the space. Nothing. He muttered a stream of curses, apparently coming to the same realization.

"There's a security system at your house, isn't there?"

"Yeah. Papa had it installed after... After."

"Good." He turned and led her to the truck, hand tight on her waist while his eyes constantly scanned the parking lot as they crossed it.

"If Collin and his family are really trying to undermine this alliance, what does that mean for the wedding? For the families?" *For us*, she wanted to say but didn't.

"I don't know," he replied, opening her door and helping her inside. "First, I'm going to take you home."

"And then?" she wondered as he started the engine and pulled onto the street.

"And then Collin Milano is going to wish he'd left you the fuck alone."

Chapter Fourteen

The sun hung low on the horizon, casting long shadows over the city as Aidan drove away from the glistening skyscrapers toward squat brick warehouses and stone buildings. Declan wanted to wait until after the wedding to implement Aidan's new inventory and distribution system, which was just as well. Arguing about Collin and the Milanos had kept them plenty occupied.

Falcone didn't see them as much of a threat. Little people talking a big game. They didn't have much power or much support in the Mafia, not enough for a full-on takeover anyway. Collin apparently got his charm from his father, who had been arrested twice for domestic violence. Giordano had greased the right palms to get him released both times.

But even with Falcone's assurances that it was probably nothing, something didn't sit right with him. It all felt too personal, too targeted at Viv specifically. Declan insisted, however, and Falcone agreed that going after Viv to break up the alliance made sense. As if she was some kind of weak link. The woman was anything but.

Aidan wanted to send this fucker a warning, but Declan

had ordered him to stand down. No need to stir up trouble with a wild card this close to the wedding. Except it wasn't Aidan doing the stirring. Collin was clearly sending a message, and their answer was to ignore him. The wedding would proceed, the marriage would be consummated, and the alliance would be sealed. That was that.

But Aidan knew demands like that didn't drift into the ether when they weren't met. Cementing the alliance on Saturday wouldn't make Collin or his family's desire to subvert it simply vanish. They'd have to respond to it eventually, and Aidan was worried the price would be much higher by the time they did.

For now, though, he'd been ordered not to touch the son of a bitch, and since he and Declan had established a tentative truce in the last few weeks, Aidan was unwilling to push him too hard on it. He'd settled for extra security at the wedding and Nico following Viv around like a hawk while she got ready for the ceremony.

He pulled into the gravel lot of one of their smaller warehouses and glanced at the clock on the dash. Sean's car was here, and he was, no doubt, already inside waiting. Probably checking his watch with that irritated scowl on his face that reminded Aidan of his father.

James pulled in as Aidan crossed the lot, jogging to catch up with him. It was still odd to see James out doing syndicate business. He hadn't been back in the field much since his wife had been murdered a few months ago. For the first time, Aidan wondered if all the wedding talk weighed on him.

"I hear you've got plans for inventory and distribution changes," James said, pulling open the side door and letting Aidan go ahead of him.

Aidan shrugged. "I haven't talked to Sean about it yet to take his temperature on it. You think he'll be pissed I overstepped?" Sean had been handling logistics since Aidan was in diapers.

"I doubt it. Okay, well, maybe a little pissed," James chuckled when he saw Aidan's raised brows. "But not because you overstepped. Because he hates change."

"The more efficient we are, the more money we make."

"Lead with that," James said, following the long hallway past the front offices and toward the storage hangars in the back.

Sean stood at the far end, clipboard in hand, running through the list as he scanned the wooden crates lining the floor in neat rows.

"You're late," he said, glancing up from his task. "It's all hands on deck to clear out the last of the inventory for buyers and get this shit off to new homes before the wedding, and we've only got a few days left."

There was a slight hitch in James's step, but he recovered quickly. Aidan could hear the strain in his voice when he asked, "Where's the rest of the team?"

"They're out back, loading the truck for the first delivery. I want to finish cataloging the rest of this, and then it should be good for the second delivery we're running tonight."

Sean shifted his gaze to Aidan. "I hear we'll be doing things a little differently soon."

"Just trying to keep profits up."

Sean's stare was unflinching before he inclined his head. "Up is the best place to keep them. Here." He shoved a crowbar into Aidan's chest and nodded to wooden crates on the far side of the warehouse floor. "Start with the ones lined up over there."

Aidan used the crowbar to pry the lid off the first crate. "Declan tell you about this Collin guy we've been dealing with?"

"He mentioned it when I saw him yesterday," James said,

stooping to brush away the packing material and count the weapons in the crate. "Said he was a guy with a big mouth and a small dick."

"While I am positive that's true," Aidan replied, pounding the lid on the crate back into place once James made his tally, "I'm not convinced that's all it is."

"Why?" Sean wondered, leaning against a concrete pillar with his arms crossed.

"There are other, better ways to poke at the alliance and push us into backing out than targeting Viv or any woman. And I'd rather be out there pummeling my fist into that bastard's face getting answers than here counting and delivering guns," Aidan added, prying off the lid to another crate.

"Aww," James crooned. "That's so sweet. We love hanging out with you too, cuz."

Aidan rolled his eyes. "You know what I mean. What kind of fuck goes after a woman to get what he wants?"

"The kind that doesn't mind smacking them around a little bit. Yeah," Sean said when Aidan bristled. "Declan told us about that too."

"I don't like the guy, and I don't think he's going to just go away after the wedding."

"Probably not. But the media is watching this wedding closely. Your article in the paper has drummed up a lot of public interest, and your brother knows the games he's playing with that shit better than we do."

"So we do nothing."

Sean shook his head. "Not nothing. Just not something right now. I'm sure Declan won't mind giving you your pound of flesh once the public has moved on to the next bit of celebrity gossip. They put Evie's life in danger too. I'm sure he hasn't forgotten."

Aidan wrenched the lid off another crate, leaning on the crowbar while James counted. "I'm counting on it."

"You ready, then?" James wondered, making check marks on the paper in his hand.

"For what? Ripping that guy's face off? Absolutely."

James pushed slowly to his feet. "No, for the wedding."

"I'm…as ready as I can be, I guess." Aidan shrugged. "I don't know. Does it matter if I'm ready or not? It's happening either way. My job is to get through this wedding and knock her up."

"And then?" Sean wondered.

"And then what?"

"Once she's pregnant."

Aidan pounded the top on the last crate and avoided his uncle's gaze while James made his final tally. "I haven't thought that far ahead. I figured I could set her up with a nanny in a nice house somewhere. Make sure she has everything she needs to take care of the kid."

"You're going to dump your wife and kid somewhere, and what? Go back to your old life?"

Aidan blew out a breath. "Well, it sounds stupid when you say it."

"Believe me," Sean deadpanned, "it sounds stupid when you say it too."

"Don't look at me like that," Aidan said, flicking a hand at them both. "You two know I'm hardly husband and father material. Never have been, never will be. Don't intend to start now."

"It's a learned skill," James assured him.

"Not for you. I hear actually wanting to be either is a much better place to start."

"You want her, though," Sean said. "Don't tell me you don't, because we all saw that kiss at the party."

"Wanting to fuck her and being in a relationship with her are two very different things. It doesn't matter anyway. She wants this about as much as I do.

James grunted. "You seem pretty sure about that."

"I am. She'll have plenty of space and plenty of cash. Hell, she can even have all the lovers she wants as long as she's discreet."

He pushed away the sudden pang in his chest as voices echoed from the back of the warehouse. Whatever his uncle had been about to say evaporated from his lips as the rest of the team joined them, and Aidan sent up a silent prayer. He wanted nothing more than to talk about anything else.

"These ready?" Rory wondered, gesturing to the crates on the ground.

Sean took the clipboard from James and scanned it quickly. "Yeah. Pull the second truck inside, and we'll load these up so they're ready for later. Then it's just a matter of waiting for word from Brogan that the drop is a go."

Eager to get away from another conversation with his uncle and cousin about his impending marriage, Aidan helped load the second set of crates into the truck. In truth, he hadn't spent much time thinking about the after of his marriage lately. He wasn't sure when he'd stopped or why.

The more time he spent with her, the less he spent thinking about their far-flung future or kids. Instead he was consumed with thoughts of her lips and her ass and the floral scent of her hair. Consumed by the way her laugh made his stomach tighten and how quick she was to match his sarcasm with her own.

Christ. He scrubbed a hand over his face, leaning back against the tailgate while they waited for the signal from Brogan. He needed to stop that shit right fucking now. This marriage was a business transaction. Business transactions didn't require emotions; even if they did, he didn't have any.

It was simply the way he was built—cold efficiency. The same cold efficiency that allowed him to shoot a guy who was blackmailing them between the eyes allowed him to fuck women senseless and not get attached. That's exactly what he needed to remember with Viv.

Fuck her senseless and don't get attached. It was the only rule he had for sex. Well, that and always wear a condom. If he was being forced to break one rule, he was determined to keep the other one.

James came by to hand him an earpiece that he hooked deftly over his ear. As soon as he settled it in, he could hear the rapid clicking of keys under Brogan's fingers on the other end. No doubt finalizing payment or running a last-minute background check on a new player. They never went into anything blind, and that was all thanks to Brogan.

Aidan suspected Brogan's anger about the night Finn died was directed as much at himself as it was at Aidan. It was proof that even when you had access to as much information as Brogan did, even when you meticulously and carefully planned out every detail and its contingencies, shit could still go wrong. And when shit goes wrong, people die.

This time it had been Finn. Next time—and there would certainly be a next time—it could be any of them. It was a risk they all accepted by living this life. Aidan would give anything to have traded places with Finn, anything so Finn was here to go home to his wife and kid every night.

"Deal closed. Ready for drop off," Brogan said in his ear, jolting him out of his thoughts. "Will confirm payment in full."

The men moved in a flurry of activity, climbing into their respective vehicles while Aidan swung up into the driver's seat of the delivery truck and cranked the engine, waiting for James to join him in the passenger seat. When Sean's arm shot out the window of the lead car, Aidan pulled onto the road behind them and followed at a distance. They always made deliveries in a caravan. A lead car to absorb the initial hit in an ambush and a tail car to provide cover support.

Not that they'd ever been ambushed. Not even the Italians had been stupid enough to take a direct hit at them. They weren't stupid enough to do it now. Their firepower, their men, their training. The Callahan syndicate was unmatched, and every criminal in the city knew it.

Which is why this alliance with Falcone was so ground-breaking. It had been more than a century since a Callahan ancestor had established dominance in Philadelphia, running blockades during the Civil War and getting a taste for the unchecked wealth that came with illegal deals and illicit agreements.

As immigration from Ireland picked up in the last half of the 19th century, the syndicate grew to what had become known as the original five until it became twelve sometime during the Prohibition era.

In all that long and sordid history, never once had they aligned with a rival organization. They hadn't needed to. Callahans had always been willing to do whatever was necessary to stay on the throne of power, no matter how bloody.

This alliance was necessary now, according to Declan. Technology and the digital age made it both easier and harder to continue their business. Declan was all too willing to adapt when he needed to, but Aidan suspected he knew that if they wanted the syndicate to continue to thrive for another century or more, they were going to have to plan for the long term.

He could respect his brother's commitment to maintaining the legacy even if he hated being the guinea pig for the whole damn thing. Especially because it left him unable to stop thinking about a certain irritatingly irresistible woman with big brown eyes, a full, heart-shaped mouth, and long legs he wanted to feel cinched around his waist. Or his head. Or both. Definitely both.

"Aidan!"

His fingers jerked on the wheel at James's shout. "Jesus! What?"

"Just wondering if you were going to miss the second turn like you missed the first and get us all arrested."

Aidan muttered a curse and slammed on the brakes in time to take the secondary entrance into the docks, coasting to a stop and throwing it in park while one of their syndicate men leaned out of the guard house window in his uniform.

"Rough day?" he wondered, holding out a hand for their papers.

James passed a folded slip that said they were delivering electronics and flicked a glance at Aidan. "Just a little caught up. Everything okay?"

"Yeah. My coworker might be annoyed I sent him on a random and ultimately pointless errand, but he's new and I can't stand the guy, so it was fun for me. Plus, he's a pain-in-the-ass rule follower. Probably best he didn't see the truck anyway."

He handed their papers back and pushed a button that made the chain-link fence in front of them glide out of their way with a buzz. They drove through the maze of one-way lanes until they reached the loading zone they were looking for, and Aidan backed the truck up to the mouth of the shipping container.

"You good?" James wondered.

Aidan watched three men emerge from the dark of the metal tube. "I'm fine. Let's go." He climbed down from the truck, leaving James to follow.

The men probably wouldn't make trouble. They wanted to take their product and go as much as Aidan wanted to get rid of it, but the weight of the gun at his back made him feel better about facing three guys built like defensive linemen.

"You have what we pay for?" the smallest man said in an accent Aidan couldn't place.

"You pay for what we have?"

The man grunted just as Brogan confirmed payment in full in his ear, and Aidan signaled to James to open one of the crates for inspection. Once satisfied, the men quickly offloaded the weapons and left the way they came.

"What the hell was that back there?" James demanded as they pulled into the warehouse parking lot, maneuvering the truck into the hangar out of sight of the road.

Aidan cut the engine but didn't get out. "Nothing. I was thinking. Distracted."

"About...?"

"About nothing. The wedding. Whatever."

James snorted. "No one in this truck believes that. Least of all me."

"It's really not a big deal. I know you hate weddings anyway."

James sighed. "I don't hate weddings."

"You should," Aidan replied. "I would if I were you."

"Why? My wedding was great. It was everything after that turned into a nightmare. You know," James said after a beat, "just because you believe you're not cut out to be a husband and father doesn't mean it's true. You might surprise yourself."

Aidan groaned and climbed out of the cab, tugging his earpiece out and dropping it into the drawer of a nearby filing cabinet.

"I'm not doing this with you. We're not going to trade stories about women and paint each other's nails."

"Of course not. That would be impossible. You don't have any stories. You've never spent more than a few hours with a woman, and I imagine you don't do much talking."

Aidan snorted. "That's the way I like it."

"Clearly. The question is, why?"

"It doesn't matter why."

117

"Sure it does," James said, following him all the way out to the parking lot and their cars. "You're about to get married, man. To a real live person who deserves more than to be dumped in some house to raise your kid. The Callahan men don't get a lot of shit right, but we get this right. We treat our women well."

"She's not my woman. She's my wife. Or she will be."

James shoved his hands into his jacket pockets against the breeze that kicked up and sent leaves scraping across the pavement. "I fail to see the distinction you're trying to make."

"Viv knows what this is. I've been very clear about that." Aidan jerked open his car door. "We'll both do our duty, Declan will get his blood ties, and I'll get to go back to the way my life was before. Case closed."

Without giving James a chance to respond, he slammed into his truck and reversed out of the parking lot so hard he showered gravel behind him. It was his own damn fault he'd lost sight of his original goal. But he wouldn't let it happen again. He'd satisfy Declan's demands and be done with it. Period. And if that thought sent a sharp stab of pain through his gut, then it was just nerves and nothing more.

Chapter Fifteen

Aidan stared at himself in the long mirror that hung on the back of the door and adjusted the cuffs of his tuxedo shirt. He wondered briefly if the mirror was always here, hung on the back of the door in what looked like a small study, or if it had been put there specifically for today so he could get one last look at himself before his freedom was vacuumed away.

"And then after the prayers, Father Michael will—"

"Evelyn," Aidan snapped. "I was there at the rehearsal last night too. I haven't forgotten the steps."

Truthfully, he hadn't been paying much attention to the ancient Father Michael last night, but he'd say anything to stop Evie's incessant nervous chatter. It wasn't like her to be this unsettled; she was as steady and stoic as Declan most of the time. But right now she was driving him crazier than usual, and he had enough to worry about today.

"Right. Okay. Of course. Do you need anything?"

"A new identity and an untraceable bank account in the Caymans."

"That's hilarious," she said with her hand on the door-knob. "Oh, I talked to Cait this morning."

Aidan's head whipped around to stare at his sister-in-law. "You did?"

"She said she's sorry she can't make it, but she didn't want to steal your thunder. And she'll be back in a couple weeks to congratulate you in person."

"Yeah," he breathed. "Okay."

"I'll send the guys in," Evie said before slipping through the door and leaving him alone.

He fingered the cuff links he wore, tracing the C etched into the silver with a fingertip. Another family heirloom that would be a part of the day. These cuff links had been worn at every Callahan wedding back to his great-grandfather. Declan had worn them a few months ago, and Finn a decade before that.

Aidan understood why Cait didn't want to come. More than pulling focus from him and Viv was the fact she'd gotten married to Finn in the same church by the same priest. Aidan felt the loss acutely today, and he knew it would be tenfold for Cait if she was here. He didn't blame her for staying away and shielding herself from the memories for as long as possible. They were crushing.

"Hey." James poked his head around the door. "Can I come in?"

"You're asking?"

"No." James eased the door closed behind him and produced a bottle of scotch from one jacket pocket and a stack of shot glasses from another. "I brought refreshments. Your brothers should be in here next. Declan was checking with the extra security he added, and Brogan was—"

"Avoiding me."

James sighed as he lined up the glasses on the low coffee

table. "He won't hate you forever. He has to forgive you—and himself—eventually."

"Clearly you don't know my brother. I'm pretty sure he's still mad at me for breaking his video game console when I was seven."

"You threw it out a window."

"I did not throw it out a window," Aidan protested. "My foot got caught on the cord, and when I tried to get it off, I kicked it a little too hard."

"Almost twenty years later, and that excuse still sounds like horseshit. Here." He pressed a shot glass into Aidan's hand. "Pre-game with me. *Sláinte.*"

James clinked his glass against Aidan's and downed his shot with a hiss as Aidan did the same, shaking his head as the amber liquid burned a trail down his throat.

"Getting started without me?" Declan asked, pushing into the room. "Christ, you're shooting Macallan? Have I taught you nothing?"

"We'll sip it later," James assured him, refilling their glasses and passing them out.

"Brogan is checking security feeds one more time and threatening Danny McBride with pain of death if he fucks something up today. He'll be along in a minute."

"The fear of God as motivation. Brogan's favorite," Aidan said.

"What's my favorite?" Brogan asked from the doorway.

"Threatening Danny McBride if he fucks up your equipment," James replied. "Come. Shots."

"How many of these have you had so far?" Brogan wondered as James raised his glass into the air.

"Enough to get me through the day without being catatonic. Not enough to embarrass myself. Promise."

"There are two photographers out there. Don't make me cut you off," Declan warned, seemingly satisfied when James drew an X over his heart. "And you." He turned to survey Aidan. "Don't get wasted at the reception."

"Wouldn't dream of it."

Declan slapped Aidan on the shoulder and raised his glass. "May the road rise to meet you."

"May the wind be always at your back," James continued.

"May the sun shine warm upon your face and the rain fall soft upon your fields," Brogan added.

"And until we meet again, may God hold you in the palm of his hand," Declan finished.

"*Sláinte*," Aidan said, clinking his glass against the others and downing the shot.

"One more," Brogan said, motioning to the bottle. "For Finn," he added when Declan protested.

Declan nodded. "For Finn."

The silence was thick as James filled their glasses once more, setting the bottle back on the table with a heavy thunk.

"For the family who can't be here with us today," Brogan said. "For Mom and Dad."

"And Finn," Aidan said quietly, his throat tight.

"*Sláinte*," Declan whispered, throwing back his shot just as music drifted through the door. "I think that's our cue."

He handed his glass to James and took Aidan by both shoulders. They shared a long look, but Declan said nothing, no parting words of wisdom or warnings not to fuck it up. When Declan released him, Aidan took a deep breath and stepped around his brother to the door.

Pulling it open, he crossed the short hall to the side door leading into the sanctuary. He gripped the knob to steady himself before pushing through. The church was packed just short of standing room only, every pew filled with people in their Sunday best.

Those expensive Brazilian flowers speared up out of bronze vases and hung in petite bouquets at the end of each pew. Evie and Libby sat with Sean in the front row, and Aidan felt Cait's absence sweep over him like a dull ache.

When they were in place, the doors opened at the back of the church, and two little girls in bright white dresses tied with burgundy sashes stepped through, carrying baskets decorated with the same ribbons. They were cousins, not sisters, and one exuberantly showered the carpet with deep red and orange rose petals while the other methodically dropped them one by one on her way up the aisle.

They reached the end and quickly ducked into the pew with their grandmother on the bride's side before the doors opened again and a little boy in a black suit stepped through. Another pang hit Aidan square in the chest. If they hadn't left for Cait's family's summer home in upstate New York right after Finn's funeral, the ring bearer would have been Finn's boy, Evan.

This boy was Leo's oldest at seven or eight, but for the life of him, Aidan couldn't remember the kid's name. The Falcones had a ridiculous number of grandchildren. The boy stopped at the end of the aisle and carefully handed the pillow with both rings tied to it over to Declan before turning on his heel and joining his parents.

The music changed and the doors opened again, and this time the bridesmaids stepped through. Sofia and two of Viv's friends he hadn't met yet wore gowns of burgundy and carried little orange bouquets up the aisle, lining up on the opposite side. Sofia sent him an enthusiastic thumbs up while he tried to ignore how his heart raced as the music changed to the wedding march.

When he glanced down the aisle, the doors were opened wide, and she was already making her way toward him. She wasn't wearing white; that was the first thing that struck him. Instead she'd wrapped herself in lace and satin the color of champagne that glittered when she moved.

It hugged every inch of the curves he hadn't been able to purge from his mind, and he found his mouth watering as she drew even closer, stopping with her father at the bottom of the stairs. She wore a long veil over curls she'd swept up to hang and drape around her neck, and she was dripping with diamonds and rubies from the family vault, including a delicate tiara that anchored her veil in place.

Her father leaned in and whispered something against her ear, brushing his lips across her cheek, and she smiled. When they both turned to him, he reached for her hand, and Falcone laid it carefully in his, catching Aidan's eye and holding it for a long beat before turning and joining his wife.

Aidan helped her up the stairs and then tucked her arm in the crook of his elbow while the priest began the ceremony.

"You clean up good, Callahan," she whispered, and he fought the urge to grin.

Turns out, Catholic wedding masses were no less boring whether you were a spectator or a participant. Father Michael might have been the syndicate's priest for decades, but he was a stickler for tradition and took them through every single second of a traditional ceremony. Probably a penance for all the sins they regularly committed and rarely confessed.

While the priest droned on about love and commitment and partnership, Aidan let his thoughts drift to the warm feel of Viv's hand on his arm and at his side, the dizzying scent of her hair, and just exactly how he was going to peel that dress off her later, inch by torturous inch, tasting every centimeter of exposed skin as he did.

He jumped when he felt a pinch on his arm, glancing down at Viv, who was turning to hand her bouquet to her sister before moving to face him, taking both of his hands in hers. He hadn't been paying enough attention to know what part came next, but the priest solved it for him with his next words.

"Do you, Aidan Montgomery Callahan, take this woman to be your wife? Do you promise to share your life openly with her, to be faithful to her in good times and in bad, in sickness and in health, to love her and honor her all the days of your life?"

He felt Viv's fingers flex in his when he hesitated, and he gave them a light squeeze. There was no going back from this.

"I do."

"And do you, Vivian Amelia Falcone, take this man to be your husband? Do you promise to share your life openly with him, to be faithful to him in good times and in bad, in sickness and in health, to love him and honor him all the days of your life?"

She tilted her head as if considering, a smile playing at the corners of her mouth before she replied, "I do."

"Now, an exchange of rings as a symbol of your eternal commitment to one another."

Aidan swallowed around the lump in his throat as he turned to Declan, palm outstretched for the rings. Eternity was a hell of a long time to be bound to a single person. Even one as enticing as his bride.

While he repeated the priest's words back to him, Aidan slid the matching ruby and diamond studded wedding band onto her finger, completing the set, then she did the same with a thick silver band.

He couldn't name the sensation that shot through him when she lifted her eyes to his, but it seared through his veins until he felt like his body was on fire from it.

When the priest finally pronounced them husband and wife, she slid her arms languidly around his neck, stepping closer and tilting her head up ever so slightly for his lips. He'd never been with a woman who matched him for height when she was wearing heels, and it turned him on more than he realized. Or maybe more than he'd been willing to admit before now.

He was under strict instructions to keep the kiss decent for pictures, but when her gaze dropped to his mouth, he couldn't stop himself from taking his time in tasting her, his tongue sliding out to drag across her lower lip, grinning when she sighed.

She broke the kiss on a laugh when the music began to play them off, and he took her hand and led her back up the aisle to cheers and applause. When they were outside, before the rest of the bridal party and guests appeared, he hauled her up against him and took her mouth again, tightening his hold on her waist when she gasped against his lips.

"A promise for later, princess," he whispered when the doors behind them burst open.

"Do we need promises for that? I thought you were a sure thing, Callahan."

When she turned to hug her sister and greet some guests, he noticed for the first time that her dress was backless, exposing her entire back from the tops of her shoulders to the dip where he liked to rest his hand. He nearly groaned out loud, his fingers itching to slip under the fabric and down to the perfect curve of her ass. Sweet Christ, he desperately needed this day to be over.

But they had hours to go yet. First he had to suffer through a receiving line shaking hands and accepting congratulations from people he'd never met before and would likely never meet again. Then he had to suffer through pictures with not one but two trigger-happy photographers who were pointing and directing and posing what seemed like every single human being Aidan had ever met in his entire life.

When the posed photos were done, Sofia and Julia surrounded Viv, carefully removing her veil and reattaching the tiara before pinning up her train with a trio of hidden buttons so it bustled behind her instead of dragged.

When they were finally done and alone for a blessed minute, Aidan reached for Viv's hand, drawing her against him where he reclined against the edge of a pew.

"Wife," he said, rolling the strange word around in his mouth. He'd never imagined he'd get to use it before today.

"Husband," she replied, draping her arms over his shoulders and leaning against his chest. "I'm already tired. If I have to keep smiling, my face is going to fall off."

"We could skip it. Go right to the hotel instead."

She straightened, a look he couldn't name in her eyes, and stepped away from him, dancing out of his reach when he tried to pull her closer again. She smiled, but her voice was guarded when she spoke.

"I spent dozens of hours planning this thing that everyone keeps calling the social event of the season, so you're not getting off that easy. You'll have to wait until later to get it over with."

"Hey." Sofia appeared at the back of the church as if summoned. "You two ready?"

"Ready!" Viv called out, turning from him and walking up the aisle, dress swishing behind her.

With a sigh, he followed them out. There would be no such thing as getting it over with tonight. He intended to take his time. And a lot of it.

Chapter Sixteen

The reception hall looked perfect, but that didn't stop Viv from wanting to compulsively double-check every single detail. More so to keep herself busy than to ensure it was done correctly. They'd hired a coordinator to see to all the last-minute things and handle any issues that might arise today, but she needed a distraction.

Aidan was being affectionate—too affectionate—and she'd be damned if she let herself get caught up in his perfect act again. Except it was easy to forget he was faking it when he pinned her with looks that shot straight to her core from across the room.

This was an act, a duty for him. She'd known that from the first night she met him. If she made the mistake of jumbling his concern over her relationship with Collin and Collin's antics in recent weeks with actual feelings for her, then that was her problem.

She only had herself to blame for not stopping the slow free fall of her stupid, traitorous heart. He'd been nothing but honest with her about this. She'd have to work harder to claw it back before he stomped on it and ruined it forever with his carelessness.

"We missed a step," Aidan said from behind her, breath caressing her cheek as he whispered in her ear.

"Did we? Which one?" She turned to peek at him over her shoulder.

"Isn't there supposed to be a first dance or whatever you call it?" he asked as he watched people join and leave the dance floor in the middle of the room.

"Oh. We decided to skip the traditional dances."

"Why?"

At the genuine curiosity in his voice, she turned to look up at him, noting the frown creasing his forehead. "Because you and I don't have a single song we've ever danced to, and you wouldn't have anyone to dance with for the mother and son dance. So we decided to skip all three."

"What if I don't want to skip it?"

She tamped down her irritation and kept a serene smile on her face when she turned away again. "There's only so much faking you're required to do today, Callahan. I think you can let this one go."

She knew he'd left only because a chill washed over her exposed back when he walked away. She was turning to take her seat at the head table when she heard the wobbly sound of the DJ's mic engaging.

"Ladies and gentlemen, if you could please take your seats so the bride and groom can enjoy their first dance as Mr. and Mrs."

Her head whipped up in time to see Aidan walking toward her. He stopped a few inches in front of her, holding out his hand. With all eyes on them, she had no chance but to lay her fingers in his and let him lead her onto the now empty dance floor.

When a song came on that she didn't recognize, he

wrapped his arm around her waist and drew her in tight against him.

"What are you doing?"

"My brother danced with his wife to this song."

Viv glanced up at the head table, where Evie was watching them with a curious smile. "Declan?"

"No," Aidan said, drawing her gaze. "Finn and Cait."

Her heart took another slow slide at the look on his face. "I'm sorry. I didn't know the first dance would mean that much to you."

His eyes searched hers. "It doesn't, really. Just this song was the first one that popped into my head. I suspect it means something to you, though."

"Why are you being so weird today, Callahan?"

"Weird?" His eyebrow lifted, and she felt his fingertips caressing the bare skin at the small of her back.

"Yeah, I didn't expect you to lay it on this thick. A much better performance than the engagement party, I have to say."

He made a noise in the back of his throat. "More photographers here this time," he murmured. "Song's almost over." He spun her out and back in, leaving her breathless. "I told them to play something for a father-daughter dance next."

When the song finished, Aidan released her. Before she could speak, her father was beside them, and the next song began. She saw something flash in Aidan's blue eyes before he turned and made his way to his place at the head table.

"You look beautiful today, *passerotta*," her father said, and she smiled.

"Thank you, Papa."

"Are you okay?"

"Of course." She tried for an encouraging smile. "It's finally done, and I can breathe. I'll worry about everything that comes next tomorrow."

"You're your mother's daughter that way." He looked

over her shoulder at where his wife sat. "She'd much rather look at things with a clear head. I wish this could have been different for you."

"I know."

"You deserve to be married to someone who would go to the ends of the earth for you."

Her chest tightened at her father's words because he was admitting what she already knew, that Aidan would not be that man for her. But if she acknowledged it today, she'd crack wide open, unable to scoop all the pieces up again.

"It'll take time, Papa. We're putting the puzzle together out of order, but we'll get there."

He didn't respond, simply twirled her around the floor until the song ended. When it did, he cupped her face in his hands like he had when she was a little girl and kissed both her cheeks, her forehead, and the tip of her nose.

"May your life be like good wine," he whispered.

"And get better with each passing year?" she finished for him around the lump in her throat. "I love you, Papa."

"I love you too, *passerotta*," he replied, leading her off the dance floor and releasing her.

She paused to talk with everyone who stopped her on her way to the head table. She felt Aidan's eyes tracking her across the room, felt the heat of his gaze on her skin like the sun. Jesus, she was teetering on the brink of insanity today.

When she finally collapsed into her seat next to him, he set a glass of wine in front of her and motioned for a waiter to bring her a plate of food.

"Is the chicken good? I ordered the steak." She reached over for his fork to take a bite, hissing when he smacked her hand.

"Get your own."

She dropped her chin into her palm at the teasing light in his eyes. This she was familiar with. This was the Callahan she could handle. The verbal sparring they were so good at felt much less constricting than the heavy weight of his direct gaze.

"What's yours is mine now, Callahan." She picked up her fork and attempted stabbing a piece of chicken again. "Wow," she said when he batted her hand away a second time. "You'd let your wife starve before you shared your food."

"You're not going to starve. They're going to bring you a plate." He made a big show of taking a bite of chicken and chewing slowly. "Mmm," he groaned. "This chicken is delicious."

She shoved at his arm, and he chuckled as the waiter appeared and set a covered plate in front of her, lifting the cloche and offering her some freshly cracked black pepper before disappearing again. It smelled divine, and her stomach growled. She'd been too nervous to eat anything today.

Watching him out of the corner of her eye while she cut into her steak, she was prepared when his hand snaked over to steal his own bite, and she smacked him with the flat of the knife, making him jump.

"I have three brothers," she said as he wiped butter off the back of his hand, "and catlike reflexes. If you're not sharing, neither am I, *husband*."

"You can have some chicken if I get to feed it to you."

She choked on her wine, coughing and shrugging his hand away when he reached up to pat her on the back.

"I don't want your food that badly, Callahan," she rasped, taking a sip of water. "You can keep it."

"Oh, come on. It'll make a great photo. And people are watching," he added, inclining his head to the guests who'd looked up at her coughs. "Do it for the fans."

She pinned him with a hard stare when he speared a bite of chicken and held it up to her lips. There was no good way to refuse now, not with people watching them and the photographer hovering just at the edge of her periphery.

Smiling sweetly, she wrapped her lips slowly around the chicken and drew it into her mouth, giving herself a pat on the back when his eyes dropped to her lips and lingered there as she chewed. He reached up to brush at an invisible crumb at the corner of her mouth, and Viv could hear the click and whir of the camera to her right. It was all an act, she reminded herself. It meant nothing.

As the evening wore on, Viv was convinced Aidan had, at some point, read a wedding magazine or something because he insisted on doing all the traditions she and Evie had decided to skip.

They cut the cake and fed it to each other, she tossed her bouquet into a crowd of single women, and when he reached under her skirt to remove her garter, his fingers grazed dangerously high on her thigh. She counted herself lucky that she'd talked him out of retrieving it with his teeth.

She should have been exhausted when they finally left the reception hall to cheers and the fizz and pop of sparklers, but the more he touched her, on her back and her arm and her shoulder and her fingers, the more electric she felt.

They took a limo to the hotel in silence, and the front desk staff congratulated them on their wedding before showing them upstairs to the sprawling two-room suite. It hardly seemed necessary for a single night, but it looked good if anyone ever asked where they stayed. Another part of the act to make it all look real.

Someone had already dropped off their bags. She could see them on the couch in the living room. Aidan thanked the bellhop and slipped him some cash, and when she heard the door close with a soft click behind her, she let out the breath she'd been holding and willed her heart to stop trying to pound its way out of her chest.

133

Chapter Seventeen

When she didn't hear any movement behind her, she turned to find Aidan reclined against the door, arms crossed over his chest, watching her. She pressed a hand to her stomach. Why was he looking at her like that?

He'd been staring at her all day like he couldn't wait to remove this dress, and now he wasn't even doing anything. Maybe he'd changed his mind or was trying to calculate the best way to get this over with as quickly as possible.

"I say we go for missionary. Quick and easy."

His eyebrow slowly lifted, but he didn't speak. He pushed away from the door, and she forced herself not to take a step back. When he stopped in front of her, he reached up to run his fingertips over the chandelier necklace she wore. The rubies and diamonds sat heavy against her neck.

His finger slid down her chest, tracing along the skin just over the top of the draped neckline of her dress, sending heat through her as his finger moved from one shoulder to the other.

She should want quick and easy because she was in very

real danger of losing herself if she gave in to everything she wanted from him. It was stupid to want him this much. But she didn't seem to be able to help it.

His hand wandered lower, stroking the side of her breast, and she let out a slow breath.

"Is that what you want, princess? Quick and easy?"

She shivered. When had that stupid nickname he had for her become a caress instead of an insult? When she didn't answer, he circled his thumb around her nipple but didn't touch it.

"No," she admitted when his eyes met hers.

As soon as the single syllable left her lips, his hands were on her, roaming over her body as if he couldn't figure out where he wanted to touch her first. He skimmed them down her back and over her ass, squeezing before he circled them up around her hips and stomach to her breasts, palming them as he finally, blissfully, dragged his thumbs across her nipples.

He canted his head, skimming his teeth across her jaw and using his fingers to tilt her head so he could drag his tongue across that sensitive spot behind her ear he liked to rub with his thumb. Her legs wobbled at the contact, and he wrapped his arm around her waist to hold her tight against him.

"I have been imagining all the ways I want to fuck you tonight."

"Have you?" she wondered, breathless, hands braced on his chest.

"Mmm," he murmured against her neck, pressing kisses down the side of her throat to her exposed shoulder. "I regret to inform you that missionary wasn't one of them. But I'm happy to add it to the list."

Her laugh quickly dissolved into a hitched breath when his fingers dipped under the shoulders of her dress and he slowly eased it down, helping her slip her arms out of the lace sleeves. When he pushed it down over her breasts, he groaned.

"You did wear something I could take off you," he said, dragging his thumb over the top of the satin bodysuit she'd worn in lieu of a bra.

"I couldn't share all my secrets, Callahan."

He leaned down to press kisses to the rounded tops of her breasts before kneeling and helping her slide the dress all the way down her legs. His hands caressed up her calves and over her thighs, fingertips sliding up her inner thighs to brush against the satin covering the slick heat of her core.

When he pushed to his feet again, he shrugged out of his tuxedo jacket and tossed it toward a chair. He studied her, eyes hungry, as he undid his cuff links and set them carefully on the table. While he slowly, torturously, undid the buttons on his shirt, she reached up to remove her necklace.

"No," he said, tugging his shirt out of his pants and letting it hang open. "I want to fuck you wearing that. Only that. And maybe those," he added, gesturing to her shoes.

She didn't wait for him to initiate contact again. She reached for his shoulders and tugged him closer, groaning against his lips when her fingers met bare skin. Pushing the shirt down his arms, she explored the broad expanse of his back with her hands, memorizing him from shoulder to waist, then down to his ass, squeezing until he ground the hard length of his cock against her hip.

His fingers slid over her stomach while he took her mouth, and he expertly flipped open the front catch on her bodysuit, giving himself just enough leverage to slip his hand in and scrape his fingertips across her nipple. She bit down on his lip at the contact, and he hissed, pinching her nipple between his fingers.

Urgently, he tugged at the satin fabric, dragging it down to her waist and dipping his head to capture her nipple in his mouth, closing his teeth around it until she gasped and arched against him, her fingernails biting into his shoulders.

Viv skimmed her hands down his chest, then further, rubbing over the bulge of his cock. Aidan groaned softly, his fingers making quick work of the rest of her bodysuit until she was completely naked and on fire from the way his eyes took in every inch of her body.

He whispered her name like a prayer while she undid the button of his pants and dragged down the zipper. His grip tightened on her breast when she shoved his pants down over his hips and freed his cock from his boxers, wrapping her hand around it and dragging her thumb over the tip.

She stroked him down and back up again, grinning when his head dropped to her shoulder on a strangled groan. It was a heady, powerful thing knowing she could make him feel as desperately needy as she felt right now.

"Need you," he murmured when she stroked him again, and he kicked his shoes off, toeing out of his pants before lifting her up and bracing her back against the wall.

She felt his thick shaft slide against her slit, and she dropped her head back against the wall with a groan. She needed him inside her like she needed air in her lungs.

"Callahan," she begged, watching him as he gripped the base of his shaft and teased the head over her clit, making the breath catch in her throat.

In one fluid motion, he slid inside her to the hilt, and she clenched around him, her legs tightening around his waist while he moved his hands to grip her ass, digging his fingers into her flesh.

He licked and sucked at her neck above the heavy necklace while he drew back and plunged into her again. Each time he did, he picked up speed until she was breathless and panting from his thrusts.

She felt him in every single nerve ending, his lips, his

teeth, his tongue, his cock. All of them drove her to the point of insanity until all she could do was cling to him, her fingernails dragging shallow scratches along his back.

"Viv," he groaned against her shoulder, lifting her enough to grind his pelvis against her clit with each thrust until her body was vibrating. "Come for me."

"Yes. Fuck. I…"

Her orgasm didn't take her by degrees; it shoved her off a cliff so she was free falling through the darkness, stars swimming in her vision.

Before Viv could catch her breath, Aidan lifted her away from the wall and carried her back into the bedroom. When he laid her down on the edge of the bed, she expected him to cover her body with his and slide inside her again. She wanted him inside her. But he went to his knees on the floor between her thighs.

He looked up at her, breath hot against her swollen lips. "I've thought about doing this for weeks," he said, holding her gaze while his tongue flicked out to drag across her slit. "Wondered what you would taste like." He swirled his tongue over her clit. "What kind of sounds you'd make."

She dropped her head back between her shoulders with a groan, lifting her hips toward his mouth until he laid a hand over her stomach and held her against the bed. He continued his slow assault with his mouth, alternating between tracing her pussy with his tongue and sucking her clit between his lips.

Each time she gasped, he circled his tongue around her clit and slowed his pace, torturing her by changing the rhythm, the speed, the pressure. Fucking hell, the man was trying to kill her.

"Stop teasing and fuck me," she pleaded, wriggling against his grip.

His gaze was sharp, hungry when it snapped to hers, and he wordlessly slid a finger inside her, making her gasp.

"I'll fuck you when you come for me again," he said, slipping his finger in and out of her pussy before adding a second one.

"Callahan," she sobbed when he wrapped his lips around her clit again, sucking as he pistoned his fingers faster.

She grappled for him, hands sliding through his hair and down to his shoulders, desperate to hold on as her orgasm swamped her, sending shock waves through her. She'd barely registered his absence before she felt his hands on her thighs, urging her legs around his waist as he sunk into her again.

"You're gorgeous when you come," he said, nipping her chin.

"I bet you say that to all the girls," she replied, arching up against him when he ground his hips into hers.

He covered the top of her body with his, bracing his forearms on the bed on either side of her, and she groaned at the feel of his chest dragging against her nipples. He scored her shoulder with his teeth, marking her skin as his pelvis ground circles against her clit.

"I saved that one just for you, princess."

He pushed up to look down at her, drawing his hips back and slamming in deep. She locked her legs tighter around his waist, pulling him in closer while his hands gripped her thighs. Sliding her hands up her stomach to cup her breasts, squeezing and tweaking the nipples gently, her eyes never left his.

He watched her play with herself, his hips moving faster the more she worked her fingers over her nipples. She could tell he was getting close when he reached down to finger her clit, rubbing it in quick, rough circles while he drove himself inside her.

She wanted to watch him come undone, wanted to see

that moment on his face, but he wouldn't relent in his pace. His fingers and his cock and those gorgeous blue eyes thrust her over the edge, and then he chased after her, her name an oath on his lips as he emptied himself inside her.

He braced his hands on the bed, breath coming in sharp pants, before rolling onto his back. She felt the rapid rise and fall of her chest under her fingers, delighting in the way her body tingled, somehow both numb and on fire simultaneously.

"I think I'm blind," he groaned. "You blinded me."

She laughed and rolled onto her side, and his eyes shot open when her breasts pressed against his arm. "How many fingers?" she asked, holding her hand up in front of his face.

He squinted. "Two."

"See? Not blind."

When she started to scoot off the bed, he gripped her wrist. "Where are you going?"

"I'm going to clean up and get ready for bed."

He released her and nodded. "Do you want me to sleep in the other room? I think the sofa is a pullout." His expression was unreadable.

"Do you want to sleep in the other room?"

"Not particularly." He watched her push away from the bed and cross to the door. "I'm not finished with you yet."

Chapter Eighteen

Aidan woke to the smell of flowers and the feel of something soft and warm pressed against his bare chest. He snuggled closer, wanting to steal a few more minutes of sleep before facing the harsh, jagged light that glowed behind his lids. He was too comfortable to move and disturb whatever dream he was having.

When he felt the feather-light flutter of warm breath on his forearm, his eyes shot open, blinking against the sunlight that fell in bright slashes across the bed. He wasn't in his bed, in his room. He was in a hotel. The day after his wedding. Completely wrapped around his wife.

She hadn't moved, still curled up in the same position she'd fallen asleep in when they'd finally spent themselves and collapsed on the king-sized bed. He'd started on the other side of it to give her space.

As much as he'd wanted to haul her up against him and drape her leg across his thigh, feel her warm wetness pressed against him, he figured post-sex snuggling sent the wrong message. But at some point in the night, he'd scooted all the way across the bed and wrapped around her like a vine. His arm slung over her waist, bare chest pressed up against her back, nose buried in the soft waves of her hair. He liked it entirely too much.

Carefully, he lifted his arm from around her middle and rolled gently back to his side of the bed so as not to wake her. He scrubbed his hands over his face. He'd never woken up with a woman before, had carefully avoided it his entire adult life. What was the protocol? Did the protocol change when the woman was your wife?

He looked down at his left hand and the brand new wedding band that sat there. He anticipated the same feeling of panic that usually sat heavy in his stomach whenever he thought about the wedding, but it didn't come. He'd examine that oddity later.

When he slid to the edge of the bed, Viv stirred, rolling onto her back, the sheet slipping down to her waist, and his mouth watered. Before he could talk himself out of it, he crawled back into bed, stretching his body out against hers and watching her face as he slowly traced his finger around her nipple.

He felt her drift toward consciousness in the way her muscles went taut and her breath sharpened and her back bowed ever so slightly. Then her eyes fluttered open and focused on him, her mouth curving into a satisfied grin as he dragged the pad of his finger over her hardened nipple.

"Morning," he said when she sighed.

"Morning," she replied, raising her arms over her head and arching off the bed to stretch.

While she did, he slid his hand down over her stomach and between her thighs, tracing her pussy lips with his fingertips.

"I could get used to waking up like this."

He dipped his head to kiss the side of her breast, fingers

toying with her clit. "I could get used to waking you up like this."

He saw it on her face the moment she let reality sink in—this wasn't something either of them would have forever—but he wasn't ready to let them drift into that reality yet. He wanted to keep her here, with him, for just a moment longer.

"Not yet," he said when she opened her mouth to speak. "Don't think too much. Just stay here with me."

He rolled on top of her, positioning himself between her thighs, rubbing his cock head up and down her slit until she was nice and wet for him. He slid inside her, rocking their hips together and loving the way she instantly wrapped her legs around his waist.

He braced one hand on the bed as he slowly slid his cock in and out of her tight, wet heat and let the other drift up her side to cup her breast, squeezing her nipple between his fingers.

"We didn't check missionary off the list last night," he reminded her. "But you won't get this one quick and easy either."

He set a slow pace, giving her every inch of his cock with every deep thrust, enjoying the way she sighed and moaned and writhed underneath him. He could live inside her and not get enough of how she responded to him, of the way her nails felt scoring his back or her teeth as she nibbled across his shoulder.

He'd nearly gone blind again when she'd wrapped her lips around his cock last night and sucked him to another orgasm. He'd thought one night would be enough to purge her from his blood, one night to give in to all the things he'd been dreaming of doing to her for weeks. But from the first moment he'd touched her, he knew one night would never satiate him.

She reached down and dug her fingernails into his hips,

urging him faster, and he knew she was desperate to come. He shifted above her, gripping her hip for leverage as he thrust hard inside her, making her groan. He fucking loved that sound. He could get addicted to it, to her.

When she whimpered, he released her nipple, sliding his hand down between their bodies to rub her clit, smiling at the way she instantly bucked against him, her pussy clenching his cock in a vise grip.

"Viv," he said, waiting for her eyes to drag open and lock on his face. "Look at me when you come."

She whimpered again, and he increased the pressure on her clit and the pace of his thrusts inside her. He knew the moment she clamped down around him with her orgasm he would follow her, but he wanted to watch her lose herself in it first. Wanted to see that haze that clouded her big brown eyes right after she came while she floated back down to earth.

She tensed just before she screamed with her release, her body bucking and shaking under him, but he didn't let up on her clit while he pounded harder, faster, deeper inside her sending her through a second orgasm while his own ripped through him.

Spent, he dropped his head into the crook of her neck, licking and kissing her skin while she rewarded him with sexy little moans and sighs.

"Missionary. Check," she said, drawing a check mark on his shoulder with her fingertip.

He laughed, rolling off her and giving in to what he'd wanted to do since last night, reaching out to pull her body against his. She froze for a minute before relaxing against him and wrapping her arm around his waist.

"You're very good at that, you know."

He let his hand slip down to her ass, drawing her closer until she finally slid her leg over his thigh. "Good at what?"

"All of it."

He chuckled, giving her ass a squeeze. "It helps to have a willing and very talented partner."

"What should we do now?"

"Sex in the shower."

She drilled a finger into his belly. "I was thinking more like breakfast. We've burned a lot of calories, and I'm starving."

"Breakfast," he conceded, reaching for his phone on the nightstand. "Then sex in the shower." He pulled up the menu for the hotel's restaurant and handed it to her. "What?" he said when she frowned at it.

"Isn't there a physical menu in here somewhere?"

"I think it's on the table in the other room. Way over there." He gestured vaguely toward the door. "I'm too comfortable to get up. Unless you want to go get it."

She snuggled closer, propping her chin on his chest. "No."

He watched her scan through the menu, brow furrowed, and Christ, if he didn't want her again already. How was he supposed to survive being married to this woman and sharing a bed with her every night? She was bound to kill him or permanently make his eyes go crossed.

"Oh," she exclaimed. "Eggs Benedict. And…one of those assorted pastry baskets. And coffee. All the coffee."

She pressed the phone into his hand and laid back down on his chest, sighing when he slipped his fingers through her hair. He should break the spell, get up, get dressed, and drag them both back into the real world. But he wanted to stay here with her pretending that things were different for just a little longer, even if he couldn't understand why.

They ate breakfast at the little table in the main room, and then he finally got to take her in the shower. He'd have to look into getting one of those waterfall shower heads installed in his bathroom at home.

He was tugging a shirt over his head when she caught his eye in the mirror as she applied mascara to her lashes.

"I realize this is probably a question I should have asked weeks ago, but, uh…where are we going to live?"

"Oh."

"I mean, I know we're going to live at the um…Callahan estate."

"Glenmore House," he supplied.

"Right. Glenmore House. I know we're going to live there for a while, but for how long?"

Unease pinched at his insides, and he couldn't meet her gaze. "Until we find the right place, I guess. Did you have somewhere particular in mind?"

When she didn't answer, he looked up to find her staring at him. The smile she flashed him was forced and didn't reach her eyes.

"No. Nowhere specific. Just curious."

She dropped her mascara into her bag and carried it into the bedroom. He tried to figure out what to say as they finished packing up the rest of their stuff, but he couldn't think of a single thing that didn't make him sound like an asshole.

He'd have to work on that. He couldn't keep his plan from her forever. Eventually he'd have to tell her. But it could wait. It didn't have to be today.

After Viv zipped her dress into its bag, Aidan threw it over his shoulder and followed her to the door. He heard the click of the latch while he gave the room a final once over to make sure they hadn't left anything important behind. When he turned to follow her out, she was frozen in place.

He stepped up behind her and noticed her eyes were glued to the floor in front of her. "What's wrong?"

He moved to her right and followed her gaze. On the floor was a long, thin flower box. The kind long-stemmed roses

146

might be delivered in. *To The Happy Couple* was written in the same slashing black lettering as the note she'd found in her jacket at her last fitting.

Setting their bags on the floor and draping her dress over a chair, he pulled her back into the room, scooping up the box and carrying it inside. The hallway was empty, but the box hadn't been there when he'd let room service in. So someone had dropped it off sometime in the last two hours. Which means they were being watched.

Easing the door closed, he crossed back to the table where they'd had breakfast and set it down gently. "Viv, come stand behind me, please."

She didn't hesitate to follow his command, immediately moving behind his left shoulder and peeking at the box over it. He reached for the lid and quickly flipped it off. It was lined with black satin, which made the stark red of the rose stand out even more.

Lifting it out, he found a plain white envelope nestled underneath. It wasn't sealed, but it had some weight to it, and when he opened the flap, he swore under his breath.

"What?" she demanded, pressing against his back to peer down at the pictures in his hands. "Oh my God."

He dropped them onto the table and fanned them out. Dozens of candid shots of Viv dating as far back as the first night they'd met and several from the wedding the night before. Any picture they happened to be in together showed his face obliterated with the same black Sharpie. A few of them had been ripped in half.

"You think this is still about the alliance?"

He scooped the pictures up and shuffled them back into the envelope before shoving them into the pocket of his jeans.

"No. I'm not sure it ever was."

Leaving the box and the rose for the cleaning crew, he turned to make sure Viv was okay. Her face was ashen, her eyes wide and staring at where the pictures had been moments before.

"Hey," he whispered, drawing her gaze. "I'm not going to let anything happen to you." She nodded, but he could tell she was shaken. "Come on. Let's get you home."

He laced his fingers with hers and held tight until they were securely in the truck and driving away from Center City toward Glenmore House. She tapped restless fingers on her knee the entire drive, and he didn't know how to ease her anxiety.

It was clear whatever was going on here went deeper than shaking the alliance. Someone had been stalking Viv for at least a month, potentially longer. And he had exactly one guess who the fucker was.

Every car was in the driveway when they pulled in, which was good. It meant he could tell them all at once and finally make them see reason this time. Collin needed to be dealt with. Aidan would not let this go unanswered a second time.

"What are you thinking?" he asked as he led her through the maze of cars and into the garage.

"That I have terrible taste in men."

He snorted, motioning for her to go ahead of him through the door. Evie and Declan were in the formal living room cuddled up on one of the couches, and Evie smiled when she saw them enter, the warmth in her face suddenly cooling when she saw their expressions.

"What's wrong? What happened?" she demanded.

"We have a problem."

He reached into his back pocket for the envelope and dropped it on the coffee table.

Chapter Nineteen

Viv sat on the floor of Aidan's closet, arranging her shoes in neat rows. Technically it was their closet, but after less than twenty-four hours in Glenmore House, she hardly felt like she could claim anything as hers. Space had been cleared for her, though, so she was intent on filling it up.

Sometime between when she'd left her parents' house for the wedding and when they'd arrived yesterday, all the things from her childhood home that she'd carefully packed into boxes had appeared stacked in the corner of Aidan's—their—room.

It seemed like magic, even if it was probably someone on the staff. Aidan said they had several live-in staff members who had rooms on the third floor.

She set a navy stiletto next to its mate and shook her head, reaching into the box for the next pair of shoes. He'd said it so casually she nearly laughed. The closest she could ever say she'd come to any sort of staff had been the once monthly housekeeper her mother paid to deep clean a house well used by five active children.

Not even married two full days, and she already felt wildly out of her depth. Surrounded by the opulence of Glenmore House with its decades of history, live-in staff, and the family that called it home. But this was her life now. All she could do was unpack and poke around to get her bearings.

She'd gotten a lot done since waking up alone with no idea where her husband was. Her clothes now lined the other half of the closet in neat rows; pants and panties and bras were tucked into built-in drawers. Her shoes took up every spare inch of the floor on her side she could find. Why the hell did she have so many shoes?

The second vanity in the bathroom was now filled with her things, neatly organized in the recessed medicine cabinet with its fancy sliding mirrors. She'd lined up her bottles of shampoos and creams in the shower and wondered if Aidan saw this as an invasion. Of his space and his privacy. Of his life.

Whether it was an invasion or the inevitable conclusion to the wedding, they had much more space to avoid each other here than they might have somewhere else. Waking up alone with no note certainly felt like avoidance.

Leaving the hotel had popped whatever bubble they'd found themselves in on their wedding night. Sex with Aidan was an all-consuming fire that ignited in her belly and spread out until she was liquid with it, desperate, needy, begging. Life with Aidan, well, that was something else entirely. And she hated that she had no idea what to expect from it.

Giving up trying to squeeze any more shoes into the space, she pushed the half-empty box into a back corner and made a mental note to look into some kind of shoe organizing solution. She could hear Aidan's quips about her sizable collection even now. He could complain all he wanted; he didn't seem to mind looking at her legs in a good pair of heels.

On her way to the door, she paused next to the bed. She'd slung the covers up loosely over the pillows when she got up, but it had been neatly made when they'd fallen into it last night, and she wondered if she should do that or not. A knock on the door drew her eyes to Evie framed in the doorway.

"Morning." Evie smiled. "Did you sleep okay?"

"I did. Thanks."

Evie surveyed the now empty corner where the boxes had been and frowned. "How long have you been up?"

"A few hours. Why?"

"I figured you weren't at breakfast because you were still sleeping. But now I'm going to assume Aidan didn't tell you about breakfast." Viv shook her head, and Evie snorted. "Figures. You must be starving."

When Evie turned on her heel and disappeared from view, Viv trailed behind her, catching the flash of a gray maid's uniform disappearing into a bedroom at the far end of the hall as she made her way to the stairs. *That* was definitely going to take some getting used to. She would have to ask Aidan how many several meant exactly.

A wide set of stairs swept down to the grand foyer while two narrower sets curved up on either side to the third floor. She wondered if there was anything else up there besides staff rooms. Aidan hadn't exactly been forthcoming with a tour or many details the day before.

Following Evie down, she knew to her right would be the formal living room, where they'd sat for hours going through all the photos, analyzing each one. Time, date, location. It chilled her to know someone had been following her for so long. It worried her more that Aidan's face had been scratched out. In some cases, whoever had left the photos had scratched at his face so violently they'd torn a hole through the paper.

In the end, they hadn't been able to come up with much.

With no digital footprint, Brogan couldn't dig anything up, and with nothing that clearly identified the photographer in the photos, it was impossible to figure out who had left them. Even the security tapes at the hotel resulted in a dead end. Whoever it was managed to stand just out of frame and slide the box in front of the door with their hand.

Which meant they knew exactly where the security cameras were and how to avoid them. It might be impressive if Viv wasn't the target. Or Aidan. They disagreed on who seemed to be in more danger. Viv was convinced it was Aidan because of the way he'd been purposefully erased, and Aidan was convinced it was Viv because she was the subject of all the photos.

Turning left as Evie had done, Viv wandered past a few closed doors and another large living room, although this one looked like it actually got some regular use with its over-stuffed couches and chairs and a well-stocked bar cart against one wall. Beyond the family room was a dining room with a long table big enough to seat twenty. It made the two tables they shoved together at her family's house for Sunday dinners look like a child's toy.

There was a door at the far end of the dining room, but she couldn't see what lay beyond it from this vantage point, and she didn't want to wander off while she was supposed to be following Evie for breakfast. She turned toward the end of the hall and stopped short in the doorway to a kitchen that took her breath away.

Gleaming, professional-grade stainless steel appliances and flawless slabs of marble countertops. A large island with a prep sink on one side and a row of stools on the other domi-nated the middle of the space. Wide cabinets went up to the ceilings, and lower cabinets with drawers to the floor lined nearly every wall save for a small sunken eat-in table.

If she were going to sit down and design her dream

kitchen, this one would be pretty close to perfect. She might tweak the layout a bit, put in a baker's pantry where the shelves lined the far wall and add a double oven instead of the beautiful French range that sat behind the island.

She salivated over getting to bake in this kitchen and wondered what Aidan would say about building or renovating something like this wherever they ended up. Assuming they ended up anywhere.

His reaction when she'd asked him where they were going to live had twisted something sharp inside her. Something that told her if he'd been honest with her instead of quickly and expertly deflecting the question, she wouldn't have liked his answer.

"You okay?" Evie asked, watching Viv with her hand on the fridge door.

"I…yes. Sorry. This kitchen is incredible."

Evie glanced around the space and sent Viv a sheepish smile. "That's what Libby always says. But since all I'm really capable of are pancakes and bacon, it's kind of lost on me. You're welcome to use it whenever you want."

"Really?" Viv breathed.

Evie chuckled, pulling covered dishes from the fridge and setting them on the counter. "Really. The staff has Wednesdays and Sundays off, so those will be your best days. Libby usually cooks dinner those nights. Or we order out."

"What did I do?" Libby strolled in with a book in her hand and hopped up on one of the stools, reaching into the bowl in the center of the island for a plum and taking a bite.

"I was just telling Viv she could use the kitchen whenever she wanted and that you usually cook when Marta and Rachel are off."

"Someone to share cooking duties with. Excellent."

"Well," Viv leaned her hip against the counter. "I'm not much of a cook, to my grandmother's great disappointment.

But I can bake all day long and not get tired of it. Breads, cakes, cookies, desserts, you name it."

"Brogan will love that. For a man as ripped as he is, he has such a sweet tooth." Libby's gaze slid to Evie. "Little early for lunch, isn't it?"

"Viv missed breakfast. I'm going to heat up the frittata and sausage Marta made. Want some? Since you also missed breakfast, but I imagine for better reasons."

Libby's cheeks flushed pink, and she shifted to toss the pit of her plum in the trash. "I could eat after burning all those calories."

Viv laughed, sliding onto a stool as Evie pulled down a couple of plates from the cabinet. "Is breakfast served every morning?"

"Did Aidan not tell you?" Libby asked.

Evie made a disappointed noise in her throat as she added food to the plates and put them in the microwave. "It's not like you have a set schedule by any means, but Glenmore House is…an institution," she decided. "And it runs like one. Breakfast is served from eight to ten in the dining room. Dinner is at seven unless someone says otherwise."

"And I can go anywhere except the west wing?" Viv asked, and Evie laughed.

"The east wing. That's where what they call the King's Suite is."

"That's her giant bedroom and its various attached rooms," Libby whispered loudly.

Viv accepted the plate of warmed food Evie passed across the island, and her mouth watered. It smelled divine. "This house is a fucking palace. How do you not get lost?"

Evie smiled. "I'll draw you a map."

"Have you heard from Cait yet?" Libby wondered, forking up a bite of egg.

Sighing, Evie leaned back against the opposite counter

and worried the hem of her sweater. "Yeah. This morning. They're coming home."

"That's good, isn't it?" Viv asked, looking from Evie to Libby. She knew Cait and her son Evan had been staying with Cait's parents somewhere in New York since Finn had been killed.

"It is. I'm just trying to figure out what to do."

"Do about what?" Viv took a bite of frittata and sighed at the explosion of flavors on her tongue. A lightly toasted slice of ciabatta would go perfectly with this. "Do you not want her to come home?"

"I do. I miss her like a limb some days. I'm just worried that…"

"That everything will feel like a bad memory," Libby finished, and Evie blew out a breath.

"Their house is across the street. It's the only place they ever lived together, and I don't know if staying there will be what she needs or be too painful. They could stay here, of course, but Finn died in the dining room and…" Evie's eyes drifted over Viv's shoulder.

"And it's hard."

Evie wrapped her arms around herself. "Yeah. It's hard."

"I suspect Cait will know what she needs. Just let her tell you."

Shoving her hair off her face, Evie sighed. "Not being able to plan everything twenty steps ahead isn't really my strong suit. But I'll try. Are you settling in okay? Need anything?"

"I either need some extra storage for my shoes or to purge some of my collection. I didn't realize I had so many high heels. But other than that, I don't think I need anything. Except maybe an update on the creep who left those pictures."

"Brogan told me about that," Libby said, rising to carry her plate to the sink. "He tried multiple cameras and angles inside the hotel, and there was no obvious culprit on any of the footage he could find."

"They blend in," Evie said. "I don't like it."

"I'm not a huge fan myself. No one has said it yet, but this is probably going to keep me in bodyguards for the rest of my life."

The look Evie sent her was full of sympathy. "Aidan was pushing for it pretty hard with Declan this morning. He's also convinced he knows who it is."

"Collin," Viv said with a nod.

"Your ex, Collin?"

"The one and only."

Libby snorted. "Too bad Leo didn't get to break his nose again at the engagement party. Fucker deserves all that and more."

"Aidan is out for blood. I guess he's partial to you not dying."

"Mmm." Viv decided to ignore the curious look in Evie's eyes. "Me too."

"They're meeting with your father in the next few days to figure out just how bloody Aidan is allowed to get."

"I suspect he won't like the answer," Viv mumbled.

Chapter Twenty

Aidan hefted another crate onto the stack meant for a buyer, his breath coming out in white puffs. He'd pushed himself at a punishing pace the last few days. Loading and unloading product, closing a few more deals, getting his new inventory system up and running.

He'd spent less time at home than he probably should have, but at this point, he considered it a bonus if only because he often found himself wanting to be at home. And that wouldn't do.

He could handle being naked with Viv, listening to her breathy moans and needy sighs as she moved under him. He liked to be the spark that set her aflame. It was everything in the light of day that was a mystery to him. So he'd made a habit of rising early and staying out late, and Declan was starting to notice.

He hadn't said anything yet, but Aidan sensed the heavy weight of Declan's disapproving stare when he dashed into the dining room for something he could eat in the car and a cup of coffee. The man should be happy. Aidan was doing exactly what had been asked of him every night. Gladly.

Playing house had never been part of the deal. Strictly speaking.

Besides, all this extra time on his hands gave him plenty of ways to imagine killing Collin Milano. He had quite the inventive list going. His favorites involved a lot of pain. The bastard had all of it coming and more for ever hitting Viv in the first place, let alone scaring her by being a creepy asshole. Milano would get every bit of what he deserved just as soon as Declan let Aidan off the leash.

The chime of his cell phone dragged him out of his thoughts, and he set the last crate into place before digging it out. Declan.

"Hello?"

"Where are you?"

"I'm at the 25th Street warehouse. Just finishing up sorting some inventory for the next few buyers. Why?"

"Almost done?"

Aidan frowned. Something in Declan's tone was off. "Just about. I sent all the guys home an hour ago, and I'm nearly ready to head out myself."

"I need you to meet us at the club."

Aidan checked his watch. "Little early for a drink, isn't it?"

"Falcone wants a meeting. Twenty minutes," Declan said before disconnecting the call.

Irritation had him rolling his shoulders. Fuck, he really hated being at his brother's beck and call sometimes, hated that Declan expected to snap his fingers and get whatever he wanted. Except he would because Aidan was interested in hearing what Falcone had to say. Viv's father seemed to be the driving force keeping Collin Milano alive, and it was starting to piss him off.

The fact that Falcone knew Collin had been hitting Viv months ago and did nothing to him had rage bubbling just under the surface. Nothing but a broken nose, and even then, that had been her brother's doing. The man was supposed to be loyal to family. If he wouldn't protect her from an abuser when she was still under his roof, what good would he be ten, twenty years from now when it counted most?

Securing the warehouse behind him, Aidan climbed into his truck. Twenty minutes was a steep ask at this time of day, but he'd do his best, and Declan would have to deal with it.

When he pulled into the parking lot of the nightclub, he was surprised to see it full with Declan's Range Rover, Brogan's Jag, and Evie's Maserati, plus two other vehicles he didn't recognize, all parked in a neat row. Must be some meeting for them all to rush over in separate cars.

He keyed in his code for the employee entrance and let himself inside. The club always looked strange in the light of day. The matte black and chrome looked much better under the sweep of neon lights and pumping bass. Not that he'd spent much time here in recent weeks.

"Not as late as I thought you'd be," Declan said, emerging from a long hallway that led to a manager's office and the bathrooms.

"You really set me up for failure with twenty minutes. Falcone finally ready to explain?"

Declan raised a brow and turned for the basement door. He unlocked the biometric lock with a mechanical whir and click, and Aidan followed him down the stairs that illuminated as they walked. He could hear muffled voices coming from the conference room in the back.

When they stepped into the doorway, Aidan saw Brogan and Evie on one side of the table, Falcone flanked by Leo and Gavin on the other. Declan moved to take a seat next to Evie, and Aidan dropped into the chair on Brogan's other side, ignoring the subtle way Brogan leaned away from him.

"Now that the gang's all here," Declan said, turning to Falcone, "what did you call this meeting for?"

Aidan could tell by Declan's tone his brother didn't appreciate being summoned. He preferred to be the one doing the summoning.

Falcone leaned his elbows on the table and steepled his fingers. "I've looked into the Milano situation, and my hands are tied."

Aidan's hand curled into a fist on the table. "They're tied, or you don't care to do anything about it?"

Falcone's jaw clenched, and he leveled Aidan with a hard stare. "What are you insinuating?"

"Nothing. I'm outright saying you should have done something about this guy months ago. The last time he posed a threat to your daughter."

"You think Giordano would have let me just off one of his men?"

"From what I heard, Giordano didn't really care who did what as long as the money was coming in."

"Then you are grossly misinformed. If I had done anything to Collin, he most definitely would have retaliated. Not because I killed Collin but because I did it without permission."

"So why didn't you get permission?"

"Because Giordano didn't see violence against women as a punishable offense. A policy I'm sure you're familiar with," Falcone added, flicking a glance at Brogan, who tensed.

Declan rubbed at his temple. "Then what is it you wanted to say, Falcone?"

"I can't touch Collin—"

"Won't," Aidan mumbled.

"Because executions without proof will hardly help me earn the respect I need to pull the Mafia up out of the gutter. Italians have been all too happy to stab each other in the back for generations if they thought they could gain something from it. That's a leadership problem."

Falcone flattened his palms on the table before leaning back in his chair. "I'm not saying I like it. No one is particularly fond of the Milanos. Collin's father, Frank, is a total prick and too drunk to be useful most of the time anyway, but they're tied to the Bellos by marriage, and the Bellos are a substantially larger family that I cannot risk alienating right now."

"So we just, what? Wait until he gets close enough to hurt her? Kill her?"

"You're saying he's untouchable," Brogan said.

"No, I'm saying I need proof. Real proof," Falcone added before Aidan could interject. "There was a black Jeep on that footage of the hit and run, but there are thousands of black Jeeps in the city, and you can't ID that one. Other than being out of line at the engagement party, we can't find him on video doing a single fucking thing."

"You think he's innocent?" Evie wondered.

"No. If he's not the one doing it directly, he's the mastermind behind whoever is, but I can't execute him without proof. I have too much on the line here. If we can find definitive proof, I'll watch while you end him. With pleasure." He turned to Aidan. "Until then, I have to think of the bigger picture."

Evie sighed and shared a look with Declan before sliding her gaze to Aidan and finally turning to Falcone.

"I have to be honest. I don't like sitting on this." She held up her hand before Falcone could speak. "I understand what you're saying, but that doesn't mean I agree. He's been careful so far. We have no reason to believe he'd suddenly get sloppy and trip up."

She sat forward in her chair. "So we need a plan B. Something that allows us to do what's necessary once things are stable. I'm not willing to put more members of this family at unnecessary risk. No matter how new. We've suffered enough loss."

Falcone pinched the bridge of his nose. "There is one thing."

"Go on," Aidan said, voice dripping sarcasm when Falcone didn't continue.

"DiMarco's restaurants."

"What about them?" Brogan asked, jaw tight.

"You did whatever you did to take legal possession of them, and I want them back."

"For what?" Evie asked.

"Years ago, Giordano ran underground casinos and gambling rings. A few fighting rings, but mostly sports betting and cards. They were exceedingly profitable, but he let them die when DiMarco came to town. We all know what they replaced it with."

"And you want to establish some more in the basements of DiMarco's old restaurants."

"And let the Bellos, and by proxy, the Milanos, run them, yes."

"Money is usually a good motivator," Evie agreed.

"That it is."

"Why does this feel like a reward rather than a punishment?" Aidan snapped.

"It's establishing loyalty. Unless you want your children to be dealing with this all over again in another fifty years, you have to give me time to rebuild."

Declan tapped his fingers on the tabletop and swept a look at Evie, whose facial expression changed the barest hint of a degree. Whatever Declan saw there, though, he agreed with, and he turned back to Falcone with a nod.

"I can agree to give you the restaurants for the casinos on one condition."

"What's that?"

"Either I run the restaurants, or I keep a cut of all profits, upstairs and downstairs."

Falcone's brows knit together. "I can't share profits with the Callahans. I'll look like a lapdog."

"Then I guess I get to run the restaurants."

"I'll still look like a lapdog, renting a room in a Callahan restaurant to do my business."

"Give me more credit than that. We run them through a shell management company. We've got plenty. They can look like yours, but they'll be mine. I'm rather partial to restaurants. That's my only offer."

The room was silent for a long moment before Falcone finally relented. "Fine."

"Great." Declan's expression was blank, but his voice was all smiles. "We'll sort everything out on our end and contact you with the details."

They rose and shook hands over the table. "My men want to put all of this behind them," Falcone said. "Move on with their lives. I want to build a better Mafia."

"We're on your side on this," Declan said, his gaze sliding to Aidan. "You'll have your loyalty from the Bellos or your proof. We'll respect your decision on this for now. I'd rather we be friends than enemies."

When Falcone turned toward the door, Aidan rounded the table and jogged to catch up with him. "Can I have a word?"

Falcone dismissed Leo and Gavin with a wave of his hand, and Aidan pulled him aside into a smaller, empty room.

"If he goes after her, I won't hesitate to kill him. I'm not asking permission. I don't care about your Mafia politics. If he takes a direct hit at Viv, he will not leave in anything but a body bag."

Falcone studied Aidan for so long Aidan was worried he

might be having a stroke or something. Finally he blinked and said, "Good. I'd expect nothing less."

Without another word, he turned on his heel and strode out, leaving Aidan alone in the doorway to the long hallway.

"What the hell was that about?" Declan wondered when Aidan caught up to them on the stairs.

"A mutual understanding. If I can't go after Collin, I want to discuss another protective detail for Viv. Any time she leaves the house."

"She's going to hate that," Evie said.

"Well, I'd rather she hate me than be dead," he replied, ignoring Evie's startled expression.

Declan paused next to his car and scrubbed a hand over his jaw. "I can't spare you indefinitely."

"I know. A rotation, a schedule. Something."

"Yeah." He studied Aidan across the hood of his Range Rover. "If it's important to you, we'll make it work."

"It's important to me."

"Then we'll figure it out. And Aidan?" Declan pulled open the door of his car. "If it's so important to you, try spending more time at home."

Declan let the meaning hang in the air before getting into his car and pulling out of the lot. Evie didn't say anything, just gave him a long look and followed Declan out.

"Are you going to give me some ominous look before driving away too?"

Brogan snorted. "You surprise me, little brother."

"With what?"

"Nothing."

"Brogan," Aidan said, waiting until Brogan looked up at him again. "Will you help me find proof?"

With an almost imperceptible nod, Brogan folded himself behind the wheel of his Jag and drove away, gunning the engine.

Aidan didn't like having his hands tied. He didn't want to wait until the other shoe dropped before he could do something about this threat hanging over them. He wanted to find the proof he needed to get rid of this fucker and protect what was his. And he wouldn't stop until he had it.

Chapter Twenty-One

Seven days, four hours, and—she glanced up at the clock on the bakery wall—twenty-eight seconds. That's how long it had been since Aidan stuck her with yet another protective detail. This time, a steady rotation of men either from the syndicate or her brothers.

It was driving her crazy. Viv tried her best not to complain. The alternative might very well be keeping her safely locked away in Glenmore House. It was big, but it wasn't that big. It wouldn't take long for cabin fever to set in if they tried to keep her cooped up there.

Aidan had been spending more time at home, Declan's influence, no doubt, with the way he seemed to carefully watch them at dinner. Proximity hadn't made it any less awkward, though. It was like the man was trying to be as wooden and stilted as possible. She'd taken to figuring out which buttons to push just to get him to do more than smile and nod.

She preferred the yelling to the uncomfortable silence, and if she pressed the right buttons often enough, they ended the night sweaty and satiated. He might not be willing to give her a decent conversation, but he was more than willing to give her his body.

Which had only, obnoxiously, uncovered a new problem for her. It's not that the sex was bad. She could hardly say that. But with their main interaction consisting of either staring at each other through strained smiles or fucking like animals, she was starting to feel like a warm body and not a wife. A very exhausted and sexually satisfied warm body, but a warm body nonetheless.

"Are you almost done?"

Viv jumped at her brother's voice just over her shoulder. Nico had been tasked with babysitting her this afternoon, and he looked about as happy about it as she felt. It was Friday night, and the kid probably wanted to be halfway to wasted with his friends instead of waiting for her to finish decorating some cupcakes for a wedding tomorrow.

"Almost. It'll go faster if you can load those bowls into the dishwasher for me." She gestured with her chin at the stack of bowls she'd used to color the frosting. "And fold up four cupcake boxes."

He grumbled but obeyed, packing the bowls into the empty spaces in the basket for the industrial-sized dishwasher and then grabbing flattened bakery boxes from one of the shelves and bending them into shape.

"How's winter training going? Feeling good about the season?"

They didn't have much in common, but Nico had taught her a love of baseball since he'd started playing little league when he was six. He was a natural with a baseball in his hand and a hell of a third baseman. He'd set the university record for recovering the most infield hits three years in a row and made the varsity team as a high school freshman before being scouted to his college team.

"It's good. Coach says there will probably be MLB scouts checking me out all season. But..."

She put the final mound of frosting on the last cupcake and reached for the sprinkle mix she'd chosen. "But what?"

"Papa keeps talking like he won't even consider it. With all the Mafia shit and everything. That we can't afford to be under the spotlight."

"That's ridiculous. The Callahans are in the spotlight all the time, and they seem to be doing fine."

"The Callahans aren't constantly trying to kill each other."

"Highly debatable." Viv showered the final box of cupcakes with sprinkles and sealed the lids with tape. "They argue with each other plenty."

"You know what I mean."

She sighed. "I know. Do you want me to talk to him?"

"Maybe?" He took the boxes of cupcakes from her hands and set them in the fridge. "He can't say no to both of us, right?"

"Probably not. I'm very cute."

Nico snorted, waiting for her by the door while she set the dishwasher to run and turned off all the lights. The night air carried that late autumn bite to it. Winter would be here soon, blanketing the city in snow and ice and the angry screaming of drivers who hated the plows. She liked fall best with its crisp tang to the air and brilliant colors.

She didn't know the way to Glenmore House by heart because she'd spent most of her time there being chauffeured, so they used GPS to follow the winding roads through the Main Line until they stopped outside the gate at the bottom of the driveway. They hit the button for guests because she couldn't remember the passcode she was supposed to use either—she'd have to write that down—and waited for the gate to swing silently in.

"Fucking hell," Nico whistled. "This is some place you got here, sis."

"I don't have any place. This is where I live for now."

"For now?"

She shrugged. "Who knows where I'll end up."

"Do you like living here?" he asked as he pulled around the circular drive.

"It's nice," she assured him. "Lots of space and plenty of people coming and going so you don't get bored. Almost like home."

"This is absolutely nothing like home. Which is now very lame and quiet without you."

"Aww, Nicky," Viv said, using his childhood nickname. "Are you saying you miss me?"

She leaned over and gave him a loud, wet kiss on his cheek, and he made a big show of wiping it off with the back of his hand.

"I'm saying you are a very loud person, and now the house is not as loud."

"Uh huh. Do you want to come in? The housekeeper let me use the kitchen long enough to make ham and cheese scones the other day. Never mind," she added when his eyes drifted to the clock on the dash. "Go out and have fun. But if it's drunk fun, call someone to come get you."

"Okay, mom."

She climbed out and stood in the driveway, watching his car pull around the circle and drive away until his taillights disappeared. She let herself in through the front door since it was the only door she had a key for and stopped short at Aidan standing at the base of the stairs.

"Hey," she said when he only stared. "Did you...have a good day?"

When he remained silent, she crossed to the stairs and began climbing them. He was always so weird around her.

169

The only time he acted like a human being capable of forming full sentences was when they were fighting or having sex. And even during sex, his sentences were short commands that turned her on far more than she wanted them to.

"Who was that guy?" He followed her up, keeping pace with her.

"Which guy?"

"The one you were kissing in the car."

She stopped short and gripped the banister to keep from tumbling backward down the stairs. "Excuse me?"

He moved two steps up and turned to face her. "I was walking past the window and happened to look out and see you lip locking with some guy who's supposed to be protecting you not...not...seducing you," he finished with a flourish.

She couldn't help it; he looked so goddamn serious. She laughed. Quietly at first, until it bubbled up out of control. She doubled over with it, tears forming at the corners of her eyes.

"You happened to look out and see me? Callahan, you cannot be serious. Do you know who was babysitting me today?" She wiped her eyes and moved around him to continue up to their room.

"It was supposed to be Liam."

"Liam got called away for something. Nico begrudgingly sat with me at the bakery and drove me home."

She slipped off her jacket and crossed to the closet to hang it, biting her cheek at the look on his face when she reemerged. She could see the internal struggle as he tried to douse the jealousy.

"I never thought I'd see the day you were jealous, Callahan. You can barely manage to string two words together unless we're naked. I didn't think you cared that much."

"I don't," he snapped, and the words bit into her with a sharp sting of pain.

"Well," she said softly, "my mistake."

She moved to brush past him into the bathroom, but he slid his arm around her waist and pulled her body in close, his forehead resting against her temple, his breath warm on her shoulder. He opened his mouth to say something but closed it again as if he couldn't find the words.

"You make me crazy," he finally murmured.

"The feeling is entirely mutual, I can assure you."

"That's not what I…let me show you."

His fingers skimmed under the hem of her sweater, sending goosebumps along her skin. He traced down over her hip and around to her ass, squeezing even though he didn't move to reposition her body flush against his.

When he shifted to graze his teeth over her jaw, she tilted her head for him, and the movement had her brushing against the already hard length of his cock. Knowing she could make him hard just by standing next to him unlocked something in her, something that made her want to take a chance.

"Callahan." She turned toward him, wrapping her arms around his neck and lightly brushing her lips against his. "I want to know you."

"You've seen every inch of me," he replied, rubbing his lips lightly against hers again while he pushed her sweater up over her stomach, stopping just long enough to squeeze her breasts through her bra before tugging it off over her head and down her arms.

"That's not what I mean," she said, sighing when his fingers tightened on the clasp of her bra but didn't release it.

"What, then?"

He was staring at her intently, but she was afraid if she made eye contact she'd lose her nerve, so instead she leaned in and pressed a kiss to the side of his throat, punctuating each word with her lips against his skin.

"I want to know more about my husband."

His hands stilled against her hips, but he didn't push her away. "Like what?"

She sucked on the skin at the base of his neck, letting her fingernails drag along his torso as she pushed his sweater up over his chest and leaned back to pull it off. God, he was perfect. Those shoulders that felt so good under her nails and the arms that effortlessly held her up against the shower wall and the chest that warmed her back before he would slip inside her in the morning.

"What did you want to be when you grew up?"

"That's what you want to know with my cock inside you?"

She bit down on his shoulder, making him hiss. "Your cock isn't inside me right now."

He tightened his hold on her ass and rocked her against his hard length. "It will be."

"Don't change the subject," she said, sliding her hands down his back and around to his belt, slowly loosening the buckle. "Well?"

"I don't know if I really thought about it. I never had any other choice but the syndicate."

Her fingers stilled on his belt, and she stepped away. "Honest answers only, Callahan. Every little boy has dreams."

He reached out to twirl a strand of her hair around his finger. "I wanted to be a rock star."

She moved closer, fingers skimming up his thighs and around to the button on his jeans. "Do you play any instruments?"

"My grandmother wanted to teach me how to play the piano. My father refused," he said, sighing as she popped open the button and dragged down his zipper.

"That's sad."

"Why?"

She kissed his lips, slowly letting him take it deeper before pulling away. "Because it was something you wanted to do."

"Piano or not, it's not like I would have actually been able to become a rock star."

"Maybe not, but that doesn't mean it couldn't have been something you enjoyed doing just for fun. Everyone needs fun things."

"What if my fun thing is sex?"

"Then I guess you've had a lot of practice."

He was quiet for a beat before he reached to pull her hands up from his waist, pressing a long kiss to both palms. He set her hands on his shoulders and moved to unhook her bra, letting it drop to hang on her elbows while he traced his fingertips around her nipple.

"What did you want to be when you grew up?"

"A ballerina," she said, releasing a shaky breath when his fingers flexed against the hard nub.

"And why didn't you?" He leaned down to pull her nipple into his mouth, making her gasp.

"I am wildly uncoordinated. I think I made it halfway through a twelve-week class when the dance instructor told my parents I was better off with more stationary hobbies."

He chuckled against her skin and sent vibrations through her body. Stripping away her bra, he backed her against the bed, sliding his thumbs into the waistband of her leggings and pushing them down over her hips and thighs, bending to help her step out of them. He pressed a quick kiss to her pussy before rising again.

"Next question? Better ask them while you can still form sentences."

She barely kept from whimpering while she watched him toe off his shoes and shed his pants and boxers.

"What's your favorite way to unwind after a hard day?"

He raised a single brow at her, his eyes raking suggestively down her body before his hands traced the same path, palming over her breasts and down her stomach to her pussy, cupping it in his hand and giving it a gentle squeeze.

"Okay," she gasped. "That was a stupid question. If you could spend a month anywhere in the world with no responsibilities, where would you go?"

"Rome," he said without hesitation, teasing his finger over her clit.

She jerked back, looking up at him. "That's not funny."

"Of course it's not funny. It's not a funny question." He leaned in to trail his lips across her shoulder to her neck, licking and kissing up the side of it as his fingers continued to work back and forth over her clit, making her breath catch.

"Are you making fun of me?"

"No." He continued his slow assault of her pussy, pushing one finger inside and making her knees wobble.

"Why did you say you wanted to go to Rome on our honeymoon?"

"Because I've always wanted to go to Rome. My grandfather went once. I begged to go, but he would only take Declan." He slid in a second finger, and she groaned, gripping his bicep to steady herself.

She couldn't tell if he was messing with her right now, not with two of his fingers buried inside her and picking up speed as he worked them in and out, his lips and teeth and tongue teasing across her neck and shoulder. She wanted to believe him, but maybe this was another act he was putting on to get what he wanted.

"I'll prove it to you later," he promised. "Right now I have to be inside you."

He slipped his fingers out and eased her back on the bed before covering her body with his own. The head of his cock brushed against her slit, and she arched her hips up in response until she felt him slide inside her inch by inch until he was finally buried deep.

"I think about you all day," he murmured against her neck, rocking his hips into hers.

"I think that's evident since I haven't gotten much sleep in the last week."

She felt his lips curve into a smile, and he slid out and back in with one forceful thrust, making her groan low in her throat.

"I think about your taste, your scent, the way your pussy grips my cock when you come." He punctuated each one with a thrust of his hips. "I think about what you're doing, who you're talking to, what you're thinking."

He covered her hands with his and laced their fingers, growling when she wrapped her legs around his waist and fitted them closer together.

"I can't stop thinking about you," he whispered, hips moving more urgently. "I don't know what to make of it. I don't even know why I'm telling you this. Other than you drive me crazy and I can't help myself."

"C-Callahan." She shuddered as he drove into her, his words opening up something inside her that would be impossible to close again. "Don't lie to me."

"I wish I could. It would make all of this a hell of a lot easier."

She met him thrust for urgent thrust, her breath coming in ragged gasps as he pounded into her, his head buried in the crook of her neck so his groans vibrated through her sternum and straight into her heart. His grip on it was tightening, and he didn't even know it. He wouldn't know how to protect it.

"Oh God." She shuddered as he rocked and ground

against her, his hips moving at a punishing speed that pushed her closer and closer to the edge.

"Come for me, Viv. Let me feel you come."

"Yes," she all but sobbed as she gave in to the blinding flash of the orgasm that consumed her.

When she felt his body go taut against her, she squeezed his hands and tightened her legs around his waist until her heels dug into his ass. His body went limp with his release, but he managed to hold himself above her to keep from crushing her. Every rise and fall of his chest brushed against her sensitive nipples and sent ripples of pleasure through her.

He finally rolled off her, laying on his back next to her on the bed, staring up at the ceiling. She was afraid to move and break the delicate thing he'd created between them with his words.

"I don't know what to do about you," he said, reaching for her hand and linking their fingers.

"I don't know what to do about you either," she admitted.

She held her breath for the inevitable rejection, braced herself for it, but after several long moments, he simply maneuvered them both under the covers, turned off the lights, and drew her back against him. He nuzzled his nose into her hair, and she heard him draw in a deep breath, as if he was drinking her in.

She had no idea what the hell had just happened between them tonight, but she knew one thing. She was falling in love with her husband, and she had no idea if he would ever love her back.

Chapter Twenty-Two

Aidan jolted awake to someone jackhammering at the door. He was spooned against Viv from behind, her head pillowed on his arm, his other arm wrapped tight around her waist. His cock was wedged against the rounded curve of her ass, and his first thought was he was going to kill whoever was pounding on their bedroom door.

"Callahan, murder whoever the fuck that is," Viv mumbled, eyes still closed.

"I'd love to."

Brushing his fingertips across the underside of her breast, he rolled out of bed and tugged on his jeans from the night before, yanking open the door to Evie's nervous face.

"What the hell do you want at this hour?"

Evie's brows shot up, and she crossed her arms over her chest. "It's eleven in the morning, and Cait is on her way home. She's early, and I'm freaking out a little. I need Viv."

"I'm up," Viv called from the bed, and he glanced back to see her sitting in the middle of it with the sheet clutched to her breasts. Fuck, she looked good enough to eat.

"I'm sorry to interrupt," Evie said, voice strained. "I'm just—"

"Don't be." Viv waved her words away.

"I definitely think you should be," Aidan grumbled.

"What my husband means to say is, we'll get dressed and be right down to help."

Evie's face was washed in relief. "Thank you. I'll be downstairs."

Viv shoved her hair off her face and smoothed it with her hand, glancing up at him when he closed the door and crossed to the bed.

"I wish you hadn't done that."

"Offered to help?"

"Promised to be right down." He reached out to pull her to her knees, eyes traveling down her body when the sheet fell away. "I wanted to keep you in bed for a little while longer."

She slid her hand up his chest and wrapped it around his throat, grinning as she leaned in to steal a quick kiss from his lips.

"I'm sorry to disappoint you, Callahan. We'll have to skip morning sex and dive right into our usual awkward exchanges over toast."

She started to get out of bed, but he held her firmly. "They're only awkward because I never know what to say to you."

"Mmm," she replied, avoiding eye contact.

Sighing, he released her. It was probably better if they retreated to their corners anyway. He'd shared too much with her last night. Not just answering her questions, though he had because he'd wanted her too much to tell her no. But confessing his thoughts while he'd been buried inside her.

He needed to say it, couldn't have stopped the words if he wanted to. He couldn't tell if she believed him or not. He'd hardly blame her if she didn't, and it was probably better that way. He didn't understand it himself. There was no way he'd be able to explain it to her. These constant foreign sensations in his chest whenever she flitted across his mind, which was far too often for his liking.

"How long has it been since you've seen Cait?"

Viv poked her head out of the closet clad in a purple bra and matching panties, and his only thought was how much he'd like to rip it off her again.

"Not since the funeral. She hung around for a few more days before heading to New York with Evan and her parents, but she kept her distance from me."

"Why?"

When she stepped out again, she was wearing a pair of tight dark wash jeans and a gray sweater that showed off every curve.

"Woman," he growled as she crossed to the bathroom. "Are you trying to get fucked?"

He watched her lips curve into a grin while she carefully brushed out her hair and twisted it into a series of elaborate braids that she wound around each other. He had no idea how she managed to do that in less than five minutes, but he wondered how long it would take him to undo them again.

She quickly swiped makeup over her features and dabbed on a little of the perfume that smelled like her. Jasmine, he'd discovered from reading the label.

"Why did Cait avoid you?" she asked, following him into the closet when he went in search of a fresh shirt.

He turned so he couldn't see her face and pulled a long-sleeved shirt off the hanger. "I made a bit of a scene right after the funeral."

"You what?"

"I accused Libby of getting Finn killed."

He tried to move past her, but she put her arm out to stop

him, and he chanced a look at her face. She didn't look angry or disgusted or even disappointed. She looked...like she wanted to understand.

"Did she? Get Finn killed?"

He almost bit off a quick confirmation out of habit, but the acid died on his tongue.

"No." He shook his head, staring over her shoulder. "No, I think I'm the one that did that."

"How?" Her voice was soft.

"It doesn't matter."

She placed a hand on his cheek and forced him to meet her gaze. "It matters to me."

"It was impossible to gauge how many guys DiMarco might have had in his house at any one time. There was never a pattern, so we made an educated guess. We guessed wrong."

He spoke quickly, clinically. It was the only way he could tell the story. "Finn had a team on the second floor. They were overwhelmed. I had a team on the first floor with two guys shooting at us after backing us into a dead-end hallway. Brogan thinks we could have overpowered them and gotten upstairs to help Finn."

He took a deep breath. "I didn't want to take a run at them and lose any men in the process. By the time we took them down and made it upstairs, it was too late. Finn had been stabbed. We rushed him home, and he died on the dining room table. Libby was the last person to talk to him."

"And you wanted it to be Libby's fault so you didn't have to blame yourself?"

Relief flooded his chest. Someone finally understood when it felt like no one had even bothered to see him or his pain or his guilt for months.

He reached up to cup her cheek, brushing his thumb over her skin. "Yeah. Something like that."

She turned her face and pressed a kiss against his palm before taking his hand and leading him into the hallway. She didn't offer any platitudes about how it wasn't his fault and he shouldn't blame himself. He wouldn't have wanted them anyway, and he wasn't sure if she knew that or if she didn't think he deserved to hear them. The thought of it being the latter was like a knife twisting in his gut.

When she moved to drop his hand as they neared the bottom of the stairs, he tightened his grip, ignoring her startled glance. Evie stood in the foyer, fidgeting restlessly with the hem of her sweater.

"There you are."

"Where do you need us?" Viv asked, rubbing a soothing hand up and down Evie's arm.

"I think we're just going to set up some easy canapés in the solarium. It's far away from the...from the dining room. And I don't want to pressure her to stay for an entire meal if she isn't up for socializing that long."

"That makes sense. Do you need any help with the food?"

Evie shook her head. "The staff is handling it. I think I'm just looking for moral support so I don't pass out."

Viv shot Aidan a worried glance. He'd never seen Evie this panicked before. He had to admit it made him uneasy.

"Where's Declan?"

"He's on his way home from the office. He had an early meeting he couldn't cancel."

"What's bothering you, Evie?"

Evie glanced at Aidan and nibbled her bottom lip before turning to Viv. "What if she hates me?"

"Why would she hate you?" Aidan wondered.

"I don't know. It hasn't exactly been a banner year since I came back to Philadelphia. I mean, look who I'm talking to." She gestured widely at Aidan. "You hate me more than anyone."

181

"He doesn't hate you," Viv said quickly.

"Well, there's no love lost, that's for sure. And I just...I don't want to lose her. Not after what happened to Maura. I can't."

Aidan dropped Viv's hand to take Evie's shoulders and give them a rough shake. "Evelyn," he said sternly. "Cait is stronger than you give her credit for. You don't have to do anything else for her except be there when she needs you."

"Right. You're right." Evie blinked rapidly. "I'm going to see if I can convince Libby to come down. She's more nervous than I am, if that's possible."

"I'll go with you."

Both women disappeared around the corner at the top of the stairs moments before Declan came through the door.

"How's everything here?"

"Canapés are being arranged in the solarium." He gestured to the back of the house with a tilt of his head. "Your wife is freaking out, worried Cait is going to hate her."

"Why is she worried about that?"

"I have no idea. She's upstairs with my wife, trying to talk Libby into coming down. Apparently Libby is worried Cait will hate her too."

Declan rolled his eyes. "I've never known Cait to hate anyone."

"Me either, although she didn't seem that interested in being around me after the funeral."

"She didn't spend much time around anyone once Finn was buried."

"She saw you. And Brogan."

"Brogan and I visited her to see if she needed anything. Did you?"

Aidan opened his mouth and closed it again. "No."

He'd assumed she didn't want to see him after his

outburst and Declan's reprimand. Assumed she blamed him for Finn's death like he'd blamed himself, like Brogan did.

At a noise at the top of the stairs, he glanced up and saw the three women standing side by side. Evie looked a little calmer, and Libby looked nervous but determined. Only Viv looked steady and sure of herself.

Something punched through him at the sight of her. Not the familiar sensation of lust he often got when he saw her across the room, something deeper, headier, stronger. He couldn't put his finger on it, but it created a warmth that spread through his body and heated him to his toes.

"They're both so nervous," Viv whispered when she joined him. "They're making me wonder if I should be nervous. I thought you said Cait was a sweet person."

"Cait is a sweet person," he assured her.

"Then why is everyone so fucking afraid of her?"

He reached up to tuck a stray curl that had come loose from her braid behind her ear. "I think they're worried about hurting her." Christ knew he was.

She nodded as if she understood and squeezed his shoulder. At the sound of a car pulling into the drive, everyone tensed.

"It'll be fine, love," Declan said to Evie, taking her hand and pressing a kiss to the back of it. "Breathe."

Libby reached for Brogan, who wrapped his arms around her from behind at the sound of a car door slamming. To steady himself, Aidan slipped his arm around Viv's waist, curling his fingers into her hip to keep himself anchored as footsteps echoed up the front walk.

Evie didn't wait for the knock to come. She swung the door open to Cait's surprised face, and everyone seemed to notice what was different all at once.

"Holy shit," Viv breathed low in his ear.

Holy shit was right. Cait stood framed in the doorway, her

bright cap of blonde hair that swung to her chin fluttering in the breeze, kind blue eyes smiling if a little tired, and pregnant. Very pregnant.

"You...you're..." Evie stumbled.

Cait looked past Evie to Libby. "You didn't tell them?"

Evie's head swiveled to look at Libby, and Libby blanched.

"*You* didn't tell them?" Libby replied.

"Because I thought you had told them already!"

"It wasn't my news to tell!"

Cait sighed, her smile wistful, and rested her hands on her round belly. "Well, I guess now I understand why you never asked me about it when we talked."

"When did you...how far..." Evie turned to Libby. "How did you...? Well, just...come in." She blew out a breath and stepped back from the door. "It's cold outside."

"I missed you," Cait said, voice cracking as she wrapped Evie in a tight hug. "There's..." her words trailed off.

Evie nodded as if she understood. "I know."

"All that worrying for nothing," Viv whispered as Cait hugged Declan, Brogan, and Libby in turn.

"Mmm," Aidan mumbled.

"Aidan," Cait said, clasping her hands so her arms framed her belly. "You've grown up a lot since I left."

He lifted a brow. "I'm exactly the same size."

Cait's gaze slid to Viv and back to him, a smile tugging at the corner of her mouth. "That's not quite what I meant."

"You're an annoying big sister," he said, eliciting a bright smile from her by using his favorite tease.

"Yeah, but I'm your favorite one."

He wrapped her in a strong hug and whispered against her ear, "I'm sorry, Cait. I wish that...I'm so sorry."

Cait pulled back, eyes serious as she searched his. "Don't do that," she said, low enough that only he and Viv could hear. "I've heard enough from Evie to know what Brogan has been saying. He's hurt."

"But I—"

"No," Cait interrupted. "I don't blame you, and I know Finn wouldn't either. So don't go blaming yourself. Okay?"

He pressed a long kiss to her forehead until he was sure his voice wouldn't shake. "Okay."

Cait released Aidan and turned to Viv, who had tears in her eyes that she was rapidly blinking back. "You must be Vivian. I've heard a lot about you."

"Good things, I hope. And please, call me Viv." Viv extended her hand. "It's so nice to meet you."

"Do you mind if I hug you instead?"

"Oh, ah, no."

Cait wrapped her arms around Viv, and Aidan noticed the small smile that ghosted Viv's lips.

"We're sisters now," Cait said when she released her. "Sort of."

"You'll always be ours, Cait," Declan assured her.

"Always," Evie promised.

"Evan is asleep with my parents across the street, so I have a few hours. What have I missed?"

Evie looped her arm through Cait's and led her back to the solarium with everyone following, but Viv gripped Aidan's arm and held him back.

"Are you okay?"

He stared at the empty spot where Cait had been standing. "I…" He felt Viv's warm hand on his shoulder and let its weight ground him in the present before he got sucked into the visions of Finn's dead body that swam before his eyes. "I will be."

Viv searched his face and, satisfied with what she saw there, gave a quick nod. He reached for her hand and brought her knuckles to his lips.

"Come on. Cait tells the best stories."

"Two questions. Does she have any about you? And is she willing to share them?"

"Yes. And eagerly."

Viv smiled as they rounded the corner into the solarium. "Perfect."

"Careful, princess," he warned, noting how her eyes softened at the nickname.

Interesting. When had she stopped hating that? When had he stopped using it to rile her?

"Careful with what?" she prompted.

"Turnabout is fair play. I'm sure your brothers could tell me plenty of stories."

"They absolutely can. And only half of them are true."

He released her when they stepped into the solarium and watched her move through his family with effortless ease. He liked the look of her there, he realized. In his home, among his people.

At some point, he had strayed from wanting to keep her at arm's length to simply wanting to keep her. Except he was hardly qualified to hold on to her heart. He was just as liable to mangle it as he was to keep it safe from harm. Maybe more so.

It would be better for her if she never let him hold it at all. He didn't know how to love someone, especially not someone like Viv. Something that had never bothered him until her. Until she'd fallen into his life with her sharp tongue and perfect body.

He wanted to keep her safe, and the only way he knew how to do that was to keep her as far away from him as possible. Even if all he seemed to want to do was pull her close and never let go.

Chapter Twenty-Three

Viv sprinkled flour on the counter in front of her and tilted the dough out of the bowl where it had been completing its first rise. The staff had the day off, and Viv was taking full advantage of having the kitchen to herself. Well, almost to herself. Libby had tasked Viv with keeping an eye on a pot of sauce simmering on the stove for lasagna later.

So far, Viv had made two dozen Linzer cookies with raspberry jam, a red velvet cake with cream cheese frosting for after dinner, and an orange ricotta cake she needed to drop off at her sister's house. It was a new recipe she'd been playing around with in her spare time.

Baking was her happy place. It was where she got out of her head and lost herself in the repetition of measuring ingredients, mixing until the batter or the dough looked just right, then baking, cooling, and decorating. She could lose hours in the kitchen.

She missed being able to pin her hair up and disappear into a recipe or two for a few hours to relieve some stress or test something new that was rolling around in her head. She liked to play with flour and sugar and vanilla and see what she could create.

She was a decent cook, her grandmother would have accepted nothing less, but baking was where she shined. At least no one seemed to mind that she and Libby took over the kitchen twice a week when the staff was out.

"There was a day," Brogan said from the doorway, watching her fingers work the dough, "when Wednesdays and Sundays meant we'd order pizza or eat whatever casserole Marta left. I can't say I mind the home-cooked food."

"Libby makes the food."

Brogan pointed at one of the cookies, the red jam showing through the hole she'd cut in the middle. "Are these not edible?"

She laughed. "They are. Butter cookies with jam inside."

He picked one up and popped it whole into his mouth, chewing with a groan. "Fucking delicious. Is my lovely future wife home yet?"

Viv raised a brow, pinching the seam of the loaf and flipping it gently onto the sheet pan she'd already prepared. "Did Libby finally say yes?"

"Not yet. She keeps saying she isn't ready."

Viv glanced up at where Brogan was staring down at the cookies. "Does that worry you?"

"No. She's already promised me fifty years, and I intend to collect. Marriage is a piece of paper as far as I'm concerned. No offense."

She smiled and carefully covered the shaped loaf with a dish towel. "None taken. I happen to agree with you."

"That so?"

Forcing herself to give a casual shrug, she set the loaf inside the cold oven to rise a second time. "You're not married to Libby, but what you have with her is deeper and more real than what your brother and I have. Whatever a piece of paper might say."

"Does that bother you?"

When she looked up, he was watching her carefully, and she realized she might be skirting dangerous ground with this conversation. Brogan and Aidan might be on the outs right now, but they were brothers, and from what she could tell so far, the Callahans put family above everything else.

"It's just...different," she decided. A vague truth.

Brogan's eyes narrowed imperceptibly. "He's not mistreating you, is he? Hitting or yelling at you?"

Unexpected temper flared at his question, and her tone was harsher than she meant it to be. "Of course he isn't hitting me." Brogan raised a brow but said nothing. "Whatever you or I think of your bother," she continued, calmer this time, "we both know he wouldn't do that."

Aidan would have to pay attention to her first. In the days since his confessions against her skin, he either ran hot or cold. In the confines of their bedroom, Aidan was warm, attentive, and passionate, although he'd been careful not to talk nearly as much as he had that night. Sometimes she'd be able to tease conversations out of him during the day, but after a few minutes, he'd clam up and suddenly have something else to do.

It seemed like every time they were finding their footing, he would sharply push her away again, leaving her dazed and off balance. It was as if he realized he was getting too close, opening up too much, so he'd move out of reach again. It was excruciating.

She looked up at the buzz from Brogan's phone in time to see him scanning the screen. She knew that look. Something was going down today. That must be why Aidan had rushed off this morning. Brogan pointed down at the cookies in silent question, and when she nodded, he palmed two and took off toward the stairs. She was going to have to start doubling her recipe.

Alone again, she began tidying up the kitchen. Loading bowls and utensils into the dishwasher and washing what was too big to fit. She grunted when she lifted the heavy container of flour onto the high shelf in the pantry and reminded herself that her dream kitchen was going to have deep drawers with all her baking ingredients inside so she never had to lug another huge container of flour again. Outside of the bakery, anyway.

When the second rise was done, she made three deep slashes across the top of the loaf, slid the pan into the oven, and set the timer. She looked up to see Libby coming down the hallway. Her face was pinched with worry, and Viv's stomach tightened.

"Is everything okay? Brogan was looking for you."

"It smells good in here." Libby eyed the cookies but didn't take one. "Bread?"

"Yeah, I thought some Italian bread to go with the lasagna." Viv nodded toward the cake she'd set under a glass dome. "And red velvet cake for dessert."

"You've been busy." Libby blew out a breath as if trying to steady herself.

"Lib. What's wrong?"

The next breath was shaky, and when she turned toward Viv, Libby had tears in her eyes.

"I went to go see my sister today. It was, in short, a disaster."

"I'm sure it wasn't that bad."

Libby's quick burst of laughter was humorless. "I've been trying to give Teresa some space because that's all she seems to want from me. She wouldn't even make eye contact with me when we first found her."

Libby ran a hand over her ponytail. "She didn't want to

live here, and I understood that. Not feeling safe with all the men in the house. I know none of them would ever—"

"I get it," Viv interrupted. "We know that, but with what she went through, I can see why she wouldn't want to stay here."

"Yeah. So we moved her in with a roommate we thought would help her adjust. Mack."

"Mack is one of DiMarco's..." Viv trailed off, unsure of how to finish the sentence.

"Victims," Libby supplied with a nod. "Yes. The only one who elected to stay and work for the syndicate. She's really great and seems surprisingly level-headed, considering everything she went through. I guess I hoped Teresa would bounce back the same way."

"But she isn't." Viv shifted to lean back against the counter. "That isn't your fault, you know. She has to heal in her own time, on her own terms."

"That's what Brogan keeps telling me, but I feel so helpless. When DiMarco had her, all I could think about was getting her out and making him pay. And now that she's free and he's dead, I have no idea what I'm supposed to do."

Libby swiped at the tears escaping down her cheek. "She won't even speak to me. Today she just stared at a spot on the wall over my shoulder. Every time I talked, she flinched." Libby's voice hitched. "What if I can't bring her back, Viv? What if because of what DiMarco did to her, she's stuck inside this prison in her own mind?"

"I can't imagine how I would feel if this happened to someone I love, but what that bastard did to Teresa wasn't your fault. You did everything you could to get her out, to give her a chance at a life worth living."

"Doesn't feel like it," Libby murmured.

"Maybe not, but all you can do for her now is be there to

support her when she needs it and love her even when she thinks she doesn't deserve it. I imagine she'll think that a lot."

"Seems that way. Mack at least says she's eating and doesn't wake up screaming as often." Libby scrubbed a hand over her face. "I don't know how to do this part."

"I don't think anyone really does. All you can do is focus on being the best sister you know how to be. Just love her."

Libby huffed out a breath, mouth tilting up in a small smile. "Thank you. You said Brogan was looking for me?"

"Yeah, but he might be busy now."

"Oh, right, that big deal they're closing today. You need any help?"

Viv shook her head. "No. This bread is about to come out, and then I have to figure out where to hide it so it doesn't disappear before dinner."

Libby laughed. "Well, if you're good here, I think I'll go take a nap before I come down to put the lasagna together."

"Absolutely. Maybe take a hot shower to clear your head."

"Good idea." Libby's smile was kind.

The timer beeped as soon as Libby rounded the corner to the stairs, and Viv slid the tray out of the oven. Perfect, as always. Her aunt's recipe for Italian bread never failed her. Just as she set the bread on a rack to cool, her phone rang from the other room, and she sprinted back for it before it stopped.

"Hello?" she said, a little breathless.

"Oh, good. I was afraid you wouldn't pick up." Sofia's voice was strained.

"What's up?"

"I need a huge favor. Bianca just called from school to inform me that I am, in fact, the worst mother ever because I forgot to drop her trumpet off on my way to the bakery like I promised her I would. Never mind that I wouldn't have needed to drop it off if she had remembered it in the first damn place."

Sofia's frustrated breath whistled in the receiver. "Anyway, we are absolutely slammed at the bakery, and I can't reach Tim. He mentioned something about being in meetings with Papa all day."

"What do you need, Sof?"

"Bianca has solo tryouts today. She needs her trumpet by three." Viv flicked a glance at the clock on the microwave. It was almost two. "Do you...can you grab it from my house and drop it off at the school?"

"Yeah, of course I can."

"Do you have someone to go with you?"

Viv sighed. "No one is technically babysitting me today. I can try to find someone, though. It'll be fine."

"Are you sure? I can just tell Bianca I can't make it." Sofia sounded dejected at the thought.

"Is this the solo B has been talking about for weeks?"

"Yes."

"Then I'll go get the trumpet. And I'm going to drop off an orange ricotta cake I want you to try. I think it would do well at the bakery, but you and Mama have a taste and let me know what you think."

"Okay. And Viv? Be safe."

"I will. I'll talk to you later."

Disconnecting with her sister, Viv scrolled through her contacts. James was the only person she knew well enough to ask for a favor, but if the Callahans were doing a big deal today, it didn't seem likely he'd be free to taxi her around. She dialed him anyway, eyes on the clock. Voicemail.

She tried the numbers of two more men who had shepherded her around in the weeks since the wedding. Nothing. Tapping her phone against her palm, she shoved away from the counter. She could make the trip to Sofia's and then to the school in less than an hour. What could possibly go wrong in less than an hour?

She passed the school on the way to her sister's house, noting the parking lot was full to bursting. Must be some kind of assembly thing or PTO meeting or something today. She let herself in Sofia's side door with her spare key and set the cake on the counter, jotting a quick note on the pad of sticky notes her sister always kept in the top drawer next to the pantry.

She found Bianca's trumpet sitting beside the door under a pile of coats and carried it out to her car. In good weather, the school was within walking distance, but she decided not to push her luck. She was likely going to get in trouble with someone over this. Whether it was Aidan or her father. Best to be as cautious as possible.

She didn't want to park in the bus lane this late in the afternoon, so instead she pulled alongside the curb and jogged through the full parking lot, waiting for the school secretary to buzz her in.

"I come bearing a trumpet for one very upset eleven-year-old," Viv said, brandishing the trumpet case like a prize.

The secretary smiled. "Oh, thank goodness. She was pretty down about that. If you want to say hi, I can call her up for you."

Viv glanced out the big windows. A few minutes wouldn't hurt. "That would be great, thanks."

It didn't take long for her niece, all brown curls and boundless energy, to come rushing into the office. Her smile faltered a bit when she noticed it was her aunt and not her mom, but she looked relieved to see the trumpet sitting on the floor.

"Thank you, Aunt Viv," she said in a rush.

"You're welcome, bug. Your mom was swamped at the

bakery, but she wanted me to tell you she was sorry she forgot and good luck at your audition."

Bianca sulked, toeing the edge of the trumpet case. "She didn't say that."

"Well, it was implied. I left some cake at home for you to celebrate with, okay?"

"What kind?"

"Orange ricotta."

"Will you teach me how to make it?"

"Absolutely. Now, give me a hug and go kick butt at your audition." Viv smiled when Bianca wrapped her arms around her waist and gave her a squeeze. "I love you, bug."

"I love you too, Aunt Viv. Bye!"

She scooped up the case and ran out the door, immediately faltering to a walk when a teacher slanted her a look in the hallway.

"I can't even remember what it was like to have that much energy," Viv said to no one in particular.

"Honey, you're telling me," the secretary said.

Viv laughed and pushed into the sunshine. When she rounded the chain-link fence and short row of stubby bushes to her car, she froze. All four tires had been slashed, and the rear window looked like it had been smashed with a baseball bat—or maybe a tire iron.

When she moved closer, she realized her driver's side door was slightly ajar. Rounding the hood, she reached for the handle and cautiously pulled it all the way open, her eyes scanning the backseat to make sure no one had climbed inside.

The glove box was open, and the various things she kept in there were tossed haphazardly onto the floor. The bottle of water she'd left capped in the console had been moved from one holder to the other, and her mirror had been bent down at a violent angle.

The thing that looked the most out of place was a white piece of paper folded up on the dashboard. Before she opened it, she knew the kind of writing she'd find inside. That chilling black Sharpie.

Are you finished playing house yet, you ungrateful bitch?

It took her a few tries to fish her phone out of her pocket with trembling fingers, but when she finally managed to free it, she punched in the first number that came to mind. When Aidan didn't answer, she tried her brother next.

"Hey, sis, what—"

"Leo." Viv couldn't keep her voice from shaking as she glanced around the parking lot and across the street to see if anyone was watching her. "Someone broke into my car. They slashed my tires and left..." She swallowed her panic. "They left a note."

"What? Where are you?"

"I'm at Bianca's school. Sofia asked me to drop off her trumpet."

"And you're alone? Why don't you have anyone with you?"

"It was a last-minute thing. No one was available."

"It's Viv," she heard Leo say to someone in the background. "We're on our way. Can you wait inside? I don't want you standing out in the open."

"I...yeah. I'll tell them my car won't start and see if they'll let me wait in the office."

"Good. We'll be there in twenty minutes."

Chapter Twenty-Four

Viv was pushing through the school doors onto the sidewalk when they pulled up. Leo was out of the car first, but Aidan was on the right side and had his hands on Viv before her brother reached them. She looked a little shaken but not hurt, and he felt his heart rate finally slow.

"You're together?" Her brow knitted in confusion.

"What happened?" Leo asked, ignoring her question.

"My car's there." She pointed to a row of shrubs. "Did you see it when you pulled in?"

"No," Aidan said. "We came from the other direction."

"I'll pull the SUV around."

Aidan nodded at Leo and reached for Viv's hand to walk across the parking lot, looking over when she leaned away instead of against him. He was going to ask her if everything was okay, and then her car came into view.

"Son of a bitch," he said, dropping her hand to inspect the damage. "Leo said you found a note."

She held it out, crumpled in her fist, and he snatched it from her, biting off a curse at the scrawled message. When

Leo pulled the SUV around to shield her car from the road, his eyes were almost black with rage. Aidan wordlessly held the note out to him.

"I'm going to kill this son of a bitch."

"Get in line," Aidan snapped.

"It's still not enough, though, is it? To prove it was him? Papa still isn't going to let you touch him," Viv said in a tired voice.

Aidan wrapped an arm around her waist and drew her in closer, pressing a kiss against her temple as much to calm himself as to reassure her, puzzling at the way she stiffened. When he released her, she stepped away, and his jaw tightened.

"We can't leave the car here. School will be getting out soon, and everyone in the neighborhood is going to see my car like this." She gestured at the damage. "This'll really set tongues wagging."

"Papa won't like that."

Viv's eyes were glued to the fractures that radiated from a small hole in the rear window of her car. "Doesn't Zara's uncle drive a tow truck?"

"Yeah," Leo agreed. "I think you're right. I'll call him and make sure he knows to put a rush on it."

Aidan watched her while they waited for the tow, while Zara's uncle hooked up the car to the flatbed truck and hauled it away minutes before buses started pulling into the school for afternoon pickup. He studied her in the rearview mirror while Leo drove them back to his truck.

It had been an hour at least since they'd pulled up outside the school, and not once had she made eye contact with him. He couldn't tell if it was because she was scared or pissed off, but the fact that she wouldn't talk to him, wouldn't let him touch her, was starting to irritate.

"What were you doing out on your own?" he said, his voice a little rougher than it should have been.

She didn't deviate from staring out the window as the trees and houses whipped past.

"I had something I needed to take care of, and no one was available. I'm not a child, Callahan."

He clenched the steering wheel until his fingers ached. "It's not like you have a protective detail because no one trusts you. It's for your safety, for Christ's sake."

"And that's something you're worried about today?"

"What in the hell does that even mean?"

She shrugged. "Hard to get a read on you most days."

Before he could ask her to explain, she bolted from the car the second he threw it in park and rushed into the house. Why wouldn't he be worried about her safety? He'd always been perfectly clear that keeping her alive was important to him. Fuck's sake, he'd been the first one to volunteer to shadow her weeks ago.

Slamming out of the car, he stalked to the door. From the moment Leo had told him what happened, he'd been worried for her. He couldn't stop the rapid beat of his heart until he saw for himself that she was all right.

Of course he was worried about her. She was his fucking wife. His irritating, headstrong wife with a razor-sharp tongue, but his wife all the same. Husbands were supposed to worry about their wives, so what the fuck was her problem?

The living room was empty when he let himself in, but he could hear the distant hum of voices, and he followed them back to the family room. He paused in the hallway and listened to Viv recount the story in full for everyone who'd gathered. Now that she wasn't talking directly to him, her voice had lost its hard edge, and that pissed him off too.

"Aidan," Declan said when he spotted him in the hall.

Aidan immediately noticed Viv's spine straighten. Evie

must have noticed too, because she passed a look between them before raising a brow at Viv, who only shook her head.

"You think this was him?" Declan asked.

"Who the hell else?" Aidan said, pulling the note from his back pocket and handing it to his brother. "He said at the party he'd wait for her to come to her senses. He's clearly not pleased that she hasn't left me for him yet."

He slid a look to Viv, whose eyes darted away the minute his landed on hers. They were absolutely going to have to fucking talk about whatever the hell was wrong with her. Soon.

"I haven't had any luck with the video surveillance around the bridal boutique," Brogan admitted. "There weren't any cameras directly where you saw the Jeep pull out from, and every other angle I can find only catches it partially in frame. Nothing to get any kind of definite ID from."

Aidan caught Viv's look of surprise when he turned to Declan. "Just let me take him out." Viv snorted, and he ignored her. "Falcone and his evidence be damned."

Declan's jaw firmed. "I can't. I gave Falcone my word. None of this means anything if he loses control of the Mafia. The first couple of casinos will be ready in a few weeks. And she'll have to stop going out without a detail."

Declan pinned Viv with a pointed look, and Aidan admired the way she met his unflinching stare with one of her own.

"She can't have someone follow her around indefinitely. What if this guy never backs off? What if he tries to hurt her?" Aidan shoved a hand through his hair. "How am I supposed to keep her safe?"

"I'm right here," Viv snapped. "Stop talking about me as if I wasn't."

"I'm sorry," Evie said. "I really do know what you're

going through. I've been there," she added, flicking a glance at Declan, who looked entirely unmoved.

"Me too," Libby said. "It's…suffocating."

"It's for your own good," Aidan said. Any softness Viv might have shown Evie and Libby evaporated when she glared at him.

"And suddenly you want me to believe you have my best interests at heart in all of this?" The venom in her tone silenced the entire room. "I need a minute."

"What did you do to her?" Evie demanded once Viv stormed out.

"I didn't do anything to her!"

"You did something," Declan assured him.

"You should probably go try to fix it," Brogan said, wrapping an arm around Libby's shoulders and pulling her back against his chest. "Unless you're as dumb as I thought."

Aidan stared at the empty hallway where Viv had been. She was obviously upset about something, but fuck if he knew what. All he'd been trying to do all damn afternoon was make sure she was okay. Waving away Evie's offer for a drink, he crossed the family room and sprinted up the stairs.

Viv was curled up in one of the chairs flanking the fireplace, staring into the flames that danced behind the grate. She didn't look up at him as he sank into the chair next to hers.

"Want to tell me what's wrong with you?"

"Not really."

"How am I supposed to fix it if I don't know what's wrong?"

"You have to want to fix it, Callahan."

He felt a headache forming behind his right eye. "And why would I be asking about it if I don't want to fix it?"

She finally looked at him then. Her eyes were angry, but there was something else in their depths.

"I'm not sure. You pick and choose when you want to care and when you don't. It's impossible to know which one I'll get at any given time."

"Explain," he bit off when the fire drew her gaze with a loud pop and she didn't continue.

"You have no problem wanting me with your mouth and your fingers and your cock. But I don't want that. I don't want only that," she amended.

"What do you want?" his voice sounded hoarse to his ears, and he couldn't stop staring at her.

"I want something you're not interested in giving me."

"Try me."

She looked at him, and that feeling he'd had when he'd seen her at the top of the stairs lanced through him again. He still couldn't name it, but it made him want to reach out and touch her.

"I want you to care about me. About all of me. And not just when we're naked or I'm in danger. I thought I could do it. I thought I could settle for what you were comfortable giving me, but I can't."

She took a deep breath. "I can't live this way. So either you want me all the way, or you need to let this marriage stand in name only."

The way she said it had his throat tightening. "Meaning?"

"Meaning you get exactly what you said you wanted from the beginning. A ring on my finger and nothing to do with me."

When she got up and moved to the bathroom, he said nothing. He couldn't make all the thoughts flying around in his head make sense enough to speak. He heard the door close and the lock slide into place. After a beat, water started running into the tub.

He sat staring into the fire while drawers opened and closed on the other side of the bathroom door. Eventually the water stopped, and he imagined her reclining against the edge of the tub with her hair piled on top of her head.

It wasn't that he didn't want her, all of her. It was that he was afraid to. For a long time, he had carefully built walls around himself to keep people out. Women, his brothers, and even his friends were never allowed to get too close. It was easier that way.

Easier than the way his father had been devastated over his mother's death Aidan's entire life. Easier than the way Evie's leaving Declan had nearly broken him. Easier than the terror Brogan experienced when he thought he'd lost Libby.

Excavating those walls to let Viv in felt dangerous. It sent warning signals to his brain. He'd never wanted this. But now that he had it, now that he had Viv, he didn't want to let it go.

Pushing to his feet, he crossed to the door and tested the knob, resting his forehead against the wood when he remembered she'd locked it behind her. He took two quick steps back, staring at the sliver of light under the door before turning on his heel and rushing from the room.

The idea of losing her made him feel like he couldn't breathe. And the idea of keeping her terrified the shit out of him.

Chapter Twenty-Five

Aidan swirled the scotch around in his glass but didn't take a sip. He'd let the guys talk him into going out tonight for no other reason than he didn't want to admit he'd rather be at home and couldn't think of a better excuse to say no.

After their discussion the other night, Viv had reversed the roles on him, and now she was the one always standing just out of arm's reach. He didn't like it. She wasn't mean; she never let his goading devolve into arguments. He would have preferred that to her icy politeness, a glimpse into how the rest of their lives might go if he didn't make a decision. He missed her fire.

"Earth to Aidan!"

On a sigh, Aidan tossed back the rest of his scotch and set his empty glass on the tabletop. He really regretted agreeing to this drink.

"Where is your head tonight, man?"

"I'm right here."

Liam snorted. "Yeah, right. That blonde over there has

been making eyes at you for the last ten minutes, and you're looking right through her."

Aidan's eyes followed Liam's nod to the bottle blonde in the too-tight dress. "That's because I'm not interested in that blonde over there."

"Trouble in paradise?" Liam asked.

"Everything is fine."

"Okay, well, that's a lie. Did you fall in love with your wife or something?" Aidan frowned and scrubbed a hand over his face. "Oh, shit."

"Don't look at me like that," Aidan growled. "I'm not in love with her. I'm...very fond of her."

Liam snorted. "You keep telling yourself that, man. I never thought she'd actually manage to trap you like that."

"I said I'm not in love with her," Aidan insisted, ignoring the dull ache radiating from his chest.

"Then go home with someone else tonight. Maybe it'll improve your mood."

Aidan's head jerked up. "What?"

"I can see at least three women staring at you right now. Not including the blonde. Go fuck one of them, and maybe it'll fix whatever this mood is that you're in."

"I can't do that."

Liam gave him a long look. "Because you're in love with your wife."

"Because she's not pregnant yet," he snapped.

The excuse tasted bitter on his tongue. He hated the words as soon as he said them, but Liam seemed to accept it. He shut up, at least.

When the waitress came to clear their empties and offer them another round, Aidan caught Liam eyeing the blonde who'd been making eyes at them.

"I'm tapping out and going home, Liam. She's all yours."

Before his friend could respond, Aidan pushed away from

the table and weaved through the crush of bodies to the door. More women waited in line outside the club, curves sheathed in short, tight dresses, hoping to impress the bouncers enough to jump the line. A few of them sent looks his way, but he ignored them as he climbed into his truck.

He rolled the window down despite the temperature, needing the fresh air to wash out the acrid taste of the lie he'd told Liam. He wasn't waiting until Viv was pregnant to sleep with someone else. He didn't want anyone else at all.

He wanted only Viv, and whether he was ready to admit it or not, she tugged at him in a way that no other woman had before. He might be playing a dangerous game, but he wanted to see if it was possible to have her and not have it all blow up in their faces.

It wasn't late, but the house was quiet when he pulled in. Brogan's Jag and Declan's Range Rover were both gone. Either the house was empty, or only the women were home. He let himself in and took the stairs up two at a time. It didn't occur to him she might be asleep until he opened the door to find the room bathed in darkness, but when he moved to her side of the bed, it was empty.

Frowning, he crossed to the bathroom. She wasn't in there either. Where the hell had she gone? He turned for the door to go in search of her when it opened, and she walked in, body silhouetted against the light from the hall. She reached for the light switch and screamed bloody murder when she saw him standing in the middle of the room.

"What the fuck, Callahan!"

She slumped against the door frame, hand over her chest as her breath wheezed in and out of her lungs. He had to force himself to bite back a grin. Seconds later, he heard someone running down the hall before Evie appeared in the doorway, gun in hand.

"Are you okay?" she asked Viv.

Viv flicked her wrist at Aidan and took a deep breath. "I'm fine. Your brother-in-law scared the ever-loving shit out of me."

"You mean your husband?"

Aidan watched Evie slip the safety back into place.

"When he does shit like that, he's your brother-in-law."

Evie chuckled. "Glad I didn't shoot him."

"Me too," Viv agreed with a nod. "What a mess that would have been."

"I'm standing right here," Aidan said, tone dry.

"Call me if you decide you want to shoot him after all," Evie said before disappearing.

"What are you doing here?" Viv set the glass she had somehow managed not to drop on his nightstand and closed the door behind her.

"It's my room."

"I mean, why are you standing here in the dark like a weirdo? I thought you were going out with the guys for a drink."

"I did. I was. And now I'm...not." Jesus. "And I'm not a weirdo."

"Debatable. I think you scared a few years off my life. I can feel gray hairs growing as we speak. Did you need something?"

"Yes."

He closed the space between them in quick strides, reaching out to grip the front of her shirt and pulling her forward until her body crashed into his. He slid his free hand up to loosely grip her throat and tilted her head up for his lips.

He didn't take her mouth gently. He needed to feel her, to touch her too much for that. Dragging his tongue across her upper lip, he growled when she opened for him with a moan and danced her tongue against his.

She fisted her hands in his shirt, and he tensed for her to shove him away, but instead she pulled him even closer, like it was impossible to get close enough. When she finally pushed him back, his eyes dropped to her lips, swollen from his kiss.

"We talked about this. I told you I—"

"I want you." Her eyes moved to a spot just over his left shoulder, and she was quiet for a long minute before they slid back to meet his gaze. "All of you." He swallowed around the lump in his throat while she studied him.

"Are you just saying that to get me naked?"

He chanced taking a step closer. "No. I don't know how to do this part, but I want you too much not to try."

When she reached for the hem of his shirt and lifted it slowly over his head, he nearly pulled her in, but something told him to let her have this moment, to let her set the pace of whatever was building between them.

Her hands roamed down his chest and over his abs to the waistband of his jeans, lingering there before undoing the button and dragging down the zipper. Her knuckles grazed his hardening cock, and he swallowed a groan.

She worked his jeans and his boxers down over his hips and thighs, and he toed off his shoes and socks so she could help him step out of them. The way she was looking up at him, fully clothed with her mouth inches away from the tip of his shaft, made him weak. When she wrapped her fingers around him, he shuddered.

As much as he wanted to feel her mouth around him, he needed to taste her more, to hear her sighs and pants and moans. He pulled her to her feet, groaning and dropping his head against her shoulder when she stroked him up, twisting her hand in the way that drove him crazy.

"This isn't going to last long if you keep doing that," he growled, nipping at the exposed skin of her neck.

"You recover quickly from a good fuck," she said, and he could hear the arousal in her tone.

"I don't want to fuck you." He wrapped his arm around her waist when she started to move away and held her tight against him while he tasted her skin. "I want to savor you."

Her breath hitched, and she leaned into him, her hand still lazily working his cock up and down while he tugged her shirt up and off, bringing his lips down against her shoulder as soon as she was free of it. Skimming his fingers up over her ribs, he brushed the sides of her breasts and circled the pad of his thumb over her nipple until it hardened through the fabric of her bra. He squeezed it between his fingers until she gasped and arched against him.

"Have I ever told you before how stunning you are?"

"I can't remember. Maybe?"

He reached up to cup her breasts through the thin fabric before undoing the clasp and filling his hands with them, squeezing gently.

"You are. Absolutely stunning. I could touch you every day for the rest of our lives and not get tired of it."

He kissed her, nipping her bottom lip with his teeth while he teased her nipples until she trembled, fingernails digging into the skin of his hip. He pinched them, and she arched under his fingers, gasping against his lips.

"These are very sensitive," he murmured while she squirmed against him when he increased the pressure.

He pulled back to watch her face as he gripped her nipple between two fingers and twisted it gently, then a little harder when she leaned into him, and her eyes fluttered closed. When he twisted again, her head fell back, and her body vibrated in his arms.

"Callahan."

She said it on a choked sob, and he wanted more from her, wanted to coax an orgasm from her with only his hands on her nipples and the feel of her body pressed against him. He increased the pressure, and her breath caught in the back of her throat.

"Come for me, princess," he murmured, tugging the sensitive bud away from her body while she writhed and bucked and moaned for him.

He pinched it again sharply, and she shuddered, her fingernails biting into his skin, body jerking under his touch while she came. When she finally went still, breaths quick and urgent, he leaned down to press a kiss to her throat, smiling against her skin when she sighed.

"How did you do that?" she panted.

"I don't know. Let me see if I can do it again."

He lifted her into his arms, groaning when she immediately wrapped her legs around his waist, the fabric covering her core rubbing against his painfully hard cock. He caught her nipple in his mouth, swirling his tongue around it while she gripped his shoulders.

"You're going to kill me," she groaned while he scored her nipple with his teeth.

"What a way to go," he said, and she laughed.

He kissed the valley between her breasts. "I want you to do that again when I'm inside you."

"Come?"

He dragged the flat of his tongue against her other nipple, making her gasp. "Laugh. Coming for me won't be optional."

The snark died on her tongue when he tightened his teeth around her nipple again, and she whimpered. Of all the sounds he could drag from her lips, that one was his favorite. He felt her orgasm building in the way she tensed in his arms, and he kept a steady pace on her nipple with lips and teeth and tongue, dragging another orgasm out of her until she went limp against him, resting her forehead on his shoulder.

"I think you've discovered an unfair advantage."

He grinned and carried her to the bed. "It's only unfair for you."

He urged her to lift her hips so he could tug her leggings and panties down over her hips and ass, peeling them off her legs and tossing them over his shoulder. Gripping her ankle, Aidan pulled her to the edge of the bed and leaned over her to press a kiss to her lips, sinking into it slowly until she was sighing against his mouth, her teeth grazing against his tongue.

He pressed a kiss to her chin, her collarbone, each nipple, and down to her stomach. When he paused there, he heard her quick intake of breath, but he trailed a line of kisses over her skin and across her hip.

"See? I was right. Stunning. I love when I'm right."

"Don't get used to it," she mumbled, and he grinned.

He sank to his knees between her thighs and pressed her legs apart, rubbing his finger over her slit.

"So wet," he murmured, circling his fingers over her clit in slow, tight circles until she lifted her hips off the bed.

"Oh God," she breathed when he slid a finger inside her.

"Hmm?" he slipped in a second finger, pumping them in and out while his thumb rubbed pressure over her clit.

"That feels..." Her hips jerked against his hand, her fingers fisting in the comforter.

"Feels what?" he enjoyed making all the thoughts tumble out of her head with a touch, enjoyed the little noises she made when he touched her even more.

"Amazing," she breathed. "Don't stop."

"Not until you come for me again."

He worked his fingers faster, his free hand sliding over her stomach and cupping her breast, pinching her nipple gently between his fingers while she writhed in his hand. She tensed, clenching around him, and he worked her faster, thumb rubbing urgent circles on her clit, fingers pumping furiously.

"Viv," he said, voice hoarse. "Look at me when you come."

Her eyes shot open, and he wasn't sure if it was his command or his fingers that pushed her over the edge, but her big brown eyes never left his while she chased her release to its peak and cried out with it.

Sliding his fingers out, he traced them around her nipples, coating them with her wetness before leaning down and licking them clean.

"You're the best kind of torture."

"I need to be inside you," he whispered, peppering kisses across her breasts and up to her lips.

"I need you inside me."

He was slowly sliding into her before she'd even finished her sentence. She wrapped her legs around his waist, arching up against him while he rocked his hips against hers, enjoying the way she squeezed and surrounded him.

Every time he was inside her felt better than the last. The way she responded to him was addicting. He loved to make her writhe and jerk with need, to stoke a fire in her that only he could put out.

"So impatient," he murmured when she ground against him, easing nearly all the way out and sliding back in to the hilt.

"It's your fault," she said, her breaths coming in raspy gasps as he fucked her slow and deep.

"I accept full responsibility." He slid his hand down between their bodies and stroked a finger over her clit, making her shiver. "Are you going to come for me again?"

"Yes…yes. Fuck."

"Good." He quickened the pace of his finger but kept his thrusts slow and deep. "I want to feel you come on my cock."

"Aidan."

He went still. It was the first time he'd heard her say his name, his first name, since the night they met. Every day since, whether they were talking or fighting or fucking, she'd only ever called him Callahan. He wanted to hear her say it again. He needed to hear her say it.

"What's wrong?" she asked, his lack of movement finally breaking through the haze in her brain.

"Say it again," he demanded.

"What? Say what?"

He slid his cock all the way out and back in again, eliciting a soft whimper. "Say my name."

Her eyes searched his until it registered, and they went cloudy with lust. "Aidan." She captured his face in her hands and brought his lips down for a kiss, quick and urgent. "Fuck me," she whispered against his mouth. "Harder. Please."

He couldn't deny her. Keeping the same torturously slow pace, he slammed his cock into her, making her groan while his finger worked over her clit. The way she clenched around him, her nails scoring his back, drove him crazy, and his hips thrust a little faster, giving her every inch of every thrust as hard as he could while she pleaded for more.

"Viv." He grit his teeth, her pussy gripping him like a vise as he pushed her over the edge of her own climax.

"Aidan," she panted, stroking his back, his shoulders, down his biceps, her hips grinding against his. "Come inside me."

Dropping his head into the crook of her neck, he slammed his cock in hard and deep and fell over the edge with her.

"Wow," she breathed, pressing kisses across the top of his shoulder, nipping his skin lightly with her teeth.

"That almost covers it."

He rolled onto his back and stared at the ceiling, waiting

for his heart rate to return to normal. She shifted onto her side but didn't scoot closer, propping her head in her hand.

"We have to go again. I forgot something."

"Christ's sake, woman. Give a man a minute to recover." He sat up and raked a hand through his hair. "What did you forget?"

She pushed onto her knees and traced her fingertips along his upper thigh. "I forgot to laugh with your cock inside me."

"Fuck, do you even understand what you do to me?"

He reached out to grip her wrist and tugged her into his lap, swallowing a groan when she straddled his thighs. He wasn't ready to take her again yet, but it wouldn't be long if she kept wiggling like that.

Apprehension flashed in her eyes, and he cupped her face in his hand, pressing his lips to hers, stroking his thumb over her cheek. "No, I wasn't lying. Yes, I really do want all of you. No, I won't change my mind tomorrow. Anything else?"

Her bottom lip poked out in a little pout, and he grinned. "No," she said. "What now?"

He wasn't sure if she was asking about Collin or their relationship, but he didn't have answers for either one at the moment.

"Right now I'm going to take you to bed."

She tilted her head. "We're already in bed."

"Yes, but we're going to sleep." He reached to pull the covers back and shifted with her in his lap so he was leaning back against the pillows and she was splayed on top of him.

She wrapped her arm around his waist and hooked her leg over his thigh in the way he liked, sighing when his fingers moved to comb through her hair.

"I'm not sure I like that you discovered that about my nipples," she said, and he could tell she was getting sleepy.

"Why? Afraid I'll use it against you?"

"Absolutely."

He laughed, giving her ass a gentle smack. "I wonder if you'd like nipple clamps. The kind with the little chain so I can pull on them while I fuck you in every position."

He squeezed her ass when she rocked her hips against his thigh, his fingers digging into the skin.

"I'm going to have to find something that makes you come undone. Level the playing field."

He reached up to turn off the light and listened to her stifle a yawn before speaking again. "Princess, I already have something that makes me come undone."

"What?" she asked, voice heavy with sleep.

He felt her fall by degrees until she was completely relaxed against him, her breath cool against his chest. "You," he whispered into the dark. "Just you."

Trailing his fingertips up and down her arm, he followed her into sleep, praying he wouldn't fuck this up and lose what he was quickly coming to believe was the best thing that had ever happened to him.

Chapter Twenty-Six

Viv stared out the window as they drove into Center City. It was the first time she'd been out of the house in days, and even though she knew having someone with her was smart, that Collin only tried to get to her when she was alone, it still felt stifling.

The syndicate was hundreds of men strong, but she imagined they were drawing straws to see who got stuck following her around at this point. When the traffic snarled the closer they got to the restaurant, she sighed and twisted in her seat.

"Everything okay?"

"Yeah. I'm sorry you got stuck with me today."

"I volunteered, actually," James said, honking at a driver who cut them off.

"Really? Why?"

"Because it made Aidan feel better to know someone he trusted was with you."

Viv's eyebrows lifted. "He doesn't trust the other guys who have been driving me around?"

James chuckled at her tone. "Any syndicate man would

lay down his life for you if it came to it simply because Declan or Aidan asked it of them. But I know what it's like to lose the thing you cherish most in the world and not see it coming. I wouldn't wish that on anyone, so he knows you're extra safe with me."

"It must have been an impossible loss. I'm sorry," she said immediately. "I shouldn't have—"

"Every time I think it's getting easier, another milestone hits me. We would've been married six months this month."

"I can't even imagine." The words sounded hollow, but she didn't know what else to say.

"I woke up last week, and she wasn't the first thing I thought of. And then I spent the rest of the day feeling guilty about that." His fingers flexed on the steering wheel. "I knew her my whole life, but I didn't really see her until a few years ago. She was just my cousin's girlfriend's friend. Sometimes I wish I'd noticed her sooner so we could have had longer together."

He pulled parallel to the curb in front of the restaurant and put the car into park. "So, anyway. I volunteered because even if Aidan can't say it out loud, he needs you. The family sees that. And we'll do what needs doing."

"That's what I'm afraid of."

She didn't want to see anyone die because of her. Except maybe Collin. She wouldn't shed a tear over him if he decided to do them all a favor and jump off a cliff.

"Do you want to come in?" She hooked her thumb over her shoulder at the restaurant she often went to with her friends when they all had time to meet up for lunch.

"You're eating at Breá?"

"Yeah, it's one of my favorites. Do you know it?"

"This is Declan's pride and joy. The first property he ever invested in. He's got offices on the third floor."

"Oh."

She turned to study the old whiskey distillery that had been converted into a bar and restaurant. It had a ballroom and a couple of private dining rooms on the second floor that she'd always wanted to see. She'd never wondered what was on the third. She shook her head with a faint chuckle. The Callahan Corporation really was everywhere.

"I won't crash your lunch, but I will hang out upstairs." He followed her out of the car, and they jogged across the street together.

"You've got my number, yeah?"

She nodded. "Yep."

"Great. Text me when you're done, and I'll come down."

He left her standing in the foyer as he disappeared around a corner. It struck her as funny that one of her favorite restaurants in the city was Callahan-owned. She'd been coming to this place for years. Their wine selection was amazing, and the food was incredible. Now she understood why Declan had insisted on running the restaurants above the Mafia casinos.

The hostess led her to a table in the back when she gave them the name for the reservation, and she took a seat facing the door so she could watch for her friends. They hadn't spent any time together since the wedding, and even before then, their conversations revolved around it. They were forever talking about the flowers and the dresses and the food. She was looking forward to catching up today, even if she was already bracing herself for questions about Aidan.

As the waiter set a glass of water down on the table in front of her Viv saw one of her oldest friends stop at the hostess stand. They made eye contact, and her friend pointed, weaving through the tables.

"You're a sight for sore eyes," Felicity said, leaning down to press a kiss to Viv's cheek before choosing a seat. "I'll have a glass of cabernet," she said to the waiter before turning to

Viv again. "First you dress me up in a bridesmaid's dress and make me catch a bouquet, and then I don't hear from you for weeks."

"I know. I'm sorry," Viv said, sighing into her glass when Felicity smiled. "Things have been nothing short of insane."

"I'm only teasing. I know you have a lot going on with settling in and what I imagine is an awkward honeymoon phase with a husband you barely know."

Guilt twisted sharply in Viv's stomach. She'd agreed not to tell her friends about what had been happening with Collin to avoid feeding the rumor mill. They weren't sure how Collin might react if there was talk. And Felicity's brother was married to a Milano cousin.

"Things are good, actually. We're finding a rhythm."

"Well, I want to hear details, but we'll wait for the others first. They should be here soon. Speak of the devil."

Viv glanced up to see Alex and Dani moving toward them and dropping into the last two empty seats. Both of them smiled brightly. They'd made a solid foursome since the seventh grade, and she hadn't realized how much she missed them until now.

"You look fabulous," Dani said after the waiter brought a basket of warm bread and took their drink order. "Arranged marriage looks good on you."

Viv laughed. "It still feels weird to say sometimes. That I'm married. I didn't get much of a chance to tell you I was glad you could make the wedding."

Dani smiled. "I was so worried I wouldn't get back from Europe in time. Next time I'll have to tell my boss to shove it."

Viv quirked a brow. "Next time? This wedding's the only one I get."

"Well, these two might settle down someday." Dani

gestured to Alex and Felicity. "Assuming someone will put up with them."

Alex rolled her eyes but bit back a smile. "You're one to talk. Why don't you tell her about Brad?"

"Who's Brad?" Viv dropped her chin into her hand and grinned. "I need to know everything."

"Brad is no one. A coworker. We're up for the same promotion." Dani made a face. "Just saying his name makes me want to punch him."

"Oh, so you *do* like him," Viv said with a chuckle.

"What? No!" Dani protested, her pink cheeks betraying her. "Besides, I am actually seeing someone."

"Really?" Felicity said, clearly surprised.

"Yeah. Maybe we'll even be at your party this weekend."

Viv turned to Felicity. "There's a party this weekend?"

"Yes, I was going to text you about it, but then I figured I'd be seeing you today, and I could ask you in person. Something small, nothing too crazy. You should bring Aidan."

"Okay," Viv said when their waiter returned, unsure if Aidan would be up for partying with a bunch of Italians in a place where he couldn't guarantee her safety. "I'll ask him if he's free."

"So," Dani said once the waiter left with their order. "How's married life? What's it like living in a real-life mansion? Is it as intimidating on the inside as it is on the outside?"

"Glenmore House is beautiful, but, yeah, intimidating is a good word for it," Viv admitted. "It's like living inside history. Plus, there are always people there. Always. Everywhere."

"Isn't it just the three couples?"

"And live-in staff."

"Dear God," Felicity sighed. "Live-in staff. Color me officially jealous."

"Are you planning on living there indefinitely?" Alex wondered. "It's really Declan's house, isn't it?"

"Technically, yes, it belongs to the heir, but..." Viv shrugged. "We haven't really talked about moving anywhere else."

"You haven't?"

"We haven't really been married that long."

"I guess that's true," Alex conceded. "Seems like longer."

"Now it's time for the good stuff," Felicity said, eyes bright with interest. "How's the sex?"

"Jesus, Felicity," Dani said with a laugh while Viv choked on her water. "Not exactly subtle, are you?"

"Oh, please. Like you two weren't both wondering the same thing. You have had sex, right?"

"Yes," Viv said, clearing her throat. "We've had plenty of sex."

"And?"

Viv leaned back with a grin when the waiter set a salad in front of her. "And I am not complaining."

"I knew it!" Dani said, punching her finger in the air. "The man was practically made for it."

"And he's had a lot of practice. Sorry," Felicity added when she saw Viv wince.

"You two are making her uncomfortable," Alex said, flicking a disapproving frown at Dani and Felicity. "Someone change the subject."

"Can't," Felicity said, glancing at the door. "The subject is walking this way."

Viv looked up to see Aidan making his way toward them. His gaze caught on her before he smiled in a way that warmed her down to her toes. He leaned down to press a quick kiss to her lips before turning to the table.

"Ladies." He rested a hand on the back of her chair.

"When you said you were having lunch today, I didn't know you'd be coming to Breá."

"I didn't know Breá was Declan's until James told me."

"A lot of things are Declan's. It's hard to keep track."

She quirked a brow at his tone, and he lifted a shoulder, indicating he'd tell her later. Whatever he'd discussed with Declan in the meeting he was leaving, it didn't sound like it went well.

"You remember Felicity, Alex, and Dani from the wedding."

"Yes," Aidan said, leaning forward to shake each of their hands. "Good to see you again."

"It was a beautiful event," Dani said. "I can't wait to see pictures."

"Me too," Viv agreed. "Evie said something to me this morning about having proofs back in the next week or two."

When Aidan's phone signaled, he dug it out of his pocket and checked the screen.

"I've got to run." He leaned down and pressed a lingering kiss to the edge of her jaw, and she had to fight hard not to sigh. "I'll see you at home. Enjoy your lunch."

The entire table watched him until he disappeared onto the sidewalk. Then every eye was on her again.

"What?" she asked when they only stared.

"Um, looks to me like things are better than good. Oh my God," Felicity breathed when Viv shifted in her chair. "Are you in love with him?"

Viv felt her cheeks heat, and she sucked in a deep breath. "I don't...I... Yes," she finally admitted. "I'm in love with him."

Alex shot her a sympathetic look across the table. "Why does that sound both happy and sad?"

"I'm not sad. It's just..." Viv pressed a hand to her belly. "It's unexpected. I didn't think I'd fall in love with him this fast." Or this completely. "It still feels so new. I don't want to mess anything up."

"You've got a lifetime to learn about each other," Felicity reminded her. "Unconventional as it is, I think maybe this happened for you in exactly the right way. And if you love him and he loves you, does it really matter how you met?"

"No," Viv replied. "I guess it doesn't."

They moved on from her sex life to catch up on everyone else's, and Viv pushed the food around on her plate, not really all that hungry. She hadn't had much of an appetite lately. Everything made her nauseous.

When Viv insisted on paying the bill, Felicity and Dani excused themselves to the bathroom, and only Alex remained. She'd always been the quiet, steady one of the group.

"Are you okay?"

"Of course. Why do you ask?" Viv counted out bills and slipped them into the folder.

"You didn't eat much. Just kind of moved things around with your fork." Alex never missed a thing.

Viv smiled. "I had a big breakfast," she lied. "But I wouldn't have missed seeing you guys for anything. It was nice to get away and just hang out with you again. Feels like old times."

Alex's smile was warm. "It does. You seem like you're adjusting okay, though. Settling in and all that."

"Yeah," Viv said, reaching for her bag when Alex stood. "It's taken some getting used to, but maybe Felicity was right, and everything really does happen for a reason."

"I think so too." Alex looped her arm through Viv's, and they wandered into the lobby. "I hope you'll come to Felicity's party. It's been such a long time since we all went to one together."

Viv hesitated but forced a smile when Dani and Felicity

rejoined them. "I don't think Aidan will be against at least making an appearance. Besides, I can't let you have all the fun interrogating Dani's mysterious date without me."

"About that," Alex said with a laugh. "Why won't you tell us anything about them?"

"Because," Dani sniffed. "I know how you three are. I want you to make your own first impressions."

"I'm hurt," Felicity said with a toss of her hair. "You make us sound judgmental or something."

Dani snorted. "Or something. Well, I've got to get back to work. Viv, you are stunning. I love this skirt, and we can't go this long before hanging out again."

"I won't let that happen," Viv promised.

They exchanged hugs all around, and Dani filed out, Alex and Felicity on her heels. Viv made an excuse that she'd left something at the table and waved as they left. Pulling out her phone to text James, she sighed.

The weight of the dishonesty sat heavily on her shoulders, even if she understood the reason for it. As soon as Collin was taken care of, she would tell her friends everything. She hated keeping secrets from them.

Chapter Twenty-Seven

Aidan surveyed the interior door to the basement under one of DiMarco's old restaurants. Declan's intention was to run the restaurants as legitimate businesses and leave Falcone to his illegal dealings downstairs. But in order to do that, they'd need entrances for anyone entering and leaving the casinos and soundproofing in case things got...spirited.

"We could put a door in directly to the casino. A private entrance," Gavin suggested as they descended the stairs to the basement. "This wall here is completely exposed."

"Mark it as an emergency exit, maybe," Aidan said with a nod. "Yeah. That could work. Declan won't want anyone coming in through the employee entrance. We won't staff the entire restaurant internally, and no matter how well he pays people, we don't want them getting suspicious."

He walked the perimeter of the space. The basement ran directly under the kitchen and had probably been used as food storage at one time, or maybe a bomb shelter. It wasn't the biggest basement of all the restaurants they'd taken from

DiMarco, but it offered the most privacy, so it was first on the list for renovations so they could get it up and running.

Declan had tasked Aidan with overseeing the project along with Leo and Gavin. An added incentive to getting everything off the ground was that the faster they established the casinos, the closer Aidan was to being able to kill the son of a bitch who was stalking his wife.

"Papa wants to use this one for poker since it's smaller. Exclusive games with big buy-ins. House takes 20 percent of the pot off the top."

"Only twenty?" Aidan wondered.

"For now," Leo said.

They spent the morning going over plans for renovations. They wouldn't need much. No one expected an underground gambling ring to be fancy. When they finished with one location, they'd move on to the next.

DiMarco had five restaurants in total sprinkled across the city, and after Brogan had killed the bastard, he'd worked up phony sales records and transferred ownership of the properties to one of the Callahan Corporation's shell companies. They were still trying to figure out what to do with the estate. Brogan wanted to burn it to the ground. Aidan couldn't really blame him.

When they pulled up to the last property on their list for the day, another car was already in the parking lot, parked at an odd angle and taking up three spaces. A black Jeep.

"Shit," Leo muttered as Aidan climbed out of his truck.

"Is that…?"

"Our buddy Collin? Yeah." Gavin replied.

"What the fuck is he doing here?" Aidan demanded, crossing the lot.

He tested the door and found it open. Idiot. They locked it behind them before making their way down to the basement. When they reached the bottom of the stairs, Collin was standing in the far corner, hands tucked into his pockets. It looked like he'd been waiting for them.

"Ah. Finally. I've been excited to hear what you're going to be doing to my casino."

"This isn't your casino, Collin," Leo said through gritted teeth.

Aidan pulled the rolled-up plans they'd been making notes on out of his back pocket and unfurled them, doing his best to ignore Collin completely.

"I hear my family is going to be running it. Exclusively. Sort of implies ownership. Doesn't it?"

"This is Falcone property," Gavin reminded him. "You're the renter. Unfortunately."

"Mmm," Collin replied. "I thought it was Callahan property." His gaze slid to Aidan, and he sneered. "The Falcones are in their pocket after all."

"No one would expect a weasel like you to understand a mutually beneficial alliance," Aidan said, drawing a rough sketch of the basement on the bottom of the page.

"Mutually beneficial for who?"

Aidan rolled his eyes. "Mutually beneficial is pretty self-explanatory, don't you think? At least to someone smarter than you."

Collin's eyes flashed, and Leo chuckled. "Tell me, Callahan. How's your pretty little wife doing? She come to her senses yet?"

Aidan tensed, and it took every ounce of willpower he had not to slam his fist into Collin's smug face. "I can promise you, Collin, my wife is none of your concern."

Collin moved closer and dropped his voice so only Aidan could hear. "Has she done that thing I taught her with her mouth yet? If not, you should ask her. It'll make your eyes roll back in your head. Viv's quite the little cocksucker."

Without pausing to think, Aidan let the papers he was

holding flutter to the ground and slammed Collin up against the nearest wall, enjoying the crack of his head hitting cement. When Collin struggled against his hold, Aidan shoved his forearm against the fucker's throat and pressed until he went still.

"Aidan." Leo's voice was a warning.

Ignoring his brother-in-law, Aidan increased the pressure against Collin's windpipe, satisfied when he wheezed out a desperate breath. "If I ever hear my wife's name out of your mouth again, it'll be the last fucking thing you say. And neither of them will be able to stop me."

Collin's eyes darted over Aidan's shoulder to Leo and Gavin, and whatever he saw there had a scowl painting his features. When Aidan released him, he doubled over, hands braced on his knees, while he gulped in rasping breaths.

"You son of a bitch—"

"Get the fuck out of here, Collin," Leo snapped. "Before I let him finish what he started."

Pushing past Aidan with a violent shove, Collin stomped up the stairs, and with a silent look from Leo, Gavin followed him up to make sure he left without incident.

"Feel better?" Leo wondered when they were alone.

"No. I'd rather be looking at his dead body. Let's get this over with so I can go home."

He heard the shower running when he stepped into the bedroom, and he crossed to the door she'd left ajar, pushing it all the way open with his hand. She had her head tipped back under the spray, eyes closed as she ran her fingers through her hair.

She startled when she noticed him, then her lips curved into an inviting smile and he was stripping on his way to join her. With Collin's words still taunting him, he was desperate to touch her, desperate to remind himself she was his and no one else's.

As soon as he stepped under the spray, his mouth was on hers, his hands roaming her body, touching whatever he could reach. She gasped when he palmed her breast and then pinched her nipple, twisting it viciously while she went up onto her tiptoes at the sensation.

"Rough day at the office?" she panted while he backed her up against the shower wall.

He didn't respond, simply bent to take her nipple into his mouth, soothing it with his tongue before biting it. He loved how she shuddered against him, and he knew he could make her come like this. He liked knowing he could make her come like this.

He switched to her other breast and pressed kisses along her skin while his hand moved to draw circles around the nipple he'd just assaulted, occasionally dragging his thumb over it and making her twitch. He closed his lips around her sensitive nub, sucking hard before biting down on it and making her whimper, then flicking it gently with his tongue.

When she trembled, her fingernails digging into his shoulders until he was sure she was drawing blood, he increased the pressure and the speed of his lips, his tongue, his fingers. He needed her to come apart in his hands, needed to feel what he could do to her.

When her back bowed, and her body went taut, desperate whimpers and moans falling from her lips, he slid his arm around her waist to keep her upright, gently licking and sucking her nipple as she came down from her orgasm.

"I really need to get you some of those nipple clamps," he said against her breast, loving the breathy laugh she rewarded him with.

"If you do, I'm afraid we may never get out of bed again."

"There are worse things."

He lifted her off her feet, biting her shoulder when she wrapped her legs around him. He pulled back to look at her while he sheathed his cock inside her.

"I love that look on your face when I slide into you."

"I love the way you feel, so I guess we're both getting something out of it."

He grinned, leaning in to nip her bottom lip with his teeth. "I might never get enough of you."

When he slid out and back in, she let out a ragged breath. "I might be okay with that."

He reached down to cup her ass, holding her tight against him while he ground his pelvis against her clit, making her groan. "I'm going to fuck you, princess. And I'm not going to be gentle."

She dropped her head back against the shower wall, but her eyes never left his. "Good."

It was all the encouragement he needed to pull all the way out and slam in again, his cock moving in and out at a frenzied pace. He wanted to mark her, to claim her, to remind her that no one would ever make her feel the way he could. He wanted to sear himself into her memory the way she had seared herself into his. Indelible. Permanent. Forever.

"You're mine," he gritted out as she clenched around him, close to the peak he so desperately wanted to take her to.

"Yes," she whimpered.

"Say it," he growled, hips slapping against hers as the hot water beat on his back.

"I'm yours, Aidan."

"Fuck!"

He slammed his cock deep inside her as soon as he felt her orgasm rip through her, his fingers digging into her ass to hold her as close as he could get while he emptied himself inside her.

He dropped his head to the crook of her neck, kissing and licking the skin there while she purred in his arms. "I'm afraid if I move I'll fall over."

"I'm in no rush," she said, lightly drawing circles over his back with her fingernails. "But don't drop me. I'm precious cargo."

He grinned and pressed a kiss to her shoulder before pulling back to look at her. "Was I too rough? I got carried away."

"Did it seem like there was anything I wasn't enjoying?"

"No." Carefully, he set her back on the shower floor, leaning down to capture her lips in a soft kiss. "I just wanted to make sure."

"I promise to tell you if you're ever doing something I don't like. I'll yell out watermelon or something."

He laughed while she turned to reach for the body wash he used, adding some to her hands and working it into a lather. He watched her fingers glide over his chest and shoulders, hissing when the soap stung his back.

She captured her lip between her teeth. "Sorry. I might have, ah, held on a little too tight."

"Don't be. I like knowing you marked me."

She worked her hands down his back and around his hips, pushing them up over his abs. "Want to tell me what happened?"

"Nothing happened. I just needed you."

"Well." She leaned against his soapy chest, her still hard nipples dragging against him. "Feel free to need me like that again later."

"Count on it."

He let her continue to wash him, realizing that he'd caught her at the end of her shower and grateful for the endless supply of hot water while he rinsed.

"You have anything else to do today?" she asked,

balancing one foot on the vanity to slather lotion over her skin.

He watched her, mesmerized, before remembering she'd asked him a question. "No. Nothing else. I met with your brothers this morning over plans for the first few casinos. That's all I really needed to do, but I'm sure Declan would have something else for me if I asked him. Why?"

"Felicity is throwing a party tonight. She invited us."

She didn't say anything else, but there was something in her tone. "Do you want to go?"

"Only if you want to."

"Viv." He waited until she looked up at him. "Do you want to go?"

She debated with herself for a minute before nodding. "Yeah. It's been a long time since I saw any of my friends. But Felicity's parties tend to either be small intimate gatherings or huge ragers. There is no in-between, and I don't know what this one will be like. It might not be…"

"Safe," he finished.

"Right."

"Is Nico around this weekend or does he have a game?"

"No game that I know of." She switched to the other leg.

"Does he normally go to parties like this?"

"Sometimes. When our friend groups overlap or the party is big enough it doesn't matter."

"I'd feel better if he was there as another pair of eyes and ears, but I'll take you either way. If you really want to go." She looked up at him and smiled, and it was worth any lecture he might get from Declan about taking her to a crowded party. "Now, if you put lotion on any more of your body, I'm not going to be able to control myself."

With a teasing lift of her brow, she reached up to grip the knot of the towel between her breasts and tugged until it slipped free and fell to the floor. She didn't get a chance to squirt more lotion into her hands before he was lifting her off her feet and carrying her into the bedroom.

He tossed her into the middle of the bed, grinning when she squeaked in surprise and covered her body with his. "When does this party start?"

"Seven," she said, swallowing hard as his hand snaked down over her stomach, and he teased his fingers over her slit.

"Perfect," he murmured before sliding a finger inside her and grinning when she groaned in his ear.

Chapter Twenty-Eight

Viv smoothed the brush through her hair as she blow-dried it. Normally she could let it air dry into soft waves, but her antics in bed with Aidan on wet hair had turned it into a nightmare. She was just about to give up and throw it into a messy updo when she saw him in the mirror, standing in the doorway.

His eyes raked over her, and she knew if he so much as hinted at staying home, she wouldn't hesitate to say yes. Even if she'd already shimmied her way into this dress. A dress he seemed to like very much.

"Is that what you're wearing?"

Giving up, she set the dryer down and reached in the top drawer for some bobby pins. "What, you don't like it?"

"I do." He stalked across the bathroom and took advantage of the skin she'd exposed at her neck, flicking his tongue across it. "I'm already imagining taking it off you later."

She bit her lip and met his eyes in the mirror, a little disappointed when he stepped back instead of pushing her further. He leaned against the wall and watched her while she continued twisting her hair up off her neck and pinning it into place.

She painted her lips red because she knew he liked the color, and it was a small triumph knowing he'd be thinking about her lips all night while she'd be thinking about his hands and his tongue. Besides, she had something she wanted to tell him later, and she wanted him to be in a good mood first.

He held her hand through the house and out to the car, releasing it only to help her into the truck and reaching for it again once he was behind the wheel. The intimacy they'd established over the last few weeks had given her some interesting insights into her husband.

She liked knowing things about him he probably wasn't even aware of himself, like the fact that he liked to hold hands and he loved to snuggle, especially while they were sleeping. The only times she didn't wake up with his arms around her or held tightly to his side were when she woke up alone because he'd gotten up early.

She also liked knowing he'd never shared either of those things with anyone else. It felt a little hypocritical thinking about that; she'd definitely snuggled and held hands with other men, but being the only one to do those things with him felt special, uniquely theirs.

He followed her directions to Felicity's house, a nice-sized single-family home in a good neighborhood. Felicity's family had done about as well as her own under Giordano. They were just loyal enough to stay alive, but not so loyal as to be caught in Callahan crosshairs.

The family owned a couple of successful dry cleaners in the city. In fact, most of the surviving families had businesses that operated outside the Mafia. Something to keep them grounded so they didn't get sucked into Giordano's depravity.

When they parked at the curb, Viv noticed people spilling onto the front lawn, and she sighed. A rager. Of course. She should have known Felicity wouldn't invite her to a nice, quiet evening with friends after being apart for so long. Felicity liked to see and be seen, and she forgot that not everyone felt the same sometimes.

"Still want to go in?" Aidan asked, reading her hesitation.

"Maybe just to say hi. We don't have to stay long."

"Nico is already here. Says it looks secure, but he'll stay out of our way. Apparently he's trying to get laid."

"Since when does he have to try?"

Aidan laughed as he climbed out of the truck and rounded the hood to help her down. He turned to lead her inside, but she hung back, tugging his hand gently until he was in front of her again.

"What is it? You'll worry yourself sick if you don't say what's bothering you," he added.

"How do you know something is bothering me?"

"You have a tell when you're upset." He reached up to stroke his thumb across her lower lip. "You pout. Tell me."

"I do not pout. What if Declan finds out and we get in trouble?" she said when he only raised a brow.

"I know that's not really what you're worried about. We both know who'll be in trouble if he finds out, and it won't be you. What is it really?"

"What if…" She dropped her eyes to stare at his shoulder, suddenly feeling entirely too vulnerable. "What if they don't like you? My friends."

He backed her against the warmth of the cooling engine and braced a hand on either side of her body. "Do you want your friends to like me?"

She nodded, grateful it was too dark for him to see the flush of her cheeks.

"Why?" She could barely hear his voice over the thump of the bass from the house.

"Because they're important to me," she said, fingers fidgeting with the hem of her jacket. "And so are you."

When he didn't speak, she moved to dip under his arm and head toward the house, but he grabbed her and yanked her back against him, fusing his mouth to hers while his hands wandered down to cup and squeeze her ass.

He lifted her slightly off the ground, enough to rub himself against her core but not high enough that she could get her legs around his waist. She shuddered as he teased her with a slow grind of his hips.

"I'm a very likable person," he murmured against her lips.

"That could be up for some debate."

"When I want to be," he amended.

"Mmm."

The corner of his mouth lifted, and she reached up to grip his throat in the way that always made his eyes drop to her lips. When they did, she pulled him closer, and he obliged, offering her his mouth and letting her take what she wanted from him.

His hand moved around to the small of her back, and he pulled her body against his, tightening his hold when she arched up to grind her hips against the hard length of his cock. He broke the kiss with a groan, but she took his mouth again, nipping his bottom lip with her teeth.

"Woman," he growled, "there are too many people around for me to fuck you against this truck, but don't think I'm not considering it."

"You started it."

When another car pulled up behind them, he reluctantly stepped back and reached for her hand. "I should never have let you out of the house in that dress. You're going to drive me crazy with it all night."

"That's the point, husband. To drive you crazy."

He laced their fingers and gave her hand a squeeze as they walked silently up the driveway. A few people lingered on the front porch, beers in hand, while music pumped out of the open front door.

"Is there anything I need to know?" he leaned down to whisper against her ear, and his breath against her skin made her shiver.

"About the dress?"

The look he sent her was pure sin. "I'm starting to question if you really wanted to come to this party to see your friends or just as an opportunity to tease me in public for several hours."

She grinned. "Why can't it be both?"

They drew gazes as they mounted the porch and moved further into the party. Some curious, some jealous, some indifferent. When a group moved to roughly push by them, Aidan shifted to shield her with his body, the length of him pressed up against her side until they passed.

"Not quite the welcome back Felicity intended, I think," she muttered.

"Question is, do they hate you or me?"

"Viv!" Felicity appeared out of the crowd that parted for her. "You made it. And you brought Aidan."

"As requested. Quite a crowd you've got going here."

"Oh, you know." Felicity waved her hand at the people behind her, some dancing, most standing in clusters talking and staring. "I mentioned you were coming, and suddenly everyone wanted an invite. I hope you don't mind. I know huge parties aren't your thing."

"No, it's fine."

"We can't stay long anyway, I'm afraid," Aidan lied, slinging an arm over Viv's shoulder. "I have a meeting later."

Felicity poked her lip out in an exaggerated pout, and Viv wondered how much she'd had to drink already.

"Well, in that case, can I steal her for a minute?"

Viv glanced up at Aidan and then tracked his gaze around the room until it landed on Nico standing in the far corner, who gave them a quick nod and a signal that everything was clear on his end.

"Yeah. I'll go grab something to drink. You want anything?" he said to Viv.

She shook her head. "No, I'm good for now."

"Okay." He gave her hip a squeeze. "I'll come find you."

He didn't immediately move from his spot, instead watching Felicity pull her into the crowd as if he didn't like the idea of her being out of his sight. She had to admit, it made her a little uneasy too.

With a party this big, it was impossible to know who was or wasn't there. When she glanced up at Nico again, he was following her path through the crowd, and that made her feel a little better about not being able to see Aidan.

Winding through the guests, Viv listened to snippets of conversation. Someone expecting and hoping her parents didn't find out, another couple getting engaged, someone cheating on her boyfriend with another woman. She turned at that one to see Aubrey Capone, worrying her lip over her infidelity. Libby would love that bit of gossip.

When they finally cleared the last of the crowd and spilled onto the patio, the cool night washed over her skin. It felt like coming up for air after being underwater. Viv recognized the group of people clustered around a fire pit that was cracking and popping. Dani with her mystery date, Alex sipping out of her own plastic cup, and Alex's brother, RJ.

"You actually made it," Dani said, pressing a kiss to Viv's cheek. "Viv, meet Paula." She indicated the curvy blonde.

"I was told I'd get to meet you tonight. It's great to finally put a face with a vague description."

"Where's Aidan?" Alex wondered, taking a sip of whatever she was drinking.

"He's getting himself a refreshment." Felicity gestured over her shoulder with her cup.

"You left him alone in there?"

Viv chuckled. "He's got a gun. I'm sure he'll be fine."

"A toast," Felicity said, raising her glass toward the fire. "I said a toast!" she chided when no one else did the same.

Once all the glasses were raised, she started again. "A toast to happily ever after and great parties and being delightfully buzzed on a Friday night."

"I think you're a little more than buzzed, Liss," Dani said, but she drank to the toast anyway.

The patio doors opened, spilling more guests and music into the night, and Dani jumped up, eyes bright. "I love this song! Come on, babe," she said, grabbing Paula's hand and leading her inside to dance.

RJ stood next. "I need another beer. Anyone need anything else to drink?"

At the chorus of no's, RJ disappeared inside again. In the silence that followed, Felicity swayed on her feet, humming along off key to the song currently playing. At the sound of a crash from somewhere inside the house, her eyes shot open.

"Shit, shit." She set her half-full glass on the edge of the fire pit. "Those drunk assholes better not be starting a fight and breaking anything I can't replace."

She took off toward the house, and Alex sighed. "She says that like she's not also drunk. I'm going to go provide backup. Are you okay out here by yourself?"

"Yeah. Don't worry about me. If you see Aidan, will you tell him where I am?"

Alex's answer was a smile before she trailed Felicity into

the house. Alone, Viv stared into the flames, suddenly regretting asking Aidan to come to this party in the first place. Everything felt so different, she felt different, and she wondered for a moment if anything would ever feel the same again.

She'd rather be at home with Aidan watching a movie than here listening to drunk people get drunker. They hadn't watched a movie together yet. She doubted he'd ever done that with another woman either. Another first for them to share. She turned to go in search of him.

"Long time, no see, Viv."

She froze at the voice behind her. Fear licked at her belly, but she schooled her features before pivoting, eyes searching for the fastest way away from him.

"Collin." She crossed her arms over her chest and took a step back. "Not quite long enough."

He took a step forward, a grin spreading slowly across his face. He liked when he scared her. He always had. But she wouldn't let him see that. He didn't deserve that kind of power over her.

"What are you doing out here all by yourself?"

The tone of his voice had her gaze traveling over the rest of the patio and realizing the crowd had mostly disappeared back inside to escape the chill even the alcohol couldn't chase off.

"Just getting some fresh air. I was actually going back inside to find my husband and leave."

She knew instantly that calling Aidan her husband had been a bad move. Colin leapt at her, gripping her arm and shoving her back against the high brick wall lining one side of the fire pit.

Viv swallowed the panic that rose in her throat and shoved at his chest. "Get off me, Collin."

"I know you've missed me, Viv." His breath fanned

against her face, and his proximity made her nauseous. "Do you think about me when he's fucking you? Wish it was my cock instead?"

He fisted his hand against her hip, and she felt the material of her dress bunch in his fingers, riding up her thigh.

He pressed his nose into her hair, inhaling deeply. "Mmm, I want you right now, baby. Can't you tell how much?"

When he moved to grind his hips forward, she stepped out of his path, and he scowled, gripping her arm and hauling her closer.

"Let go of me, Collin. Now." She hated the tremble in her voice, but he seemed to delight in it.

"I don't know why you're being such a bitch. You used to beg for it. Beg me to use you."

"If that's how you remember it, then you're delusional. At worst, I laid there until you were finished. At best, I faked an orgasm so you would get off me."

He pulled her forward and shoved her back against the wall so hard she had to blink against the stars that formed in her vision.

"You lying slut. If you've forgotten how good I was to you, then maybe you need a reminder."

He moved in again, and she darted her eyes over his shoulder. It was enough of a distraction for him to turn slightly away from her, and she seized the opportunity to ram her knee into his crotch. Sprinting away when he reached down to cradle himself, she yelped when he recovered fast enough to grip her hair and tug her backward.

He hauled her back against his chest, cinching one arm around her waist and squeezing her breast roughly with his free hand. "Just for that," he snarled in her ear. "I'm not even going to be gentle when I fuck you."

Sucking in a deep breath, she slammed her heel down

onto his toe, running as soon as he released his hold. "Aidan!" she screamed, panic lacing the single word.

She saw a body moving quickly through the crowd before Collin caught up with her and prayed it was Aidan's. Collin had his arm wrapped around her neck when Aidan burst through the wall of people, gun already drawn at his side.

"It would be a very good idea for you to let go of my wife."

"Hello, Aidan. Tell me," Collin dragged his fingers over the side of her breast, and she saw Aidan's fingers tighten on the gun in his hand. "Do you like to watch?"

"I'm going to kill you, Collin. You get to decide how much time there is between now and then."

"Viv, baby," Collin said, gripping her arm and shoving her to the side. "Do me a favor, and wait right there while I kill your husband."

Collin cracked his neck with an audible pop and drew a gun from the waistband of his pants. But before he could raise it, Aidan rushed him, slamming his elbow into Collin's face.

Collin's head snapped back, and he nearly dropped his gun. He recovered quickly, but Aidan was faster, catching Collin's wrist between his forearm and bicep when he raised his arm to shoot and shoving his other hand against Collin's upper arm.

The result was a sickening crunch of bone and Collin's scream of pain. When Aidan released his arm, Collin stumbled back, and the gun fell to the ground. Viv dove for it, scrambling out of Collin's reach when he tried to grab for her ankle. With practiced hands, she popped out the magazine and threw it over the brick wall into the yard.

"Viv," Aidan said, his voice deadly. "You okay?"

"Yes," she replied, even though her voice sounded thin to her ears. "I'm okay."

Aidan advanced on Collin, who had straightened, his injured arm hanging limp at his side. "I told you what would happen if you said her name again."

When Aidan raised his gun, Collin crouched down and reached for something at his ankle, but he was too slow. A single shot rang out, and Collin crumpled to the floor. Aidan put another bullet dead center in Collin's chest before bending to retrieve the gun from the ankle holster he'd been going for.

"Vivian," he said, his voice desperate as he pushed to his feet. She jumped into his arms, burying her face against his neck while he wrapped around her. "You're okay. It's okay. I've got you."

She could hear someone approaching them rapidly, and she jolted when Aidan set her quickly on her feet and pushed her behind him. His body relaxed just before she heard Nico's voice.

"Papa's on his way. He wants you to get her out of here."

"Nico—"

"Don't worry about this. Me and about two dozen people saw exactly what happened. I'll make sure Papa knows you had no other choice."

She felt them grip each other's hands in the jerk of Aidan's body, and then he was scooping her up and carrying her around the outside of the house to the driveway to avoid the crowd. When they reached the truck, he quickly helped her inside and sprinted around the hood to climb in.

Once the doors were locked, he punched on the overhead light, and his hands were on her, skimming over her tangled hair, across her cheeks, gently down her throat where Collin had squeezed. He mapped every inch of her he could reach before he was satisfied she was unharmed.

"Christ, Viv." His voice broke, and she wanted nothing more than to climb into his lap, so she did. "I'm sorry," he murmured into her hair. "I was looking all over for you. I didn't even think to check outside. I'm so sorry."

She wound her arms around his waist and pressed her face into his neck. "You found me. I'm okay."

"Did he hurt you? Do you need…do you need a doctor?"

"No." She shook her head. "I just want to go home."

He eased her gently back into her seat and reached to buckle the belt around her, planting his hand on her thigh as if to reassure himself she was still there as he started the car and drove toward home.

Whatever fallout there was from tonight, she wouldn't feel bad that the man who'd plagued them for months was finally gone. Despite the rapid beat of her heart, it felt like a weight had been lifted off her chest. They were free. Now she and Aidan could finally get on with the rest of their lives. She was eager to get started.

Chapter Twenty-Nine

Aidan spent days making sure she was okay, and Viv was happy to let him. Once the adrenaline from facing Collin wore off, she'd crashed and slept for twelve hours straight. Each time she woke up, Aidan was with her, always touching some part of her body like he was afraid that if he let go, she'd disappear.

She'd recounted her version of events first to her father and then to Declan, and Aidan had done the same. In the end, there were plenty of eyewitness accounts to back up that Collin had attacked Viv, threatened her, and Aidan had done what was necessary to keep them both alive.

The only Milano family member who had spoken out against what happened that night was Collin's father when he showed up at her parents' house in a drunken rage and heaved empty beer bottles at the garage door. Even the Bellos had distanced themselves from the Milano family to side with the Falcones.

Apparently no one wanted to be subjected to the wrath of Adrian Falcone or the Callahan syndicate in the aftermath of attacking a Callahan bride. Declan, at least, was pleased with the success of the first test of their new alliance, though Aidan would have preferred Collin dead and buried long before he'd ever put hands on her.

With the weight finally lifted off them, it felt like they could really look ahead and plan for the future. Because the future was fast approaching. She'd mentioned moving out of Glenmore House a few times, and when Aidan didn't immediately balk at the idea, she took that as a good sign. She was ready to build a life with him.

Rolling onto her back in the middle of the bed, she stretched out her sore muscles. It hadn't taken too much convincing to get him to make love to her again. He'd touched her reverently, coaxing some of the most intense orgasms she'd ever had from her body while he worshipped her.

It had taken some convincing that she wasn't breakable, though. That she loved when he fucked her senseless. She'd finally gotten through to him last night, and now she was delightfully sore in all the right places. She still wasn't sold on the nipple clamps, however. The man was too good with his hands already.

She could hear the splash of the shower from the bathroom and thought about joining him when his phone started buzzing incessantly, signaling a string of incoming text messages. She rolled to grab it from the nightstand in case it was something important enough from Declan to interrupt Aidan's shower and caught her name and pregnant in the flurry of message previews.

When the messages finally stopped, she hit the button to expand them all. She felt a little guilty reading through his private messages, but she wanted to know if he knew already. And if he did, why he told some guy named Liam.

Heard about what happened the other night with that Collin asshole. Shit, man.

According to Liam, the murmurings through the syndicate were that Aidan should have drawn it out and made Collin suffer. That had a grin tugging at her lips.

Remember the blonde from the club last week?

She paused, chewing her bottom lip. She didn't really want to hear about Liam's sexual conquests, but she hadn't hit the message about her supposed pregnancy yet, and she had to know.

She's got a hot roommate. Leggy brunette with great tits. As soon as Viv's pregnant, let me know, and I'll set you up with her.

The words had her heart plummeting into her stomach. Her throat tightened, and she threw the phone to the end of the bed to stop herself from reading any more.

After everything he'd said, everything he'd done, Aidan was still just waiting to knock her up so he could be done with her. All these weeks since she'd asked for more from him, since he'd agreed to give it, since he had given it, had been an act. A game. A lie.

She pulled her knees up to her chest and dropped her forehead against them. He'd always been good at pretending. This time he'd put on a show so good he fooled her too. But she didn't want to play his games anymore. She couldn't stay here and willingly let him trample all over her heart.

When the shower cut off, she slid out of bed and crossed to the closet. Hopping into a pair of jeans and pulling a sweater over her head, she grabbed a bag and began filling it with clothes. By the time he emerged from the bathroom, she was packing the last of her things from her nightstand.

His eyes dropped to the open bag on the bed in front of her, and he frowned. "What are you doing?"

She bent over the end of the bed and grabbed his phone, lobbing it at his chest so hard he grunted. The only display of emotion she would allow herself. Any more and she was liable to scream until her throat stopped working.

"Your friend Liam texted."

"Okay," he drew out the word and looked down at his phone.

"I wouldn't normally read your texts. It's not really my style, but I thought maybe it was something important from Declan." She was annoyed with herself that she felt the need to explain why she'd invaded his privacy after what she'd read, but she pushed it away. "Liam had much more interesting things to say."

Still frowning, Aidan unlocked his phone and scrolled through the messages. She knew he landed on the one that cracked her heart in two when he paled and his head jerked up. She zipped up her bag and lifted it from the bed.

"Wait," he said before she could round the bed for the door. "I can explain."

She set it carefully back on the mattress and crossed her arms over her chest. "Explain then."

"What I said to Liam. I didn't mean it." He shoved a hand through his hair. "That night we went out for drinks. He kept accusing me of being...out of it."

"Out of it," she repeated, not at all convinced those been anything close to Liam's exact words.

"Yeah. He wouldn't drop it. Kept egging me on, trying to get me to pick up some random woman and go back to her place." His Adam's apple bobbed, and he took a tentative step forward. "I wanted him to drop it, so I told him I was waiting to make sure you were pregnant before I...." He winced like the memory of it hurt him. "Before I slept with anyone else."

"Don't," she said when he took another step.

"I regretted it as soon as I said it."

"But not enough to correct yourself. Not enough to tell him you didn't mean it."

"I...no."

"I'm going to leave now," she said, surprised at how calm her voice was even though she felt like she was breaking apart. "Please don't touch me. Please don't try to stop me. Please don't contact me. If I'm ever ready to speak to you again, you'll be the first to know."

"Viv. Please don't go. I didn't mean it. I swear. I—"

"The problem is, Callahan, I don't believe you."

She glanced down at the open drawer to the nightstand and reached for the only secret she'd ever kept from him.

"Besides, this is good news for you. I'm pregnant." She dropped the pregnancy test on top of the nightstand with a snap. "You've successfully fulfilled your purpose." She nearly choked on the word, the one he'd used that first night when he'd brutally slapped her back into place. "So you're free to have all the leggy brunettes you can stand."

Lifting her bag off the bed, she crossed to the door, a mix of grateful and heartbroken that he didn't try to stop her. She felt the stranglehold she had on her control slipping as she jogged down the stairs, and she quickened her pace. She was nearly free until Brogan pulled into the driveway behind the rental car she'd been driving while they waited to replace her old one.

Viv tried to play it off, but when Libby got out of the passenger seat and saw the bag in her hand, her smile faltered at the obvious concern on her friend's face.

"Viv?" Libby asked. "What happened?"

If she explained it, if she uttered even one word about what happened upstairs, she wouldn't survive it. It was too raw, and the pressure building in her chest was suffocating.

"Ask Aidan."

Yanking open her door and tossing the bag on the front seat, she climbed in and started the engine, peeling out of the driveway before either of them could stop her. Rolling the windows down, she let the cold air stream over her face to keep her thoughts at bay a little longer. It stung her eyes, and tears gathered there, but she much preferred the physical pain to the maelstrom that swirled behind her rib cage.

She didn't even realize where she was driving until she pulled up to her parents' house. Nico was at school, and her parents were gone, so she let herself in through the garage and trudged up to her bedroom with heavy steps.

The door swung in on the same room she'd left not that long ago. Bed neatly made, the few belongings she'd left arranged precisely on top of the dresser. Dropping her bag on the floor and toeing off her shoes, she crawled under the covers, hugged a pillow to her chest, and finally let the pain swamp her.

Chapter Thirty

Aidan stared at the empty space where Viv had disappeared. Pregnant. His head swiveled to the piece of bright white plastic on top of the night-stand, and he crossed to it, his heart pounding.

He fisted his hand to keep it from shaking and reached for the test, turning it over in his fingers. Two pink lines. A confirmation. He sank onto the edge of the bed and stared at the proof in his hands. His body was numb.

Seeing those messages on his phone from Liam must have broken her knowing she was already carrying his child. His child. A baby. They were going to have a baby. Assuming she ever wanted to be in the same room with him again.

He wanted to hurl the test across the room just to throw something, but it felt precious, sacred, so he set it gently on the table and dropped his head into his hands, pressing the heel of his palms against his eyes.

Everything he'd always said he never wanted had just walked out on him. He should feel relieved. This had been his plan from the beginning. Get her pregnant, set her up nicely, go on with his life. When had he stopped wanting that? When had she become the only thing he wanted?

Easy. That night she'd asked him for more. He'd been halfway gone for her but still clutching the ledge of what he could control by fingertips. He hadn't really known why he was still holding on at that point other than it felt familiar and comfortable.

Then she'd told him that if he wanted to keep her, she needed all of him. He'd been more than willing to give it. Like her request had finally given him permission to admit what he'd been too scared to accept. He wanted her and the life they could have together if he just let go.

At a noise from the doorway, he shot off the bed, stumbling as he spun. Viv. He could apologize, make her see that he was truly sorry. But it was only Brogan, standing there with his arms crossed and his face impassive.

"Whatever you're here to yell at me for, it'll have to wait. I'm not in the mood."

"Why did Viv run out of here with an overnight bag looking like being here was physically painful for her?"

Aidan glanced at the test and then up at his brother. "Probably because being here was physically painful for her."

Brogan took a step into the room. "What did you do?"

"I told her I was waiting to sleep with other women until I got her pregnant."

"You did what?!"

"Or rather, I told Liam, and she found out."

"Jesus fucking Christ, you're an idiot. Do you even know how good you have it with her? She's the first person you've ever met who actually made you commit instead of acting like some base-level primate that humped anything that moves."

"I know."

"Here I thought she was finally teasing something that

253

resembled real emotions out of your cold, dead heart. And all this time, you've been plotting and planning to break hers. "

"Fucking hell, Brogan. I didn't mean it. I might have meant it two months ago when Declan first told me about all of this. It felt like a way to maintain control when everything was spinning. I was going to fake my way through whatever I had to get through until it was done and Declan had what he wanted. A new generation."

"But?"

Aidan shoved a hand through his damp hair and gripped the back of his neck. "But somewhere along the way, I stopped pretending, and I fell in love with her. I didn't even realize it happened. I wasn't sure I was capable of falling in love with anyone."

"What?"

"It's not exactly an emotion I'm familiar with. My cold, dead heart, remember? Isn't that why you think Finn's death meant nothing to me?"

Brogan's mouth thinned into a hard line. "I never said that."

"No. Only that it was my fault." Aidan chuckled, but there was no humor in it. "And what was it you said a week after the funeral? That you wished it was me instead?"

Brogan flinched and rubbed a hand over his face. "I'm sorry, Aidan. I didn't mean what I said about that any more than you meant what you said about Viv. I was hurt and angry, and you made an easy target."

"I always have."

"Explain."

Suddenly too tired to stand, Aidan moved to one of the chairs flanking the fireplace, and collapsed into it. "Do you know what it's like growing up as the kid who killed your mother?"

He didn't look up when Brogan leaned against the back of the other chair, his eyes glued to the dark, empty fireplace.

"No," Brogan said, "And neither do you because you didn't kill her."

"Too bad no one said that to Dad when he was still alive. Losing Mom when I was born devastated him. It was easier for him to blame me than it was to blame anyone else. He was hurt, he was angry, and I made an easy target."

"Aidan…" Brogan began.

"He never remarried. He loved her that much, I guess. Then there was Evie and Declan. He was never the same after she left."

"Is that why you hate her so much?"

"Yes," Aidan admitted. "Then you almost lost Libby, watching Cait lose Finn. Why would I want to willingly sign myself up for that kind of avoidable pain? It was so much easier to be cold and dead."

"Until you met Viv."

"She's the first person who didn't make me feel cold and dead. I knew I was going to fuck it up, and I was right."

"You should go talk to her. Apologize and—"

"She's pregnant. And she made it very clear she wanted me to leave her the fuck alone."

"So that's it then? You finally realize what you want, and you're going to give it up without a fight?"

"That's what she asked me for. How do I make this right, anyway? She's probably better off without me."

"Is your kid better off without you too?"

"I'm sure it is. I doubt I'd be any better at being a father than I am at being a husband. It's better for both of them this way. If I try to fix this, I'll only hurt her again. And the kid too."

"If you really believed that, losing her wouldn't hurt so

much." Brogan straightened, and his voice was stern when he spoke. "I'm disappointed in you."

Aidan snorted. "Oh, goodie. Can't wait to hear why."

"Your entire life, all you've ever done is fight for exactly what you want. Right or wrong, win or lose, you ram head first into the problem until it caves or you end up concussed. The one time you have the opportunity to fight for what really matters, and you've given up before you've even tried."

It was silent for so long Aidan didn't realize Brogan had left until he glanced up, and the room was empty. He wanted to believe letting her go, letting her raise their kid to be a better person than he was on her own, would be the right thing to do. But the idea of not having her, of never hearing her laugh again, never feeling her next to him in bed and never seeing their kid grow up twisted something sharp and painful inside him.

Shoving out of the chair, he crossed to the closet and pulled on a sweater. Viv was worth fighting for; there was no question about that. He had and would do whatever it took to keep her safe. He could learn not to hurt her, learn to be better. Whatever he needed to do to be the man she deserved, he'd do it if she gave him another chance.

Right or wrong, win or lose, he'd never stop trying to be the man she needed him to be.

Chapter Thirty-One

Viv laid in bed, legs propped up on her headboard, staring at the ceiling. She felt empty. She wished she could stop crying.

Every time she thought she was out of tears, someone made an offhand comment, or she smelled something that reminded her of Aidan, or she saw him in her dreams, and there they were. Streaming down her face and coating her pillow, leaking from her eyes and dampening the hair at her temples like they were right now.

She'd let the pregnancy hormones take the blame for this if she thought it was true. Mostly she was heartbroken. Occasionally she felt stupid. She should have known this was coming, should have known Aidan would do and say anything he could to get what he wanted.

The man deserved an Oscar for the way he'd fooled her over the last few weeks. It would be truly impressive if the result didn't leave her feeling like an exposed nerve. One wrong move from exploding into unimaginable pain.

And if that wasn't enough, now she had a baby to think

about. His baby. A little person who would look like him and remind her every day of the man she loved who couldn't love her back. At least their baby would love her, and she could pour every ounce of love Aidan didn't want into their child.

Someone knocked on the door, and she turned her head to see Sofia peek around the frame.

"I still don't want to see him, Sofia."

Aidan had been coming by nearly every day since she'd left him standing in their—his—room at Glenmore House. A few times, she'd been able to hear his voice drifting up from the bottom of the stairs while he argued with Sofia, who'd assigned herself the role of official gatekeeper. One she seemed to delight in entirely too much each time she turned Aidan away.

"Not Aidan. I haven't seen him today, thankfully. But you have visitors who are worried about you."

Sofia pushed the door open all the way, and Viv saw her three best friends standing in the hallway. A fresh wave of tears washed over her at the sight of them, and they all rushed in.

Immediately they climbed onto the bed, exactly like they would have done in high school, Felicity on one side, gripping her hand tightly, Dani on the other, and Alex at her head, stroking a hand over her hair.

"We've been worried after what happened at the party with Collin," Felicity said.

"You haven't been answering our texts," Alex added.

"But this is more than that," Dani finished. "What happened, Viv?"

Viv inhaled a deep, shaking breath. "Collin has been stalking me."

"He what?" Alex gasped.

"For months. He's sent me pictures, left notes on my car, called me names, threatened me. I guess Felicity's party was his next escalation."

"Is that why you suddenly started going everywhere with Aidan?" Alex asked, threading her fingers through Viv's hair.

Viv nodded. "Collin showed up at the engagement party and did everything but outright threaten me. When we left later that night, he'd vandalized our cars. Aidan insisted on a protective detail whenever I wasn't at home, and he was the first to volunteer."

"Why didn't you tell us?" Dani wondered, rubbing Viv's arm gently.

"I wanted to, but my dad asked me not to. He's trying to do right by the Mafia. We've been so broken for so long. Giordano would have—"

"Done absolutely nothing," Felicity said, anger in her voice. "Because you're only a woman."

"Or ordered his execution. Depending on his mood."

"Papa wanted evidence it was really Collin. So it didn't look like he was executing Collin for no reason or for some vendetta. And we didn't have any. He was too good. Hiding from the cameras, never leaving anything behind that we could definitively identify him with."

"Until the party," Dani said.

"Right. I think he would have tried to rape me if I hadn't put up such a fight. Or if we'd been somewhere my fighting wouldn't have mattered."

Viv felt Felicity squeeze her hand at the same time Alex's fingers stilled in her hair. The reality of that admission, that Collin would have raped and probably killed her given the chance, had sat like a heavy weight on her shoulders. The reality of how close she might have come if not for Aidan.

"But if Collin is dead, why are you here?" Felicity wanted to know.

"And why are you so sad?" Dani added.

259

"Because Aidan and I..." Her breath hitched. "I don't think it's going to work out between us after all."

"What do you mean?" Alex resumed combing through her hair. "What happened?"

"This whole time, he's been faking it. Making me believe he was falling in love with me so he could get what he really wanted." Viv wanted her voice to sound bitter. She wanted to be angry about it instead of hurt. Anger felt like an emotion she could harness to move on instead of being saddled with this burden of grief.

"What did he really want?" Dani's voice was soft.

"To get me pregnant to solidify the alliance so he could go out and sleep with other women."

Felicity sucked in a sharp breath, and her voice was hard when she said, "That bastard."

"I wish he would have told me from the beginning. It would've been easier if he'd let this be a duty for us both. Why did he have to lie? Why did he have to make me believe he loved me?"

"Maybe he wasn't lying?"

Viv glanced up at Alex's upside-down face. "I found out because one of his friends was texting him about it. He'd apparently mentioned it just a few weeks ago."

Alex's face fell. "I'm so sorry, Viv. He doesn't deserve you."

"Maybe not, but I don't know what happens now." She laid a hand on her stomach, fingertips rubbing over the flat plane. "Because I'm pregnant."

"Oh, honey." Dani curled into Viv's side, laying her head on her shoulder. "How far along are you?"

"I don't know. I only took one of those at-home tests. How do you calculate that?"

"I think by the date of your last missed period," Felicity

said. "That's what I remember the doctor saying when I had that scare last year."

Viv scrunched up her nose and tried to think back. "Six weeks, I think?"

"Jesus. That had to be right around your wedding night. Strong swimmers," Dani murmured.

"Actually," Alex said. "A recent study suggests the egg chooses the sperm it wants by sending out a chemical signal to the...and that is not helpful," she finished, cheeks pink.

"Yeah," Felicity agreed. "Definitely not helpful. Does he know?"

Viv nodded. "I told him. Right before I left."

"And have you talked to him since?" Dani reached up to brush a tear off Viv's cheek. "About what happens next?"

Viv shook her head, not trusting her voice.

"You'll have to talk to him eventually, honey. You're both going to be parents. Don't you think he wants to be in his baby's life?"

"I know I have to talk to him," Viv whispered. "But it hurts too much to think about all that right now. I've got eight months left to figure it out."

"Nine," Alex said. "It's technically forty weeks gestation, which is ten months total and nine to go. Well, eight and a half. Sorry!" She added, holding her hands up in defense when they all looked at her.

"Why do you even know any of this?" Dani mumbled with a roll of her eyes.

Alex shrugged. "I like to read."

"He comes by almost every day asking to talk to me."

Viv turned her head to look at the clock. He'd normally have been by already, but Sofia mentioned she hadn't seen him today. Part of her wanted him to leave her alone because it felt easier to be mad at him, but another part of her, the stupid part that had fallen in love with him in the first place, liked that he was still trying.

"Next time he comes, you should actually go downstairs."

"But make sure Sofia doesn't answer the door," Felicity added.

"Yeah," Dani agreed. "She was scary when she opened the door until she realized it was us. I've never seen a real live person snarl before, but she managed it."

Viv laughed, wiping at her wet cheeks. "I'm glad you guys came by. I've missed you. And I'm sorry I didn't tell you about Collin. I wanted to."

"We understand," Alex assured her. "If you'd told Felicity and she blabbed to half the Mafia, it could have gotten ugly. Collin was a loose cannon. He was always going to go off at some point."

"I do *not* blab," Felicity pouted.

"Keep telling yourself that, cupcake," Dani replied, reaching over to pat Felicity's arm. "Do you want us to go so you can be alone?"

"No," Viv said after a beat. "Stay and distract me with something. How's Brad?"

It was dark when her friends finally left, but Viv felt lighter. She got out of bed for the first time in days and took a shower, changing into fresh clothes and stripping the bed so she could put on clean sheets. She already missed the luxury of a live-in staff. She hadn't thought about making the bed or changing the sheets or putting out fresh towels in weeks.

On her way downstairs, she added her things to the washing machine and set it to run. Tomorrow she'd clean her room, give her hands something to do while she worked out exactly what in the hell she was going to say to her husband when she could face him again.

She didn't know if she could ever forgive him for lying to her, for manipulating her so well for so long. But she was carrying their child. The entire point of this marriage was growing inside her, and he deserved to be part of that child's life.

No matter how they ended up, this kid deserved to be loved by both of its parents. Even if seeing Aidan and not being able to have him for the next eighteen years would be excruciating.

Chapter Thirty-Two

Aidan sat in Declan's office underneath Reign, finalizing the renovation plans he'd drafted with Leo and Gavin. They'd taken a second pass at each location to ensure they weren't missing anything. Spending time with Viv's brothers had been exhausting.

Aidan wasn't sure if Viv had told them what happened, but they didn't seem overly pleased to be in his presence, and they spent the entire day communicating in grunts and pointing fingers. The work was getting done at least, and, for now, that was all Declan cared about. So far his brother hadn't broached the subject of Viv's absence or asked what happened.

Maybe he already knew and was still deciding the best way to make Aidan pay for fucking it up so royally. And wasn't that going to be something to look forward to? Brogan had already told Libby if the way she glared at him in the hallways or over dinner was any indication. He hadn't seen much of Evie in the last week, but he imagined she'd look at him with equal amounts of disgust and disappointment too.

It didn't help that every attempt he'd made to try and

apologize had been rejected. Not by Viv. He hadn't seen her since she walked out. The devastated look in her eyes when she dropped the pregnancy test on the table played front and center in his nightmares.

He knew he wouldn't be able to make it go away until he talked to her, but Sofia was busy guarding the gate. It didn't matter what time he dropped by her parents' house; Sofia was always there, ready to snap at him and force him to leave. And he'd tried every time of day he could think of outside of throwing rocks at Viv's window in the middle of the night.

The last time he'd been by, he only wanted to know if she was okay. Something in his eyes or his voice or his general pitiful demeanor had Sofia softening just enough to tell him that Viv was safe and as well as could be expected. Then she'd slammed the door in his face.

It had only been a week, and he missed her. He hadn't known it was possible to miss someone that much. She hadn't sent for any of her things—something he was taking as a slightly positive sign—so the room still smelled like her. He woke up thinking about her, and he went to sleep thinking about her, and he was starting to feel like one of those pathetic, lovesick assholes in movies who couldn't get their shit together.

"...and then I think we'll be good to get started."

Aidan's head jerked up to look at Declan. "Get started with what?"

Declan gave an aggrieved sigh. "Have you been listening to anything I've been saying?"

Aidan rubbed his fingers over his eyes and then pinched the bridge of his nose. "Not really. No."

Declan tapped his pen against the desk, and Aidan felt his brother's eyes boring into the top of his skull from across the room. He braced himself for a lecture. Which is why Declan's next words were so damn surprising.

"Why don't you go home?"

"Because we have a ton of work to do."

"And we'll have to do it all twice if you're not paying attention to any of it. Go home."

"That's it? You're not going to yell at me to get it together or punish me for ruining the alliance?"

"You haven't ruined the alliance yet." Declan shuffled the papers they'd been going over into a stack. "Falcone is as keen to work together as ever. I imagine he hopes the two of you will sort this out eventually. Which is what I'm also hoping for. I'm sure I could manage to yell at you for something, though. Do you have a preference?"

Aidan snorted and leaned his elbows on his knees. "I don't know what to do if she won't talk to me."

"She'll come around eventually. She's pissed now, hurt too, but she's carrying your child, and even I know Viv well enough to know she won't keep you out of the baby's life. Give her time."

"How much time?"

"As much as it takes. Now go home before I really do start yelling."

Before Declan could change his mind, Aidan shoved off the couch and retreated to Glenmore House. By the look of the driveway, only Brogan and Evie were home, and avoiding them would likely be easy. He'd been on better terms with Brogan the last few days, but it wasn't perfect, and Evie, well, things would probably always stick a little there.

He'd nearly made it safely to his room when Evie caught him as she left her own. He'd successfully avoided her for the most part since Viv left. He simply didn't have the energy to get into it with her right now.

"I have something for you if you don't mind waiting."

She didn't wait for an answer, and he rolled his eyes, leaning against the frame of his bedroom door when she turned and started back toward her room. When she returned, she held out a small, black thumb drive.

"What is this?" he asked, taking it from her outstretched hand.

"They're still finishing the portraits, but the photographer sent over the edited candid photos from the wedding. I thought you might like to see them."

"Oh." He stared at the black rectangle in his palm. "Thank you."

"Aidan." Evie's voice was hesitant. "Can we talk?"

"Why the hell not," he replied, opening his bedroom door and gesturing her through. "This week couldn't possibly get any worse."

She walked a few paces into the room and stopped. "I wanted to say I'm sorry."

"You talked to Brogan."

Evie turned, brow furrowed. "Talked to Brogan about what?"

"This." He gestured between them. "He told you what I said the other day, and now you're here apologizing."

"I have no idea what you're talking about." And it was clear by the look on her face she didn't.

"Okay, then, I'll bite. Sorry for what?"

"For whatever I did to make you hate me so much. I don't know what it was. But I wish you'd tell me so I could make it right. We were never best friends, but you didn't hate me...before."

"Before you left and pulverized my brother's heart into a million pieces?"

Evie flinched like he'd slapped her. "Is that it? You hate me because I hurt him?"

"Something like that. What does it matter at this point?"

"It matters because I love Declan and Declan loves you. It matters because *I* love you. I've known you since you were two years old, Aidan. I held you when you cried at your grandmother's funeral. We have a lot of history together, even if I missed ten years of it."

She clasped her hands in front of her. "And one day, Declan and I are going to have kids, and I don't want you to hate them because they're mine."

His eyes dropped to her stomach. "Are you...?"

"No." She shook her head. "But we're trying. I'm sorry, Aidan. I was young and angry and stupid. Declan hurt me, and I did the only thing I could think of in that moment. Run away from the pain. And when I did, I hurt people too."

She looked up at him, gaze unflinching and full of remorse. "More people than I realized. And I'm sorry I hurt them. I'm sorry I hurt you. I will spend every day of the rest of my life making it up to Declan and to Cait and to you, if you'll let me. But how much longer do you plan on punishing me for something I have regretted every day for the last ten years?"

"I can't snap my fingers and make it all go away."

"Right." Evie nodded, moving past him to the door. "Do you regret what you did to Viv?"

"Every fucking minute of every goddamn day."

"And if you reconciled with her tomorrow or next week or ten years from now, if she forgave you and you got to start over, would you want her family to hate you for the rest of your life because of one mistake? I wouldn't want that for you, Aidan."

"Evie," he said when she turned to go. "Thanks for the pictures."

She gave him a small smile before disappearing around the door. It felt foreign to see Evie and not be angry. He could summon it if he wanted to, but ultimately, she was right. He needed to stop punishing her for something that happened a decade ago. He could no more hate Declan's kids than he could hate his own, but seeing Evie in them would be difficult unless he could let his anger toward her go. Another problem for another day.

He pulled his laptop out of the bottom drawer of his nightstand, plugging in the thumb drive and bringing up a series of folders labeled things like Bridal Suite, Ceremony, and Reception.

He double-clicked the one marked Bridal Suite and instantly saw rows and rows of Viv in the thumbnails. Getting her hair and makeup done, posing with her bridesmaids in satin robes, getting fitted into her dress, and attaching the veil and tiara.

He clicked out of this folder and into the one marked Ceremony. These were mostly of their back as they went through the motions of the wedding mass. He vaguely remembered the photographer getting close enough to take photos of them exchanging rings. He clicked quickly through these until he got to one that took his breath away.

It was after the ceremony, after they'd taken all their posed photos and were waiting around for the limos to arrive to take them to the reception. He'd pulled Viv back into the church to get a bit of privacy. He'd just wanted to look at her for a minute.

He was leaning back against a pew, and when he slid his arm around her waist to pull her in against him, she'd leaned against his chest and wrapped her arms around his neck. Her head was tilted up for a kiss, and she had the beginnings of a smile playing on her lips. The photographer had captured the moment perfectly.

It was the first time he'd called her wife. He'd been testing the word on his tongue, and she'd responded by calling him husband. He didn't realize it then, but that had been the moment she'd become so much more to him. He only wished now he hadn't resisted it for so long.

Saving that photo to his personal files, he pulled up the ones from the reception. These were a lot of the same photos in rapid succession, so he clicked through them quickly until they started to look oddly familiar. He scrolled through their first dance, the cake cutting, and the bouquet toss until it hit him.

Jumping up, he crossed to the desk in the far corner of the room and pulled open the top drawer, fishing out the pictures the stalker had sent them. He dumped the contents of the envelope onto the desk and spread the pictures across the surface, picking out the ones he recognized.

They were the same shots, the same moments, but from different angles than the photographer captured. In some of the printed photos, he could even see the photographer's elbow peeking into the frame or the strap of the camera as it dangled in the corner.

Except…Collin hadn't been at the wedding. After the engagement party, security had been tight at the church and the reception hall. You had to show both an invitation and ID to get into either one, and Collin's name and photo had been on a red flag no entry list. If he'd even tried to get in, they would have alerted Declan and Falcone.

There was no way Collin could have taken any of these photos, and Aidan had no idea why the hell none of them had put it together before now. Probably because he seemed like such a perfect culprit. But he was getting ahead of himself. Collin could have just as easily paid someone to help him take the photos.

Aidan selected all the photos that matched the ones from the stalker and clicked to enlarge them in a slideshow, paging through each one. The first few didn't strike him as odd, but after the third or fourth photo, the same person was in the background of every single shot, phone in hand.

In some, they were obviously taking a photo during a moment other people were also capturing with their phones. In others, they were doing their best to remain inconspicuous, their phone aimed at odd angles or partially obscured by objects. These seemed to match up with photos that were a little fuzzy or weirdly cut off.

He tried to zoom in, but it blurred out the face too much. Ripping the thumb drive free, he sprinted up the stairs to Brogan's lair. Surely his brother had some kind of technology that could clear up this image so he could see who the fuck had been taking photos of Viv from across the room.

When he burst into Brogan's lair, his brother and Evie jerked around to stare at him. "Brogan. I need your help." He threw the thumb drive at him. "The photos on this drive, in the folder marked Reception. I need you to enhance one of them."

"Why?"

"Because I think Viv's stalker is in them."

"You think Collin got into the wedding somehow?" Evie wondered.

"No. I think if Collin was the stalker, he had help. And if he wasn't—"

"Then they're still out there," Evie finished as Brogan quickly plugged in the drive and brought up the folder.

"These," Aidan said, pointing at the pictures he'd been looking at downstairs. "They're in all of them. The one in the back, holding a phone."

Brogan brought up a program on a different screen and dropped the first photo Aidan indicated, drawing a square over the face of the person in the background holding a phone half hidden by a planter. Pixels moved and shifted over the image until it cleared up ever so slightly, but it still wasn't the best shot.

"Let me try another one. Something with better lighting and less contrast between the fore and background."

Another series of clicks and the pixels were undulating over the image before it produced a much clearer result.

"Shit."

"Is that—" Evie peered at the screen.

"Her friend Alex. She was a fucking bridesmaid."

"She could have just been taking pictures of her friend's wedding," Evie said, but Aidan could tell by her tone she was tracking his suspicions.

"And all the same shots happened to end up in a box outside our hotel room door the next morning?" He turned to look at Evie. "Didn't they use some pictures from the engagement party in the article for the paper?"

"Yeah." She nodded. "I think they did."

Aidan didn't have to ask; Brogan was already pulling it up in search and saving the photo to run it through the scanner. It didn't even need cleaning up. You could clearly see Alex's face at the edge of the frame in three out of the four photos used, each one with her cell phone raised to snap a picture.

Fear shoved his heart into his throat, and he scrambled to dig his phone out of his pocket. Taking deep breaths to steady himself, he punched in Viv's number.

"Come on, Viv. I need you to pick up," he muttered as it rang in his ear.

When her voicemail clicked on, he disconnected and tried Sofia instead. Nothing. Pacing the floor of Brogan's lair, he dialed again, nearly groaning with relief when she actually answered.

"Sofia, where's Viv? Is she at your parents' house right now?"

"I can say with one hundred percent certainty that wherever my sister is or isn't is none of your damn business."

"Sofia—"

"She's asked you to leave her alone, Aidan. Haven't you hurt her enough? Just let her move on in peace and go to h—"

"Sofia!" Aidan shouted, unable to keep the panic from his voice. "I know you hate me right now. You have every right to. But Viv might be in trouble, and I need to know where she is. I need to make sure she's safe."

"Safe from what?" He could hear the wariness in her voice.

"The stalker."

"But Collin is—"

"It's not Collin. Or it's not only Collin. It's Alex too. Please."

"You're sure? You have to be sure, Aidan."

"Sofia. You know I wouldn't lie to you about this. Whatever you think of me, I would never compromise Viv's safety. I'd never put her in danger."

"Oh God." Sofia sounded terrified, and Aidan gripped his phone with white knuckles. "Aidan. She's with Alex right now. Alex said she had a...a surprise for the baby."

He muttered a string of curses under his breath as he sprinted into the hallway and took the stairs down two at a time. He barely registered the sound of Brogan's pounding feet behind him. She was going to be okay. She had to be. He needed her to be.

"Send me the address. And Sofia? Don't stop calling her."

Chapter Thirty-Three

Viv glanced down at her phone as it buzzed in her hand again. A fifth call from Sofia. What was her sister's problem today? Sofia knew she was coming over to see Alex. It was the first time she'd left the house in a week, and while she figured Sofia might be concerned Viv would break and go find Aidan, the incessant calling was a bit much.

Setting the phone on silent, she slipped it into her purse just as Alex came through from the kitchen carrying a tray. Her friend smiled as she set it on the coffee table.

"Have any crazy cravings yet?" Alex asked, handing Viv a glass of lemonade.

"Not yet. But I can't get enough of berries right now. Raspberries specifically. I can eat a whole pint by myself in one sitting. Multiple times a day." Viv rubbed a hand over her belly.

"Is it weird?"

Viv looked up. "Being pregnant?"

"With everything else going on, yeah."

"A little." She set her glass on the table, missing Alex's

disappointed frown. "Everything happened so fast. Getting married, falling in love with him, the baby. Part of me feels like I'm still trying to catch up."

"It'll take some time, but I'm sure you'll figure out what's best for you."

"I've been going over and over what to say to him in my head."

"Say to him?"

"About the baby. We'll have to figure something out when it comes to dealing with the pregnancy. I don't know if he'll want to go to doctor's appointments. Then there's co-parenting…"

"You're going to let him be in the baby's life?" Alex set her own glass down with an angry snap. "After what he did to you?"

"Of course I am. This is his child too. Family is important to him."

"It didn't seem that important to him when he was bragging to his friends about fucking other women." Viv winced and Alex sighed. "I'm sorry. That was a low blow."

"It's not like I asked for any of this. Every second of the last few months was directed by someone else. I get to be in control of this. He may not be interested in having anything to do with this baby, but I won't feel right if I don't at least make the offer. Let him know the door is open."

"You're right. I'm sorry. You're a good person, Viv. You've always been the best of us."

Viv smiled. "I thought that's what they said about you?"

Reaching for her glass again, Alex laughed. "How are you feeling about everything else? Everything that happened with Collin?"

"Relieved, honestly. On some level, that feels awful to say because he's dead, but…"

"The bastard deserved it."

"Right." Viv huffed out a laugh.

"I still can't believe he did all those things. Calling you an ungrateful bitch just because you wouldn't leave your marriage and satisfy whatever ridiculous fantasy he'd conjured up in his head."

Viv faltered as she reached for her glass. How did Alex know what one of the notes said? She'd never given her friends any specifics.

"I know," Viv said slowly. "At the party he kept saying he could tell how much I wanted him. How much I missed him."

Alex rolled her eyes. "Please. How delusional. I don't know how you tolerated dating him before. He was never good enough for you."

"No, he wasn't. What about that guy you're seeing? The one Felicity told me about?"

Alex's eyes drifted to Viv's face, and she cocked her head at something in Viv's tone. "We stopped seeing each other. He was interested in someone else."

"That's a shame. I hope it was on good terms at least." Viv tried to keep her voice light, fingers clutched tight around the glass in her hand. "Who's the someone else? Do I know them?"

Alex studied her for a long moment, and Viv read her suspicions in the way her eyes narrowed and her mouth thinned into a hard line.

"You might. They've been away for a bit. Playing house."

The glass slipped from her fingers and crashed to the carpet, spilling cold lemonade over her shoes. "It was you." Alex's mouth split into a sinister grin. "The whole time?"

"Not the whole time. Collin was responsible for the accident and the thing at the engagement party."

"But everything else. Everything after. That was you?"

"Guilty."

"But why?"

Eyes darting around the room, Viv tried to identify the best escape. Alex sat between her and the front door, and there was no guarantee Viv could make it to the back door before Alex caught up with her.

"You've always had horrible taste in men, Viv. Remember the guy you gave your virginity to in high school?"

"Robbie?"

"Yes. He flopped around on top of you for two minutes, and he was done. Then there was Kyle. A total idiot."

"I thought you liked Kyle," Viv said, edging her hand into her purse to see if she could find her phone.

"I'm surprised he didn't flunk out. Who was after that? Oh, right. Greg with the bad breath. I mean, really, the list could go on. You get my point."

"Yes," Viv agreed, her heart pounding. "I see what you mean. Collin was the worst of them, though."

"No, he wasn't," Alex snapped.

"Who was worse?"

"Aidan fucking Callahan."

Viv blinked in surprise. "Worse than Collin?"

Alex leapt out of her chair so fast Viv squeaked, shoving to her feet and moving behind the chair to put distance between them. She silently cursed herself when her purse fell to the floor with a thunk and her phone with it.

"Of course he was worse. You were trapped! In a loveless marriage with a man who only wanted to breed you." Alex's lip curled. "I was trying to save you. But then you went and did what you always do."

Viv swallowed at the fury in Alex's eyes. "What's that?"

"You fell in love with him. It would be sweet if it wasn't so pathetic," she spat. "Because all he did was turn around and hurt you like all the others. I would never hurt you like that, Viv."

When Alex took a step forward, Viv took one back, glancing down the hall. "Of course not, Alex. You're my friend."

"We could have been more than that. But you wouldn't notice me."

Viv's breaths went ragged, and she tried to fight off the panic threatening to choke her. She had to keep her head and figure out how to get out of here. She had no idea what Alex was capable of.

"I've always loved you," Viv promised. "As a friend. As a best friend."

She took another step back and felt the tickling brush of the plant Alex kept against the back wall of her living room. One more step and Viv would be flush with the wall, all but backed into a corner. On instinct, she took a slow step to the side, forcing Alex to pivot to stay in front of her.

"We could have been more than friends. I know you would have loved me the way I love you if you had only given me a chance. We could have been great together."

"I'm sorry, Alex." She took another step to the side and tried to think of the right thing to say while her pulse pounded in her ears. "You're right. I should have seen you sooner. How much you loved me. But I was afraid."

Alex's brow furrowed, and she shifted. "Afraid of what?"

"Afraid that if you found out how I really feel, it would ruin our friendship."

"How you really feel about what?"

Viv swallowed hard. Fuck, she hoped she was saying the right things. "About you. I wasn't sure if you loved me as much as I loved you. If you noticed all the little things I did just for you."

Viv took another step toward the door, eyeing the knife on the tray next to Alex. No. She had a better chance of making a run for the door. She just had to get a little closer.

"Things like what?" Alex demanded.

"Like wearing your favorite color." She could hear the tremor in her voice, but Alex didn't seem to notice, her eyes brightening. "Blue, right?"

"You wore blue to the restaurant when we all had lunch." Alex's voice lost its hard edge and filled with hope. "You did that for me?"

"Of course I did. I only married Aidan because I had to. But now that we're finished, what if we tried to start over? Just you and me."

Alex's face lit up in a smile, then her eyes dropped to Viv's stomach, and the smile fell away, replaced by a hatred that made Viv's heart squeeze. "We can't," Alex spat.

"Why not? I...I want to." God, a few more steps, and she might be able to make it.

"Because!" Alex gestured wildly at Viv's stomach. "You're pregnant with his brat. And I would do a lot for you, Viv, but I won't raise *his* baby." She paused, and the thoughtful look Viv knew so well smoothed out her brow and scrunched up her nose. "If you want this to work, you'll have to get rid of it."

"What?" Viv jerked to a stop, hands flying to her stomach. "Get rid of it?"

"Yes," Alex said with a curt nod. "Get an abortion, and then we can start over."

"You know I can't do that. This baby is innocent."

"That baby is tainted," Alex said through clenched teeth.

"Alex," Viv said, taking another hesitant step toward the door. "We can talk about this. We don't have to decide right now."

"We don't need to talk about it. My mind is made up. God, after everything I've done for you, you can't do this one little thing for me. You're so selfish!" Alex stomped her foot against the carpet.

"You're right," Viv replied, mouth dry. "I...I'll do it. For you, Alex."

She squeezed her eyes shut at the idea of aborting her child and reminded herself she was only saying what Alex wanted to hear. When she opened her eyes, Alex was smiling again. It looked too wide for her face, and it was edged with madness.

"See? Now was that so hard? There are other ways to have kids. We can try something else if you really want them."

"That's a good idea. Definitely something to consider."

"You know," Alex said, tapping her finger against her lip. "I didn't think we'd ever get to be together like this. You wouldn't lie to me, right, Viv?"

Alex looked dejected at the thought, and Viv quickly shook her head, pulse pounding in her ears. "Of course not. I'm just glad it's all out in the open now."

"Me too. Oh!" Alex clapped her hands in excitement. "We're going to be so happy together. Just wait and see. I feel like we need to celebrate! I think I have some champagne. We can get drunk and then see where the night takes us."

Viv's stomach twisted, but she forced herself to smile and nod. Once Alex was in the kitchen, she'd have at least a few minutes to grab her purse and get out. As soon as she was away, she'd call someone. Her dad, her brothers.

At the sound of footsteps on the porch, they both glanced at the front door seconds before someone knocked.

"Are you expecting someone?" Viv asked.

"No. Wait here."

Alex bent to retrieve the knife she'd never used to cut the pound cake, gripping it tightly.

"Alex? Are you home?"

Alex spun to face Viv, face contorted with rage. "What the fuck is he doing here?"

"I don't know." Viv shook her head as Aidan pounded on

the door again. "He has no idea I'm here. I haven't talked to him in a week."

"You lied to me!" Alex shrieked. "You couldn't wait to go back to him and be his whore!"

"Alex, of course not. I would never lie to you."

"He can't have you. You're mine."

When the frame splintered, Alex surged forward, shoving Viv into the wall, causing pain to radiate from her shoulder down her arm. Aidan rushed in, Brogan fast on his heels, and Alex immediately wrapped her arm around Viv's shoulders, holding the knife point to her throat. When she swallowed, she felt it dig into her skin.

"I knew you would fuck this up for us again. But you're too late," Alex said. "She said she wants to be with me now."

Aidan glanced at Viv, his gun still trained on Alex, and she could read the confusion in his gaze.

"It's true," Viv said, unable to keep the tremble from her voice. "We're going to be together now. I'm sorry, Aidan."

"Don't call him that," Alex hissed, tightening her grip on Viv's shoulders. "You don't deserve her," she said to Aidan.

"You're right," Aidan replied. "I don't. She needs someone who can take care of her."

"Exactly," Alex agreed. "And I'm the only one who can do that."

"You'll take great care of her and the baby."

On a snarl, Alex dropped the knife to Viv's stomach, and Viv couldn't help the whimper that escaped her.

"We're not going to raise your spawn. Maybe I should end it for her while you watch. Then we won't even need an abortion, will we, sweetheart?"

"If you do that, you'll hurt her," Aidan said, voice thick. "And we both know you don't want to do that."

Alex considered it for a beat before she moved the knife back up to Viv's throat. "That's true." She pressed a kiss to

Viv's cheek, and Viv had to force herself not to recoil at the touch. "You can go, Callahan. We don't need you anymore. Viv has made her choice."

"I can't do that until you put the knife down."

Alex's laugh was a harsh bark. "I'm not stupid. I know the second I put this knife down, I'm dead. Like you said, I won't hurt her. So get out of here. Once you're back in your truck, I'll let her go so we can live happily ever after. And forget you ever existed."

Viv could tell Aidan was searching for some other excuse to stay, but Alex was losing her patience, the knife twitching in her fingers.

"A...Callahan," Viv corrected when Alex jerked. "You have to let go," Viv added, praying he caught her meaning. "Drop it so we can move on."

Viv reached up to gently touch Alex's arm around her shoulders, breaths coming fast when her hold loosened. "You can't hold on to me forever."

Aidan gave a slight nod. "I understand. Of course. You'll be safe now."

At the last word, Viv wrenched herself free from Alex's grip and dropped to the floor, pressing herself flat against the carpet as gunshots exploded overhead. She saw the knife fall from Alex's fingers and reached for it, throwing it into the corner.

When she looked back, Alex's body was stretched out on the floor next to her, lifeless eyes staring at nothing. With a strangled scream, she shoved to her feet and spun toward the door, straight into Aidan's arms.

"Hey, hey, it's me," he said when she fought against his grip.

"Aidan," Viv said, breaking down into sobs and wrapping her arms tight around his neck. "How? How did you know it was her?"

"I'll tell you later." He stroked her hair. "Are you hurt?"

He pulled back to look at her, wicking away a dot of blood from her neck with his fingertip.

"She got a little shaky with the knife there at the end."

"McGee's on his way," Brogan said from the doorway, and Viv jumped. She'd forgotten he was there.

"I should call Papa."

"I called him," Brogan said. "Declan too."

"Let me take you outside. We can wait for them there. No, don't," he said, gripping her chin and forcing her eyes forward when she turned to glance down at Alex.

He shifted so his body shielded Alex from view and led her away from the house. His truck was parked haphazardly against the curb, and he led her around to the passenger side, opening the door and blocking the wind from licking at her skin.

"I was so afraid I was going to lose you again," he said, pressing his forehead against hers. "Both of you." He rested his hands on her stomach.

Viv squeezed her eyes shut against the sharp sting of tears. "I'm not ready to talk about it yet. But soon. I think... however things end up between us, you should be part of this baby's life."

"I'll never be able to say sorry enough, Viv. I didn't...I never wanted to hurt you."

He leaned back to look down at her, reaching up to cup her cheek and rubbing his thumb across her lower lip. When he kissed her, she fisted her hands in his shirt to push him away, but she couldn't. Instead she pulled him closer, sighing when his arms encircled her waist, molding their bodies together.

She jerked at the sound of slamming car doors, breaking their connection, and when her brothers rushed over, raking

Aidan with cruel glares, he reluctantly released her and stepped back.

He gave her the space she'd told him she wanted while she took her father, brothers, and Declan through the story of what happened, but his eyes never left her. She felt him watching her, wanting her, but not pushing.

When her father finally asked Leo to take her home, she glanced at Aidan over her shoulder as her brother led her to his car. Leaving him felt like leaving a piece of her soul behind, but she didn't know how to soothe this ache he'd written on her heart. She worried it might not be possible.

Chapter Thirty-Four

Aidan glanced at Viv sitting in the passenger seat of his truck and then up at the black and white photo tucked into his visor. His child. Their child. A staticky blob of light with a healthy heartbeat. That steady pulse had nearly brought him to his knees when he heard it in the doctor's office this morning.

She'd called him a few days after he found her at Alex's place to ask if he wanted to go to the ultrasound appointment to hear the baby's heartbeat. It hadn't even been a question.

It was the first time he'd heard her voice since that day. When he thought he'd lost her forever. Today was the first day he'd seen her face. It healed a little part of him to know she was okay, to see for himself what Evie, Cait, and Libby had already confirmed.

She agreed to let him pick her up, something else that felt like progress, but she hadn't encouraged much conversation, giving him one-word answers until he finally gave up. He had so much he wanted to say to her; if she didn't want to talk, she could listen instead.

She didn't realize they were driving in the opposite direction of her parents' house until he pulled onto a dirt lane and followed it through a dense copse of trees that opened onto a stretch of barren land.

"This is a field."

He climbed out of the truck and rounded the hood, reaching in to help her down. She hesitated but ultimately took his hand and hopped to the ground. When she was clear of the truck, she dropped his hand and put distance between them.

"What are we doing here?" she asked, crossing her arms over her chest.

He surveyed the thick grove of trees ringing the knee-high grass. He hadn't been out here in years.

"My dad left this plot of land to me when he died. Told me to use it to build a solid foundation. I had no idea what the fuck he meant. I thought it was some stupid, cryptic message about basements."

He turned to study her profile. "Then I met you."

"Callahan..." she sighed.

"You've let me apologize, but you won't let me explain. I'm not sure if it's because you don't care enough to hear it." He blew out a breath at that possibility. "Or if you won't believe whatever I say. But I need to say it. You don't have to say anything. You can just listen."

She waved her hand, indicating he should continue, but her face gave nothing away about what she might be feeling.

"I didn't want you." When she moved to return to the truck, he dove to the side to block her path.

"This is hard enough, Callahan. There's no need for you to rub salt in the wound."

"I'm not doing this well."

She snorted. "I'll say."

He raked a hand through his hair and tried to organize the jumble of his thoughts. "I didn't want marriage or commitment. With you or with anyone. It's so much easier to be alone."

His fingers itched to reach out and touch her, but he kept them at his sides. He had to get it all out first.

"But ever since you sat down at that damn table at Scarpetta, there was something about you. Something that pulled at me. I thought it was lust because God knows I feel plenty of that for you. But even then, it was more. I just didn't know what it was."

He swallowed hard. "I've been falling in love with you since the first moment I met you. With your eyes and your laugh and your brain and your smart-ass mouth. I love how you call me on my shit and how you know what I'm thinking before I even say it."

His gaze darted over her shoulder at the trees swaying in the breeze. She tugged her jacket tighter around her, but he couldn't bring himself to look at her. He might not be able to finish.

"I've been falling in love with you, and I didn't know it. I didn't think I was capable of it. And when I realized what it was, it scared me. Because it meant you could hurt me. It meant I could lose you."

He was quiet for a minute before whispering, "Maybe I already have."

"I didn't want you either."

His gaze snapped to her face, but he didn't see rejection there. The softness in her eyes gave him hope.

"When Papa told me about all of this, I laughed—literally —in his face. Once he made it clear it would happen whether I was a willing participant or not, I decided I'd try to make the best of it. I figured maybe we could find some common ground. Be friends."

She blew out a breath. "You set fire to that idea pretty much right away."

"Viv, I—"

"Wait. You said yours. Let me say mine." He nodded. Shoving his hands in his pockets. "After that dinner, I sort of hoped you'd take a long walk off a short pier." She chuckled. "There was lust there. Obviously. I mean, look at you."

It took everything he had to keep his hands in his pockets when she dragged her eyes down his body and back up to his face.

"You were practically made for sex. And you're very good at it."

"Uh, thank you?"

"Don't get cocky, Callahan." Her voice was stern, but her mouth quirked up at the corner. "Do you want to know the moment I started falling in love with you?"

"Yes," he whispered.

"At the engagement party. After Leo hauled Collin away and I freaked out. I expected you to snap at me to pull it together, but you didn't. You asked me what I needed, and then you gave it to me. I don't think you even realized what you did for me. How you grounded me."

He hadn't. He didn't even understand it himself at the time.

"I tried to move you back to arm's length again after that. I was scared too. Scared you wouldn't be able to take care of my heart if I gave it to you. But there was something about you that pulled at me," she said, borrowing his words.

"When I asked you to go all in and you did, I thought this is it. This is our turning point where we finally both figure this out together. Finding those messages from Liam…they drilled into my worst fear. That this was all an act for you. Like the party, the interview, the wedding. That you were pretending to love me."

"I should never have said that to Liam. It might have been true once, but it hasn't been for a long time, and it wasn't when I said it to him. I don't want anyone else. Only you." He chanced taking a step closer, reaching up to run his hands up and down her arms when she didn't back away.

"It's not just that I want you, Viv. I need you." He took a deep breath. "I want to fight for you. For us. For our family." He laid his hands over her stomach. "If you'll let me. I want to start over. Right here. With you. Let me build us a solid foundation. Let me spend every day of the rest of our lives making it up to you."

She turned to look out over the empty plot of land. "I have two conditions."

His heart beat fast in his chest, and he tightened his hold on her arms. "Only two?" he swallowed a chuckle when she raised a brow. "What are they?"

"First. I want an obscenely large kitchen. I'm going to be very picky about it. This is a deal breaker."

He tucked a strand of hair behind her ear, cupping her face in his palm. "You can design this entire house to your exact specifications. Whatever you want, as long as it takes. What's the second thing?"

Her eyes searched his for a long moment before she said, "I want you to be honest with me every day. No more games, no more lies, no more half truths. If we're in this, we're in this all the way."

"You deserve all of that and more. I mean it, Viv. I'm going to spend every day of the rest of our lives showing you how much."

"Well, then. I guess you better kiss me to prove it."

Grinning, he reached down to wrap his arm around her waist, drawing her up onto her tiptoes to bring her face even with his and sliding his hand around to cup the back of her neck. When his lips met hers, she sighed, and for the first time in his life, he knew what coming home felt like.

Epilogue

8 months later

"**I** hate everything about you. I never want to touch you again," she vowed, even as she grappled for his hand when another contraction set in. "This is all your fault."

"It takes two to tango. But you're right," he added when she sent him a scathing glare. "This one is all on me. It'll never happen again."

"Shut up," she panted, collapsing back against the pillows as the contraction subsided.

He opened his mouth to speak, and she silenced him with a warning look.

"I swear to Christ, Callahan, if you are about to tell me I've never looked more beautiful, I will cut your dick off and beat you over the head with it."

The nurse who came in to check Viv's vital signs chuckled. "Things sound like they're going well in here."

"Swimmingly," Aidan said. "What if it is true?" Aidan wondered once the nurse made notes on the chart at the end of the bed and left. "That you've never looked more beautiful."

Viv slanted him a look out of narrowed eyes. "Then I'd say you're a liar."

He leaned down to kiss her forehead. "Mmm. Well. Agree to disagree."

It was true, though. She was beautiful when she cursed his very existence as the contractions got closer together and became more intense. She was beautiful when he climbed onto the bed behind her to support her when she pushed. She was beautiful when the doctor laid their daughter on her chest. She was everything.

The room was a flurry of activity while he cut the cord and the nurses cleaned, weighed, and measured the baby. Aidan had never seen someone so perfect, with her ten tiny fingers and ten tiny toes. When the nurse laid his daughter, swaddled and staring, in his arms, he marveled at how he could love someone so completely he'd only just met.

"She's got your nose," he said when they were alone, heart squeezing in his chest when his words drew his daughter's gaze.

"And your eyes," Viv added, watching them with a dreamy smile. "I hope she keeps them."

"I think the Callahan blue eyes are our strongest trait."

"Really? I thought that was stubbornness."

With a laugh, he leaned down and kissed her before carefully settling the baby back in her arms. Leaning his hip on the edge of the bed, he reached up to cup the back of her neck, rubbing his thumb over that spot behind her ear while Viv counted the baby's fingers and toes for the millionth time.

"I don't want her to be pushed aside for boys," she murmured. "I want her to know she has as much of a place in the syndicate as any of her brothers or cousins. And not only for making the next generation."

"I don't think that'll be a problem. Evie is already advocating with Declan that the girl she's carrying be the heir. And he's halfway to agreeing with her. We'll help them build something new. Something stronger."

"Good. If anyone can do it, Evie can. Why should the boys get to have all the fun, right, baby girl?" Viv cooed.

Aidan glanced up at a knock on the door to see Evie poke her head in.

"Feeling up to a visit? The nurses said it was okay to come back."

"Absolutely," Viv said, smiling as Declan filed in behind Evie, followed by Brogan, Libby, and Cait.

"You look beautiful," Evie said, leaning down to press a kiss to Viv's cheek, supporting her heavy belly as she stood. "Tell me it's not as bad as it sounds. I remain unconvinced by Cait's effortless deliveries."

"It wasn't as bad as I was expecting. Still hurt like a bitch, though," Viv admitted. "Don't be a hero. Go for the epidural."

"Noted," Evie said, rubbing her hands over her stomach. "This little angel seems worth it."

Evie glanced up at Aidan when Viv laid the baby in her arms, returning the smile he gave her. They had a long way to go, but they'd get there. He suspected his niece growing steadily inside her would do a lot to close the gap between them. Evie ran her finger over the baby's cheek.

"So soft," she murmured, nuzzling her nose into the baby's hair.

"Have you picked out a name yet?" Cait wondered.

"No, we're still arguing over the right one."

"Actually. I'd like to name her Siobhan." Viv glanced up at Aidan. "After your mom. Unless you guys were thinking of that for your girl," Viv added with a look to Evie and Declan.

Evie had tears in her eyes, but Declan shook his head. "No," he whispered. "I think it's exactly right."

"Okay," Libby said, holding her hands out. "My turn."

"Excuse me," Viv said, finger darting out to point at the ring glittering on Libby's left hand. "What is that?"

"Oh. Ah. I didn't want to…we're not…we don't want to steal your thunder," Libby finally finished.

"Elizabeth Giordano," Viv said. "Did you finally say yes?"

Libby blushed, and Brogan laughed, wrapping his arm around her shoulders and pressing a kiss to the side of his fiancé's neck. "She did. Finally."

"Do yourself a favor and don't plan a wedding in anything less than six months."

"A year is better," Evie agreed, handing Siobhan to Libby.

Once Aidan's family filed out, Viv's family filed in, passing the baby from hand to hand. Things were still strained there; forgiveness took time, but it had gotten better. The baby helped, with all the women cooing over her and all the men slapping Aidan on the back as if he'd done something.

When visiting hours were finally over, and the room was silent again, he stretched out next to Viv on the bed, the baby swaddled and fed and sleeping soundly. He had everything he wanted right here in this room, and life had never been more perfect.

"I thought I loved her when she was inside you. How is it possible it's so much more now that she's here?"

"I don't know," Viv said, voice thick with tears. "She's incredible. We made this."

He looked down at their daughter and gently traced her little clenched fist with his fingertip, his heart stuttering when her fingers opened reflexively to grip his.

"I don't know how to be a father. What if I fuck it up?"

"I don't know how to be a mother. I suspect we'll figure it out. We're in this together."

It struck him suddenly that those were the words she'd

said to him the first night they met. When she glanced up at him, he could tell she remembered it too.

Except this time, instead of pushing her away, he pulled her close, captured her lips in a kiss that was soft and sweet, and whispered, "Always."

A Note for the Reader

Dear Reader,

From the very bottom of my heart, thank you. I couldn't do this writing thing I love so much without you. As Aidan came to life in *Sweet Revenge* and *Bitter Betrayal* I knew there was more to him than meets the eye. He's a complicated, lovable asshole and one of my favorite characters. I hope that you fell in love with him as much as I did as you got a peek behind his tough exterior and watched him fall head over heels for Viv. I am deeply grateful that you took the time out of your life to come along on Viv and Aidan's journey.

If you enjoyed this book, I would really appreciate a little more of your time in the form of a review on Goodreads or Amazon or wherever you purchased it.

Next I'm sharing James's story with you in Book Four of the Callahan Syndicate Series. Look for *Dark Secrets* coming in October 2022 to Kindle Unlimited, ebook, and paperback.

For sneak peeks, bonus chapters, updates, release dates, and more, sign up for my newsletter at https://meaghan pierce.com/newsletter or follow me on TikTok.

All my love,
Meaghan

tiktok.com/@meaghanpierceauthor

Also by Meaghan Pierce

Callahan Syndicate Series

Sweet Revenge

Bitter Betrayal

Acknowledgments

Beta readers make the world go 'round. I met some incredible new people while writing this book. Thank you so much to my betas Kate, Ali, Caoimhe, Jill, and Alyse. Alyse, you answered so.many.questions. and I appreciate your thoughtful responses to each one!

To Caoimhe and Paula, my soul sisters. I couldn't begin to express my thanks for your love, support, opinions, real talk, and screenshot evidence when I get too in my own head.

For Chelsea. You're the best sister I could ever ask for. You don't read much but you've read every word I've ever written and I appreciate your love and support more than you could possibly know.

The Group Chat. Y'all don't even know what you do for me on a daily basis. Thank you for always celebrating me and, more importantly, reminding me to celebrate myself. You're all so incredible and you encourage me to keep going.

To my editor, Mo. Thank you times a million for your time and your talent. I love you more and more with every book we work on together. And to my proofreader, Holly. I TOLD you you'd fall in love with Aidan. You're welcome.

Lastly, thank you to all the readers who were skeptical that Aidan was worth redeeming. Your doubt pushed me to peel back his layers and make him come alive on the page. I hope you fell as hard as I did.

Printed in Great Britain
by Amazon

10592371R00176